# FOUNDATION FOR LOVE

The sound of his pager broke the spell and Christine angrily stepped away. "How dare you?" she said, agitated that se had allowed herself to be drawn to him so easily.

"How dare I what?" he asked, confused at the sudden change in her attitude.

"How dare you come in here," she answered, pacing the floor in front of her desk like a trapped lion, "asking me personal questions, making me feel . . ."

Noticing the hesitation in her voice, Damian decided to push it. "Making you feel what, Christine?"

"It doesn't matter," she answered, reaching for the notes she took of their meeting. "The relationship between us is business, and I would appreciate you sticking to that topic."

Suppressing his irritation, he decided to abide by her request . . . for now. "OK, Christine. We'll play it your way."

"Fine, Mr. Ware," she said.

Gathering his briefcase and jacket, he headed for the door. "I'll use the phone in the lobby. And Christine," he continued, curving the corners of his mouth, "please call me Damian."

After making sure he was gone, Christine shut her door and plopped unceremoniously into her chair. Reaching for a strand of hair, she closed her eyes and relived the moment that almost happened. Never in her life had she felt such raw attraction for a man. If his pager hadn't gone off, she would have kissed him! She hardly knew the man. As a matter of fact, she didn't know him at all. She should have never allowed him to take such liberties with her, but the sound of his voice, the intoxication of his cologne, and the heat radiating from his body were too much to take. How was she going to make it through this project? She would just have to remember that this was strictly business. Whatever physical attraction she felt toward Damian would definitely fade in time. She just had to let it run its course, and then everything would be fine. . . .

# FOUNDATION FOR LOVE

## DOREEN RAINEY

**BET Publications LLC**
http://www.bet.com
http://www.arabesquebooks.com

ARABESQUE BOOKS are published by

BET Publications, LLC
c/o BET BOOKS
One BET Plaza
1900 W Place NE
Washington, DC 20018-1211

All Kensington Titles, Imprints, and Distributed Lines are available at special quantity discounts for bulk purchases for sales promotions, premiums, fund-raising, and educational or institutional use. Special book excerpts or customized printings can also be created to fit specific needs. For details, write or phone the office of the Kensington special sales manager: Kensington Publishing Corp., 850 Third Avenue, New York, NY 10022, attn: Special Sales Department, Phone: 1-800-221-2647.

First Printing: May 2002
10 9 8 7 6 5 4 3 2 1

Printed in the United States of America

*To my heavenly Father, who makes all things possible.*
*I am nothing without You.*
*To my husband, Reginald Rainey. Thanks for your*
*support. You make pursuing my dreams easy.*
*To my parents, Alice and Elbert Smith. You both have*
*always been there for me, and I am forever grateful.*
*To my sister, Sandra Gammons. Your life continues to*
*inspire me.*

# ONE

"What a great turnout," Stephanie Jackson said, glancing around the ballroom. The sophisticated Tidewater Room, located inside the Hyatt Regency in Washington DC, was tastefully decorated with small cocktail tables, fresh flower centerpieces and white twinkling lights.

"Yes, it is," Christine Davenport answered with pride. "Davenport & Associates is finally a reality. I had my doubts . . . three months ago I wanted to forget about my own interior design firm, but looking around this room today, I'm glad you convinced me to stick to the plan and open on time."

"I had to," Stephanie replied, a trace of laughter in her voice, "I needed a job." Scanning the room, she picked up a glass of champagne from a passing tray and said to her best friend, "I'm going to go mingle."

Christine, pleased at the number of people who had come out for the reception, admired the attendees dressed in their evening best. Leaving the design firm where she had worked for several years was definitely a risky move, but thanks to referrals from her previous clients, she finally took the plunge and her business was off to a good start. However, Stephanie's idea to invite clients to an appreciation reception and asking that they bring others seeking design services served as a fantastic marketing strategy.

"Christine, what a wonderful affair."

"Thank you, Mr. Dilliard." Christine answered, smiling warmly.

Robert Dilliard, owner of fifteen shoe stores in the mid-Atlantic region, was Davenport & Associates' first client. Almost sixty years old, his distinguished dark suit, salt and pepper hair and small framed glasses perched on his nose, gave him a regal and successful appearance. Hearing of her work from a former client, he was happy to let Christine handle the decorating of his new corporate office. It was his encouragement and promise of business that gave Christine that extra bit of confidence to move forward with her plans to open her own business. "Things are going well. Thanks to you, our client list is on the rise."

"Well, I hope you have room for at least one more client. I have someone I want you to meet," he said. "He's the son of an old college buddy. He's not here yet, but he owns a construction company and is moving his headquarters to a larger facility. The space needs a complete overhaul. I'll be sure to introduce you when he arrives."

"I'd appreciate that," Christine answered, as she suddenly noticed Stephanie frantically waving from across the room. "If you'll excuse me, I'm being summoned. Enjoy the evening."

As he made his way through the lobby of the upscale downtown hotel, Damian Ware wondered if he should have canceled his evening plans. The wrong grade of lumber had arrived at one of his job sites that day, and he had spent the afternoon trying to straighten out the situation. Now he was going to have to spend the evening talking to someone about color schemes, fabrics and drapes. He cringed at the thought and wondered why he hadn't asked Tanya to attend in his place.

Shaking his head from side to side, the corners of his mouth curved into a slight smile. He knew why. Robert Dilliard had invited him and that man rarely took "no" for an answer. Robert made it clear that he expected Damian to show up. If Robert wasn't his father's good friend, Damian probably would have stood him up.

Checking the engraved invitation, he found the Tidewater Room and stepped inside. Quickly surveying the room, he paused and wondered if his mind was playing tricks on him. Staring intently, he realized it was no illusion. The stranger that had haunted his dreams for the past three months stood less than thirty-feet away from him.

The day that he had first laid eyes on her, three months prior, was forever etched in his mind. His younger brother, Brandon, had sprained his ankle showing off on the basketball court. When he had gone to the hospital to offer him a ride home, Brandon had happily declined, claiming that he was well taken care of by his latest girlfriend.

*As Damian walked through the hospital lobby, she breezed by him, the soft click of her heels and the seductive scent of her fragrance lingering in the air. He watched her move swiftly outside through the parking lot and cross the street to a small park. Sitting down on a bench, she stared straight ahead.*

*A young woman, hurrying her small white poodle into her car, and an elderly couple rushing to enter a café, seemed to go unnoticed by her. She didn't turn around to see the man packing up his hot dog stand, and she never noticed the people making quick dashes from their cars to the entrance of the hospital. Obviously unfazed by the darkening sky, she began to rub her temples, as if to counteract the pounding in her head. Lowering her head, she slowly rocked back and forth.*

*As he made his way to his dark blue pick-up truck labeled with his company's logo, he glanced her way several times. Raising a newspaper over his head to protect himself from the drizzle that had begun to fall, he slid into the driver's seat and turned the key. He gave the parking booth attendant a quick wave as the automatic gate lifted, and then turned onto the street next to the park.*

*Watching her intently, he wondered why she sat without protection from the rain. Slowing his car, he leaned over the passenger seat to take a closer look. Her shoulders began to shake and he realized she was crying. Before questioning his reason, he pulled over, grabbed his umbrella and a jacket and sprinted over to her. Ignoring the pellets of water seeping into his pullover cotton shirt and well-worn jeans, and the splattering of mud on the heels of his beige work boots, he reached her in an instant. Kneeling beside her, he asked, "Excuse me miss, but are you all right?"*

*Receiving no response, Damian raised the umbrella and laid his jacket across her shoulders. Sitting beside her, he stared ahead stoically, as her cries blended with the sounds of the raindrops hitting the ground. Wanting to comfort her, Damian gently pulled her to him and she fit snugly into the circle of his arm. As she continued crying, his body stiffened and his breathing increased. A strange inner spark took root deep inside the recesses of his core being. Minutes passed, and so did the storm. As she pulled away from him, Damian watched her closely with a look of somber curiosity.*

*Even though her drenched hair was matted to her scalp and shoulders and a colorful collage of make-up and black mascara streaks was smeared across her cheek, he found her amazingly beautiful. Her deep mahogany skin reminded him of dark chocolate. Staring into her brown eyes, he was struck by the depth of sadness reflected at him. It stirred in him the need to protect her and hesitantly, he reached up and gently pushed stringy, strands of wet hair off her face. Immediate warmth coursed through his body as his fingers made contact with her skin.*

*As she slowly stood and struggled out of the jacket, Damian also stood up. His eyes dropped to her wet white silk blouse before trailing down the outline of her camisole that highlighted the curve of her breasts, the flatness of her stomach, and the slimness of her waist. Subconsciously, he photographed everything about her. Feeling his body react, he quickly raised his eyes back up to her face.*

*"Are you all right?" Damian asked again, softly.*

*Offering him a reassuring smile, she walked slowly past him and back across the street. He remained motionless as she got behind the wheel of a car and maneuvered it out of the hospital parking lot, barely acknowledging the attendant who handed her change.*

*At that moment, another burst of thunder clashed in the air and heavier rain began to fall. Seeing the woman brush away more tears moved Damian into action. Concerned about her safety, he got back into his truck and followed her car as it headed out of Washington DC and into the suburbs of Maryland.*

*Sitting at a light, Damian heard the angry blow of a horn, signaling her failure to notice the light had turned green. Watching the windshield wipers swing at top speed, he prayed she would be able to concentrate on her driving.*

*As she pulled into the garage of a single-family home, Damian watched from across the street as the automatic door eased down to the ground. He saw a light come on a few minutes later on the second floor of the brick colonial. Not quite sure what to do next, he just sat and waited. About ten minutes later, the lights went out, and Damian assumed she had turned in for the night. Hooking a U-turn, he headed back down the street toward his home. He doubted she had even noticed anyone following her in order to assure her safe arrival home.*

As his mind moved back to the present moment, he thought of all the unanswered questions swirling around his head since that strange encounter. He had spent a significant portion of time wondering who she was and what had transpired that day to cause her such pain and sadness. He had felt an immediate and total attraction to her but he fought an inner struggle about whether or not to contact her. He lived just twenty minutes from her and thoughts of checking on her had crossed his mind on several occasions. Was she married? Involved with someone? Would she welcome his intrusion into her life? Would she even remember him?

Needing a moment to recover from the shock of seeing her again, Damian shifted his focus to finding the man who had invited him tonight. Since his parents returned to their childhood home in California several years ago, Robert had taken on the role of surrogate dad to Damian. Offering him business advice, sharing Sunday football games, and welcoming Damian into his home at any time, day or night.

As he stepped up to the bar and ordered a club soda with lime, Damian questioned why the woman would be here. Was she a client of this firm or did she work for the company? Contemplating whether to approach her, he wondered if she had thought of him at all since that day. He had spent many sleepless nights lying in bed, reliving the calmness he felt when she was cradled in his arms and wondered whether she had done the same.

"There you are," Robert said, making his way toward Damian. "I've been looking for you all evening."

"How are you, Robert?" Damian answered, giving him a hug.

"Just great. Listen, I know your time is limited tonight, but I want you to meet the young lady who is responsible for turning my drab office space into a corporate paradise. You know she is single?" he asked with a sly grin.

Damian ignored that last remark. Robert had tried to set him up on several occasions, without success. The last thing on his mind was getting himself involved in another fix up.

"I almost decided not to come," Damian said. "Between the new job we started this week and a problem I had with one of my suppliers, the last thing I wanted to do is socialize. I should have sent Tanya."

"Well, I'm glad you came. You know what they say about all work. . . . oh . . . there she is," Robert said, as he began to wave someone over. Scanning the room, Damian followed Robert's eyes until they rested on her.

*It can't be!* She couldn't be the one Robert had been raving about these past few months.

The crowd of fifty or so gathered in small groups around the buffet table, near the bar, and around the tables set up throughout the room. A three-piece jazz ensemble played smooth sounds in the background, but Damian noticed nothing but the woman's vision of beauty. Dressed in a simple black dress with a scoop neck and long-fitted sleeves, she moved with style and grace. The floor-length gown just grazed the floor, as the side slit gave a peek-a-boo view of her leg. The only difference in her appearance was her hair. Three months ago, her auburn locks hung past her shoulders. Now, her hair was only a few inches long and framed her face in wavy ringlets. Damian swallowed deliberately to keep his mouth from hanging open. If he had thought that she was gorgeous with wet hair and smeared make-up, she was breathtaking now.

What would he say? How would she react? It had been a long time since a woman had affected him this way. Not since . . . *Danielle*. That name hit his mind like water to a fire, immediately cooling his reaction to her. The sting of his relationship with his ex-fiancé still had the power to affect him and pierce his heart. What was he doing? He had to get his emotions under control. Damian had promised himself that he would devote his attention to his business and that everything else would be secondary. His company was expanding and he had new bids on the table. The last thing on his agenda was getting involved with a woman . . . no matter how beautiful she was.

Robert noticed Damian's initial reaction and was pleased. Turning toward Christine, Robert thought about all that Carlton had shared with him about his son over the years. He knew about Danielle and the lies and deceit that had ended their relationship. Robert also knew that Damian had not been serious with anyone since that relationship ended three years ago. And at thirty-six, Robert felt it was time to get the man he viewed as his son back into the game of love. Robert believed Christine and Damian had something to gain by getting to know one another.

As Christine made her way toward them, Robert turned back to Damian and was immediately taken aback by what he saw. What had been definite interest on Damian's face a moment ago, had turned into an air of aloofness and indifference. Confused, Robert went ahead with the introductions.

"Christine Davenport, I'd like you to meet Damian Ware."

"It's nice to meet you, Mr. Ware. Thank you for coming to our reception," she said, taking hold of his hand.

*"It's nice to meet you, Mr. Ware!"* his mind screamed. *She doesn't remember me!*

"It's good to finally meet you. I have heard nothing but great things about you and your company," Damian answered, accepting her hand. He stared at her for several moments, hoping to see any sign of recognition in her eyes. That was a mistake. Her sultry eyes, highlighted by elegant shades of eye shadow and surrounded by long dark lashes were hypnotic, casting a spell over him that he could not break.

"Mr. Ware . . ." she said for the second time.

"I'm sorry, what did you say?" he answered, embarrassed that he was caught daydreaming.

"I said can I have my hand back," she said, agitation in her voice.

"Of course . . . my mind just wandered to a project I am working on," he lied as he released her hand and immediately felt the loss of touch.

"Mr. Dilliard tells me that you are moving office locations?" she asked.

"Actually, we are staying in the same building but just moving to another floor with more space. The lease was signed this week. I hope to have things up and running in

three months. I would be very interested in having you . . .
I mean your company . . . decorate."

"Well, call my office on Monday and we can set up a
time to meet," she answered. "Now, if you will excuse me,
I must speak with a few more guests." She turned quickly
and walked away.

*Strange,* Damian thought, as he watched her walk away.
She didn't talk with anymore guests, but instead, headed
straight for the exit.

Walking quickly down the hall, Christine found the ladies'
room and nearly knocked Stephanie over going inside.

"Whoa girlfriend, where's the fire!" Stephanie said as she
followed Christine back into the bathroom.

Stopping in the lounge, Christine flopped down on the
sofa. "Sorry, Stephanie, but I just had to get out of there."

"What happened?" Stephanie asked, her face frowning
with concern.

"He's here."

"Who's here?"

"HIM." Christine said, looking directly into Stephanie's
eyes.

"HIM him," Stephanie asked with a look of recognition.

"Yes, HIM."

"OOHHH," Stephanie squealed. "This is great. Come on
girl," she continued, grabbing her hand and heading for the
door. "I have got to meet the man who has dominated our
conversations for the past three months."

"Not so fast," Christine said, stopping before they reached
the door. "He didn't recognize me."

"So what," Stephanie said with a look of mischief in her
eyes. "Just go out there and say 'Hi, you may not remember
me, but I think you are the sexiest man alive and I have done
nothing but talk about you to my best friend for three
months . . . What do you say we get married . . . I'm free
Thursday, what about you?" She held her side as laughter
filled the room.

"That is not funny!" Christine snarled through gritted teeth. She now regretted ever telling her best friend about her strange encounter.

"Come on, loosen up," Stephanie said, subsiding to a giggle. "What's he doing here anyway?"

"Oh, you'll love this," Christine answered sarcastically. "He's one of Davenport & Associates' newest clients."

"This is perfect," Stephanie answered, smiling. "So tell me, is he as handsome as you remembered?"

Christine thought about the moment she saw him at the reception. When Robert waved her over, she recognized the man immediately, and almost stumbled as her heart jolted and her pulse pounded. She was glad to walk across the entire room to get to them as it provided her an opportunity to get her emotions under control. He looked exactly as she remembered: gorgeous. Over six feet tall, his custom-made gray four-button suit was a vast difference from the worn jeans and casual shirt he'd worn that day in the park. Fitting perfectly across his broad shoulders, he looked tantalizingly perfect from head to toe. In the park, he had looked rugged and strong, but tonight, he looked the part of a charming prince. His rich bronze skin was a sharp contrast to his hazel eyes. His short, cropped hair was faded lightly on the sides and his thin moustache sat atop full lips. She immediately wondered how they would feel pressed against hers.

"Earth to Christine," Stephanie said with amusement. "The answer must be 'yes' judging from that faraway look in your eyes."

"It doesn't matter what I think," Christine said, agitated that Stephanie was able to read her thoughts. "He could be married, attached, gay, a mass murderer . . ."

"Or free and single," Stephanie said.

Exasperated, Christine looked at her friend who had seen her through both the good and the bad times. Stephanie knew what happened the day Christine met him and the significance behind her dramatic new hairstyle. Understanding that her best friend only had her best interests at heart, Christine still could not allow herself to become involved with anyone. The pain would be too great. Mr. Ware was a great fantasy, but now that he was here and in living color, Christine knew there could never be anything between them. "It doesn't matter. I'm never subjecting myself to a painful relationship."

"Christine, I know it's difficult for you to see, but everybody is not Henry. It's time to move on," Stephanie said softly. "All relationships aren't the same as your parents."

"It doesn't matter," Christine answered, heading for the door. "I will never give my heart to anyone."

Stephanie knew that determined tone in Christine's voice. Contemplating whether to address this now or later, Stephanie decided later would be better. "Let's get back out to our guests."

For the remainder of the evening, Christine played the perfect hostess; talking and greeting everyone before things began to wind down.

Trying not to be too obvious, Damian watched her from across the room. Saying good-bye to Robert almost an hour before, he had stayed under the pretense of wanting to confirm his appointment. The approving expression on Robert's face told him that he wasn't fooled by that lame excuse. But Damian's anxiousness soon turned to frustration, as he realized that every time he made a move toward Christine, she somehow managed to get into a conversation with someone else.

He was at a loss as to what to do. It was becoming obvious to him that she didn't remember him, and he wasn't sure he wanted to bring up what was obviously a painful period in her life. Deciding he was only torturing himself, Damian stood to leave. Standing a few feet from the exit, he was stopped by a soft voice from behind.

"You remember, don't you?"

Damian froze as the words pierced his ears. It wasn't

Christine, because he could see her across the room talking with the other guests.

"It's OK," the voice said softly. "She remembers too."

Turning around, Damian came face to face with the woman who had returned to the reception with Christine after their initial meeting.

"Excuse me?" he replied, surprised. "What are you talking about?"

"I'm talking about a man who is watching my best friend's every move, while trying to look like he isn't, and a best friend who is doing everything in her power to avoid coming within twenty feet of anyplace he's standing."

Not knowing how to reply, Damian said nothing.

"Stephanie Jackson," she offered, along with her hand. "The official bean counter for Davenport & Associates."

"Damian Ware," he answered, hesitantly accepting her hand.

"It's nice to meet you, Damian. I'm sure you know my good friend Christine," she said.

"What makes you say that?"

"Well, you see, my dear Damian," she continued, with a playful smile, "Christine and I have been close friends for a very long time. We share *everything.*"

"Is that so?" he asked, sensing that she was enjoying this exchange with him.

"You know . . . things like the places we go, the things we do, the people we meet . . . in good and bad weather."

There was another awkward moment of silence as Damian studied Stephanie. He thought she was just as beautiful as Christine, but seemed to possess a totally different personality. While Christine wore a conservative black gown, Stephanie had opted for a red dress with a v-dip open back and decorated with multicolored sequins throughout. Her black hair was pinned up in a French roll with soft tendrils cascading down the front and sides. Stephanie was obviously outspoken, while Christine seemed reserved. Damian knew that Stephanie's outspokenness would help him if she approved of him, but would be a definite hindrance if she didn't.

"You know," Stephanie continued, rubbing her hand under her chin, as if in deep thought, "for the brief encounter you two had, the effects were definitely long-lasting."

He began to relax as he sensed her approval.

"Questions?" she asked with a raised eyebrow.

"Shoot."

"Married?"

"No."

"Attached?"

"No."

"Gay?"

He smiled. "No."

"Mass murderer?"

He laughed outright. "No."

"Stephanie, there you are," Christine interrupted as she hurried over to them. "I've been looking all over for you. I have someone I want you to meet." Reaching for Stephanie's arm, she hoped to steer her away from Damian and find out exactly what her friend had been saying to him. She knew Stephanie well and figured she probably had good reason to be embarrassed.

"What's the rush, Christine?" Stephanie asked, turning to face her with a slight grin. "Things are winding down and I've met everyone I needed to meet tonight."

"Well," Christine said through clenched teeth, "perhaps it's time we thank everyone for coming and end the evening."

Turning her attention back to Damian, Stephanie said, "Damian, you remember Christine, don't you?"

As Damian looked into Stephanie's eyes, all doubt of her intentions faded. He had an ally. For whatever reason, Stephanie was doing her best to put him together with Christine.

"Yes, as a matter of fact I do," he answered, flashing a smile that almost made Christine lose her balance.

Christine immediately understood that he was referring to their meeting three months ago, and she mentally began the process of planning Stephanie's death. *What had she said to him?*

"Well," Christine answered, flashing a lethal look at her friend who just stood there with an expression of calculated innocence. Hearing the band say good night, she said, "I guess that's our cue." Turning to Damian, she hesitated. "Um, it was nice seeing you . . . um, again." Facing her friend again, she continued with little patience, "let's go."

"Oh, no, I almost forgot," Stephanie drawled with a dramatic flair. "The catering manager offered me a free room tonight, and I think I'm going to stay."

"You never said anything about a free room when I agreed to ride with you." Christine said, trying to calm herself down. *What game was she playing now?*

"What can I say?" Stephanie said, shrugging her shoulders. "I forgot."

Damian stood there, not knowing whether to leave or stay. Obviously, something was going on. He just didn't know whether that something included him or not. Fortunately, he didn't have to wait long to get his answer.

"I got it!" Stephanie exclaimed as she snapped her fingers. "Since I'm not leaving, maybe Damian could take you home."

Damian and Christine both stood there dumbfounded. Christine found her voice first. "I'm sure Mr. Ware did not plan on this reception monopolizing his entire evening. Besides," she continued with a pleading look in her eyes, "even though Mr. Ware is a new client, we still don't know him well enough to impose on his time."

Stephanie could see that Christine was irritated, but not angry. They were as close as sisters, and she would know if she was overstepping her bounds. And while she was teetering on the line, she hadn't quite crossed it.

For three months now, all she heard was talk about this mystery man who had comforted Christine at the lowest point of her life. She had heard how fine, strong, and sensitive he was as he offered her comfort. Besides, Stephanie had spoken with Robert earlier in the evening and knew that Damian was someone who could be trusted. Her positive gut reaction to Damian gave her the encouragement to nudge Christine in his direction.

"Well," Stephanie answered, ignoring Christine's obvious agitation and looking at Damian, "I've had a chance to find out some things about Mr. Ware this evening . . . and . . . um . . . let me see . . . he's not married . . . not attached . . . not gay . . . and hasn't murdered anyone."

Christine's face grew warm as she realized what they had been discussing before she had arrived.

"Did I leave anything out?" Stephanie asked, feeling victorious.

"That about covers it," Damian answered, with a slight smile. Looking at Christine, he continued, "And taking you home would not be out of my way. I only live about twenty minutes from you."

They both stared at him in surprise.

Christine took a step forward while moving Stephanie to the side. Standing to her full five-feet six inches, her eyes pierced directly into his, and she asked, almost in a whisper, "How do you know where I live?"

Glancing at Damian, Stephanie gave him a look that said "you're on your own brother," and headed for the coat check.

Damian looked back at Christine and stared into her eyes. He read questions and confusion in them, but not fear. "Come with me," he said, gently grabbing her hand and leading her out of the ballroom. Walking in silence, they exited the hotel lobby and moved into the courtyard. There were a few couples lingering in the garden, so he led her to a gazebo which was completely deserted. He reluctantly let her hand go as they turned to face each other. Immediately, he missed the warmth her touch gave him. They stood facing each other for what seemed like an eternity. The darkness in the cool October air was naturally lit by the landscaping of white flowers. Damian took off his jacket and wrapped it around her shoulders. As she slid her arms through his coat-sleeves, he pulled her close. He could feel the stiffness in her body and the pounding of her heart.

"I remember," he whispered into her ear.

His warm breath gave her tingles as it mixed with the cool air and the intoxicating scent of his cologne. He felt her body relax, and her breathing become deeper. She wrapped her arms around his waist and rested her cheek against his chest.

"How could I forget someone as beautiful as you?" he continued, gently caressing her back. "Your face has haunted my thoughts by day and my dreams at night."

Pulling back, she looked up into his eyes. "How did you know where I live?"

Embracing her once again, he said, "I was worried about you. I thought you were in no condition to drive, especially in that weather. I followed you to make sure you got home safely."

Appreciating the sincerity reflected in his voice, she asked, "If I was in your thoughts and dreams, why didn't you contact me?"

"Because I don't want to get involved with anyone ever again." The words were out before he knew it.

She pulled completely out of his embrace. The spell was broken. He just canceled her thoughts that they should get to know each other.

"Christine, I . . ." he pleaded.

"Please take me home now," she said, removing his jacket and walking past him.

Damian silently cursed himself as he followed her through the side door and back inside the hotel lobby. Catching up with Christine at the coat check, he held out his hand for her ticket. She reluctantly gave it to him and moved toward the front entrance. Retrieving their coats, Damian helped her into hers and then they walked to the garage in complete silence.

Stopping in front of a late model Mercedes-Benz, Damian opened the passenger side door and helped Christine inside. Buckling himself in a few moments later, he started the engine and headed out onto the busy streets.

The silence in the car was unbearable for him, but she did not seem to mind. She just stared out the window, like she hadn't a care in the world.

"Do you mind if I turn on some music?"

"It's your car," she answered, without turning to face him.

The smooth jazz sounds of Jeff Majors soon filled the speakers.

Damian couldn't believe he had let those words come out of his mouth. After the deceit of Danielle, he promised himself he would never give his love to anyone again. Complete devotion was too painful. For the past three years, that promise to himself had been easy to keep. Of course, there were women who vied for his attention, but he always managed to walk away. His work had always filled the void in his life, but lately, he wondered if that was going to be enough. His business was thriving and he was enjoying the fruits of his hard labor, but now he began to think that sharing it with someone would make him complete.

Steeling a glance at Christine, Damian could see where these new thoughts came from. Holding her in his arms gave him a sense of peace he had never felt before. He knew there was something special about her from the moment he sat beside her in the park. Gripping the steering wheel, his breathing suddenly became labored as something clicked in his mind. He realized the reason he never sought her out after that fateful rain-filled day was not because he *didn't* want to get involved with anyone, but because he *did*. He wanted to get involved with Christine.

Damian also wanted to know what happened that day they first met. Why was she crying? But his questions didn't stop here. What made her laugh, what did she like to eat, and where did she like to go? He wanted to know about her family, her childhood and her relationships. The revelation hit him like a ton of bricks, and it scared him to death.

Pulling into her driveway, Damian cut the engine and waited for Christine to speak. Realizing she wasn't going to, he got out and went to the passenger side and opened her door. As they walked in silence to the door, he held out his hand for her key.

Opening her mouth to protest, she decided against it. Her emotions had been on a roller coaster ride tonight and all she wanted to do was go to sleep.

After unlocking the door, Damian pushed it open and stepped aside. Christine stepped inside, disarming her alarm system, before she turned to him and said, "Thank you for the ride, Mr. Ware. Good night."

"Christine, what I said in the gazebo . . . I want to explain."

"Don't worry about it," she interrupted, with the wave of her hand. "It's been a long day, and I just want to get some rest."

Resigned to the fact that the evening was over, he decided on another approach. "Fine, then I'll see you Monday, say ten o'clock?"

Christine looked confused.

"Davenport & Associates is still my interior design firm, and I believe that I was to meet with the president on Monday. So how about it Ms. President," he said with renewed sense of confidence, "is ten o'clock OK?"

She sighed, weary of continuing any sort of conversation with him. "Fine, Mr. Ware."

"One more thing," he said, with a sly smile as he made his way back toward his car, "Call me Damian."

Christine shut the door and, leaning against it, used it for support as she heard his car disappear down her street. Unable to move for several minutes, she replayed the evening in her mind. Just seeing Damian again excited feelings in her that she had worked to suppress over the years. But being held in his arms was almost more than she could stand. Resetting her alarm, she headed upstairs to what she hoped would be a restful night. However, with visions of a certain man flashing through her mind, she knew it was going to be anything but that.

# TWO

Entering the sanctuary a few minutes before the church service was set to start, Christine spotted Stephanie, made eye contact, and purposely turned the opposite direction and took a seat. A few minutes later, Stephanie came over and sat beside her.

"I know you aren't still mad," she said sarcastically.

When she did not get a reply, Stephanie continued. "I checked him out for you. He wasn't married, attached, gay or a mass murderer. What more could a girl ask for?"

Christine turned and stared at Stephanie as if she had lost her mind. "I'm not speaking to you," she said in an angry whisper.

"For how long?"

"What?" Christine asked, trying to keep her voice low so as to not draw attention to them.

"I want to know how long it will be before you start speaking to me. That way, I'll know when to expect the details from Friday night. Especially," Stephanie continued in a mocking voice, "since you never returned my calls yesterday."

Christine thought she should have been used to Stephanie's antics by now. Stephanie was definitely the more outgoing of the two of them. She had a passion for adventure, and Christine, with her naturally conservative demeanor, spent many days squashing some of Stephanie's craziest ideas. Sometimes, however, she threw caution to the wind and joined her in her escapades. Christine recalled Stephanie convincing her to climb Dunn's River Falls on their trip to Jamaica, as well as proving that parasailing along the coast of the Bahamas wouldn't cause permanent body damage. But Christine drew the line at skydiving. For that adventure, Stephanie had been on her own. However, Christine was on the ground waiting for her when her feet touched down.

But Stephanie's meddling with Damian was too much.

"Stephanie, you should have let me handle it. You practically forced him to spend time with me."

"If I had let you handle it, you wouldn't have said another word to him that night," Stephanie replied.

Reaching for a strand of hair, Christine quickly drew her hand back, remembering the eighteen inches that were no longer there.

Noticing the motion, Stephanie knew immediately what Christine was thinking. Reaching out to touch her friend's hand, she continued, "It's OK if you want to take a chance on a man. You have to believe that your parents' relationship was the exception. Everyone is not Henry and you're stronger than Ruth. Let it go and move on."

Looking into her best friend's eyes, Christine saw the sincerity and allowed herself a small smile.

"Friends?" Stephanie asked, stretching out her hand.

"We'll talk after you buy me dinner," she said, smiling widely for the first time that day.


Christine arrived at the office just after seven on Monday morning and spent most of that time convincing herself it was to get a jump start on her day, and not in anticipation of seeing Damian Ware again. Just because she had tried on four different suits before settling on the dark green suit with emerald buttons, did not mean that she was eagerly awaiting her ten o'clock appointment. However, she had also taken extra time with her hair and makeup. Walking down the hall to the small kitchen, she got a cup of tea and headed back to her office to begin reviewing swatches of material for pillows for a small bed and breakfast in western Maryland.

After working a couple of hours, the office began to come alive as her staff began arriving for work. It was difficult for her to concentrate on the swatches as her mind kept wandering to what might happen the next time she saw Damian. She decided to take a break and walk over to her window. Glancing down from the fifth floor, she inhaled deeply and enjoyed the reason she had chosen this ten-room office suite as the location for her business. The bare trees and hydrangea bushes surrounded a small pond that separated her building from the one next door. The light ripples in the water, visible year round, always soothed her nerves whenever she needed a quiet moment.

She thought about her past and what had brought her to this place in her life. Now, as she sipped her tea, her thoughts moved from issues of the past, to those of the present. Today's issue had a name: Damian Ware.

The phone rang and Christine stopped her reflecting and returned to her desk. "Christine Davenport."

"Christine, it's Douglas Murphy."

She closed her eyes and took a deep breath. She knew this call would come again. She had just hoped it wouldn't come so soon.

"Christine . . . are you there?"

"Yes, I'm here," she said.

"I know this has been difficult for you, but it's been three months now. We have to take care of this."

"I know . . . it's just . . . it is so difficult. I haven't been to that house in years, and with the new company . . . my time has been limited."

"I know it's not easy losing your mother, but there are still things that need to be taken care of . . . the house, her personal belongings . . . her bank accounts."

She heard the concern in his voice, and knew that he was

not only her mother's lawyer, but was also trying to be her friend. At the mention of her mother, Christine felt tears welling up in her eyes. It had been like this for months. Her emotions were so overwhelming at times when she thought about her mother, which was a contrast to when Henry, her father, died over a year ago. She hadn't shed one tear. "I know Mr. Murphy, and I appreciate your patience," she said, reaching for an invisible strand of hair. "I have a very busy week," she continued, glancing at her calendar, "but I will meet you this week to take care of my mother's financial issues, and I'll definitely go to the house in the next few weeks."

"Christine, we've made arrangements before . . ."

"I know, I know," she answered, "but this time it's for sure. I have to move on with my life."

"Fine. Why don't we tentatively plan to meet next Saturday? Let's say one o'clock?"

"Sure, one o'clock will be fine."

Christine hung up and leaned back in her chair, closing her eyes. She'd met Mr. Murphy for the first time at her mother's funeral. She was surprised when he introduced himself as her mother's attorney. Ruth had been married to Henry for over thirty years, and Christine had assumed her mother retained Mitchell Jones, Henry's attorney. Speaking with Mr. Murphy briefly during the repass, she got the feeling that he was extremely familiar with her mother and her affairs. Christine wondered how long the relationship between them had been going on . . . and exactly what type of relationship they had. She also questioned whether Henry knew about Mr. Murphy.

Christine began rubbing her temples. Every time she thought of Henry, her pulse accelerated, signaling the beginning of a headache. Growing up, she never understood why her mother stayed with him. The day she left for college, she gave up trying. Since then, their mother-daughter relationship stretched almost beyond repair. When Henry died,

Christine sent her condolences, but had no intention of attending the services. The day before his funeral, her mother called and begged her to come. She went, but her heart was cold and her eyes were dry.

Rising from her chair, Christine sought out peace from her favorite view, wondering if she had the strength to get through this. She hadn't been back to that house since she left for college. She couldn't bear the memories.

Although Henry never got violent with Christine, his verbal abuse was enough to terrify and intimidate her to the point that she would have preferred a physical blow. Christine wondered why her mother allowed her only child to suffer from his vicious verbal attacks.

She had posed this question to Ruth on many occasions and asked her mother for the last time the day she left for college.

*"Mama, I don't understand why you won't come with me?"*

*"Sweetheart," she answered, cupping Christine's face in her hands, "I can't go with you. This is your chance to live. You don't need your ol' mama hanging around. Besides, your father needs me."*

*"Why do you stay with him?" she begged, biting her lip to keep from crying. "He treats us like . . ."*

*"Watch your mouth, young lady," she said forcibly. "You're too young to understand. I love him dear . . . I love him."*

"Love," she whispered, continuing to gaze out the window, "who the hell needs it."

"Is that a rhetorical question?"

Turning around, her breath took a sharp intake as Damian's arresting good looks captured her full attention. Never had she felt such an immediate attraction to someone. That day in the park, she felt a connection to him the moment he sat beside her. She often dreamed of meeting him again, and now that he was back in her life, she didn't know what she wanted to do with him. When she saw him at the reception, she tried to convince herself that she didn't care about getting to know him. But when he held her in his arms in the gazebo, her resolve began to dissipate and the thought of getting to know him better grew stronger. But his declaration of not wanting to get involved with her served to jolt her back to reality. But even so, she hadn't been able to erase him from her mind.

Dressed in dark blue slacks and a white button-down shirt, his casual stance was attractive and alluring.

"I'm sorry for just walking in, but I saw Stephanie getting off the elevator, and she directed me to your office and told me to go right on in."

"The jury would never find me guilty . . ." she whispered under her breath.

"I heard that," he said with a smile. "I'm sure she was just trying to be helpful."

Motioning him to the conference table, she said, "I would never try to guess Stephanie's motives. Anyway, we can get started."

The next hour was spent reviewing the vision Damian had for his office. Christine found herself caught up in his excitement as he talked about his plans for not only the design of his office space, but his company in general. She liked to ask her clients many questions to get a feel for their personality, style and flavor.

She envisioned a contemporary style with bright colors and comfortable seating; the reception area and the individual offices would make their own statement. However, the overall theme of colors would blend naturally. Damian wholeheartedly agreed with her vision and made some suggestions that could add a personal touch to the offices. They agreed the next step would be to tour his facility to see the layout.

"Now that we've almost wrapped up, can I ask you a question?" he said.

"You want to know how much this is going to cost you?"

she asked with a smile, rising from the conference table and heading toward her desk.

"No, I just want to know why you don't need love," he asked casually, rising himself and following her.

Taken aback by his question, Christine decided to turn the tables.

"The same reason you don't," she replied, facing him.

"Who said I didn't need love?" he asked, moving a step closer toward her.

"You did, on Friday night."

Remembering his comment that had destroyed the bond they had begun to form, he said with confidence, "I've changed by mind."

"Excuse me?" she asked, obviously startled by his response.

"I said I've changed my mind. I do need love," he said intently.

"Well, good for you. I hope you get it," she said smartly, annoyed that he stood so near, causing an unwelcome stir of excitement in her.

"So, why don't you need love?" he asked again, taking another step closer.

Christine thought of a smart reply, but then decided to be honest. "Love is sacrifice, all consuming, losing yourself to another, relinquishing who you are . . ."

"I say," he interrupted in a low and purposely seductive voice, "love is sharing, caring, giving, taking, trusting, happiness, joyfulness, and definitely sexually satisfying."

Captivated by his voice, she took a deep, unsteady breath and stepped back, only to find that she was up against her desk.

Leaning forward, he whispered in her ear, "Have you ever been in love, Christine Davenport?"

She had no idea how sensuous her name could sound until she heard it coming from his lips. Barely able to shake her head from side to side, she swallowed deliberately, shaken by the emotions his nearness stirred.

"So, how do you know?"

Suddenly anxious to escape from his disturbing presence, Christine stepped around him and walked over to the window and gazed down at the pond below, hoping to gather her thoughts. Betrayed by her body's reaction to him, her mind fought for control. Taking a deep breath, she asked, "Have you ever been in love?"

Putting his hands in his pocket, he answered honestly, "I thought I was."

"And how would you describe it?"

Remembering Danielle's deception, he cursed under his breath.

Turning to face him, Christine insisted, "Well, I'm waiting, Mr. Fairytales."

Not wanting to lie, he said quietly, "It was just as you described it, but . . ."

"No buts, Mr. Ware. You proved my point," she said, somewhat disappointed. Somewhere deep inside, she wanted to believe all the good things he said about love were true.

Understanding about her touched him, as he saw her disappointment. Moving toward her, he reached out and gently touched her arm which sent a quiet shiver through him. "I did forget one thing about love."

"And what would that be?" she asked, trying to ignore the goose bumps rising on her skin from his touch.

He nudged her closer, trailing his fingers lightly up her arms. "It has to be with the right person."

Continuing in a soft, seductive voice, he said, "It could be that we just haven't met them yet."

Feeling his gaze bear into her in silent expectation, Christine was powerless to break the spell. She stood still, allowing his hypnotic voice to take control of her.

Leaning forward, just inches from her lips, he continued in a broken whisper, "or maybe we have."

The sound of his cell phone ringing broke the spell and Christine angrily stepped away. "How dare you?" she said, agitated that she had allowed herself to be drawn to him so easily.

"How dare I what?" he asked, confused at her sudden change in her attitude. Ignoring his phone, he waited for a response.

"How dare you come in here," she answered, pacing the floor in front of her desk like a trapped lion, "asking me personal questions, making me feel . . ."

Noticing the hesitation in her voice, Damian decided to push for an answer. "Making you feel what, Christine?"

"It doesn't matter," she answered, reaching for the notes she took of their meeting. "The relationship between us is business and I would appreciate you sticking to that topic."

Suppressing his irritation at being given the brush-off, he decided to abide by her request . . . for now. "OK, Christine. We'll play it your way."

"Fine," she answered curtly.

"What time should I pick you up this afternoon?"

"Pick me up?" she repeated, confusion in her voice.

"Yes, we agreed that you would view the office this af-ternoon but we just needed to confirm a time."

"Fine, Mr. Ware," she said, taking a quick glance at her calendar. "Four-thirty is good for me . . . and I have the ad-dress so I'll meet you there as I normally do with all my clients."

Damian gathered his briefcase and jacket as he headed for the door. "I'll use my cell phone in the lobby. And Christine," he continued, curving the corners of his mouth, "please call me Damian."

After making sure he was gone, Christine shut her door and plopped unceremoniously onto her chair. As she reached for a strand of hair to play with, she closed her eyes and relived the moment that almost happened. Never in her life had she felt such raw attraction for a man. If his phone hadn't rang, she would have kissed him! She hardly knew the man. As a matter of fact, she didn't know him at all. She should never have allowed him to take such liberties with her, but the sound of his voice, the intoxication of his cologne, and the heat radiating from his body was too much to take. How was she going to make it through this project? She would just have to remember that this was strictly business. Whatever physical attraction she felt toward Damian would definitely fade in time. She just had to let it run its course and then everything would be fine.

Damian tried to get his emotions under control as he made the thirty-minute drive to his office. While his mouth ached from being denied the opportunity to kiss Christine, he also knew it was too soon. There was something going on with her that he was not aware of. The anger she displayed in her office could not have been about the kiss, or even about him. Something else caused that reaction . . . or someone. Could she have been hurt before?

Turning into the garage of his building, he realized he still did not know what happened that day in the park. Did she lose someone? A husband? A boyfriend? Or a child? At these thoughts, Damian squeezed the steering wheel so hard his knuckles turned white. Feeling his fingers go numb, he released his hold and silently berated himself for not realizing that Christine may need time to recover from such a tragic event. Patience would be the key to winning Christine. He decided to take his time and show her that she had a friend in him. He knew gaining her trust and confidence could take a while, but he knowingly smiled to himself. Christine Davenport would be worth the wait.

As he road the elevator up to the tenth floor, Damian felt a surge of pride course through him. The growth of his company had been phenomenal. After recovering from a setback his third year in business, he'd secured contracts to carry him through the next seven years, and had several bids out for more business. As he moved through the space that was now filled with gray walls and carpet, he visualized the changes that Christine would make. She would add color and brightness to these rooms, and possibly, his life. Checking his watch, he decided to go down to the deli in the lobby and grab a late lunch before his appointment with Christine.

Stephanie paused at the door when she saw Christine was on the phone, but entered her office and took a seat after Christine waved her in.

"Yes, Ms. Vanderpool, I know we agreed to have the fabrics for your drapes today, but I have no control over the traffic. The delay is caused by a major accident on the beltway. The courier is stuck," she answered in her most professional voice. "It's only two o'clock now, but I expect delivery by close of business."

As she watched her, Stephanie knew she was getting a lecture on proper business practices. Cynthia Vanderpool, another referral from Mr. Dilliard, had a completely different personality from him. They belonged to the same country club, and Cynthia, who had always used a well established firm to handle her decorating needs, decided to give Davenport & Associates a try. She constantly referred to this project as their audition.

Christine rolled her eyes heavenward as she listened to the retired school superintendent. Feeling like a schoolgirl in the principal's office, she answered, "Delivering the fabrics today will not be possible, as I already have appointments scheduled. Why don't I bring them to you first thing tomorrow, say ten o'clock?"

Hearing the lull in conversation, Stephanie retained a chuckle. Judging by the scrunched-up expression on Christine's face, she knew she didn't like what she was hearing.

"Well, since eight o'clock is 'first thing' for you, I'll see you then."

Hanging up the phone, Christine made a sound that was a cross between a groan and a sigh. "That woman's sole purpose in life is to make mine difficult."

"Well, this is the final stage of her project. Once the drapes are finished, we can kiss the wonderful Cynthia Vanderpool good-bye," Stephanie said with a smile.

Moving to the conference table, the two spent the next hour reviewing the financial statements for the month. As usual, Stephanie had everything in order. When they first met in college, most people thought that they were too different to become anything more than acquaintances, but something between them clicked, and they quickly hit it off. While Stephanie got a degree in accounting, Christine finished with a B.S. in business. Stephanie went on to work for a large marketing company and quickly rose to the position of chief financial officer. Christine graduated and went straight on to design school. They had always joked about working together, running their own business and taking on the world. Now, it was a reality. Christine smiled. Things were finally looking up.

"What's that look for?" Stephanie asked, pleased to see her friend smiling. "It wouldn't have anything to do with a handsome new client?"

At the thought of Damian, her expression faltered. "Mr. Ware and I met this morning to talk about his decorative vision for his office. We'll be meeting this afternoon to take measurements and discuss preliminary color schemes."

"Your mouth speaks professional, but your eyes say personal," Stephanie replied knowingly.

"Speaking of personal, whatever happened to you and Nathan?" Christine asked.

"Don't even try to change the subject," Stephanie answered sternly. "We are not talking about my personal life. We are talking about yours."

"Well, it will be a very short conversation because when it comes to Mr. Ware, there is nothing personal to discuss," Christine said, looking down at her notepad and doodling in the margin.

"Ah-hah!" Stephanie yelled, causing her friend to jump out of her seat.

"What!"

"Every time you . . . how do I say this . . . lie . . . you can't look me in the eye and you either start doodling or twist your hair," Stephanie said triumphantly. "So spill the beans on you and Mr. Ware."

"What are you talking . . . you can't judge my truthfulness by a few unrelated actions."

"After I broke up with Kevin in college, I got drunk and couldn't go to work. I asked you to call my boss and tell him I had to go home for an emergency. The whole time you were speaking to him, you looked down at the floor and twisted your hair. When I begged you to tell my English professor that I couldn't do my oral presentation because I had a case of laryngitis, you never looked her in the eye, and you scribbled on your notebook cover the entire time you talked. Then, when I asked you . . ."

"OK, OK," Christine said laughing. "It's a wonder you ever graduated from college. But fortunately, I have an appointment, so we'll have to continue this conversation at another time."

Joining in the laughter, Stephanie gathered her files and headed for the door. "I'll let you get away this time, but next time . . ."

Easing behind the wheel of her four-door Lexus, Christine headed north, toward Damian's office. Observing the darkening skies, she turned on the news and confirmed that a storm was headed their way. She laughed after hearing the report. It was as if storms and Damian went hand-in-hand.

Following Damian's instructions, Christine found the building easily. The modern glass exterior looked impressive. Exiting the elevator on the tenth floor, she immediately took inventory of the reception area. The gray carpet would have to go, the wood reception desk was outdated, but the chairs, if reupholstered, could be saved.

Hearing voices coming from down the hall, she followed the sound, hoping to find Damian. As she came closer to one of the offices, two people emerged, laughing at a private joke.

Stopping short in surprise, she watched as Damian strode toward her, his arms locked through the arms of a very attractive woman. She thought their behavior familiar, and while she hated to admit it, she felt a twinge in her stomach that strongly resembled jealousy. Reaching for a strand of hair for comfort, she cleared her throat to gain their attention.

"Christine," Damian said with a smile, "we didn't hear you come in."

"We did have an appointment," she said in her most professional voice. "So, here I am."

"Let me introduce you. Christine Davenport, this is Tanya Kennedy, my contract administrator."

*Contract Administrator?* Christine had not thought about what type of staff Damian might have, especially if they included attractive, female employees. Her cinnamon-brown hair rested on her shoulders, and her golden-bronze skin was smooth and clear. She wore a stylish silk pantsuit that would have been about two sizes too small for Christine, who wore a size ten. Feeling ashamed of what she was about to do, she was helpless to stop herself. She averted her eyes quickly to the woman's left hand and noticed no ring. Immediately, warning bells sounded in Christine's head. She was checking out the competition for a contest she didn't know if she even wanted to be in.

Putting her best face forward, she shook hands with the woman. "How nice to meet you, Ms. Kennedy."

"Oh, please," she said with the wave of her hand, "call me Tanya." Turning to Damian, she passed a secretive smile and said, "See you tomorrow . . . nice meeting you, Christine."

Trying to control her newfound emotions, Christine turned away from Damian's penetrating gaze before he could say anything and headed in the direction from which she'd come. "Why don't we start the tour in the reception area?" she suggested.

Taking large steps to catch to catch up with her, Damian asked, "Is there a problem?"

"No problem, Mr. Ware. I just want to complete the tour and take my notes so I can be home before the storm." When she didn't get a response, she continued, "Shall we begin?"

# THREE

There was definitely a problem, and Damian knew it. They had viewed almost all of the offices, and while Christine had vigorously taken notes, jotting down measurements, sketches and color schemes, she said little else. Their final stop was slated to be Tanya's office. He watched her walk around and stop in front of a window. Not quite six o'clock, the sky was dark as midnight and the faint sounds of thunder could be heard in the distance. He was pleased with all her ideas, but after several minutes in this office, she had yet to speak.

Leaning against the door, he took this opportunity to study her. She looked elegant in the green business suit with matching pumps. Her skirt, stopping just above the knees, showed off long, well-toned and sexy legs. Her jewelry consisted of diamond earrings and a matching pendant. He watched her reach her hand up to her hair, and then she abruptly placed her hand back at her side. She shook her head, as if clearing her thoughts. He had so many unanswered questions about her. *Would she ever open up to him?*

"So what do you think of this space?" he asked, moving toward her.

When she turned to face him, he felt the now expected tightening in his stomach. She had to be the most beautiful woman in the world. She stood about five-feet six inches and was a perfect fit for him. He had to remind himself to be patient and understand that the first step would be to gain her friendship.

"Are you sure that Tanya wouldn't prefer to decorate her own office? Most women enjoy adding their own personal touch."

"I engaged your services for the entire office. Besides, I have several women who work for me. If I was going to let each one of them add 'their own touch,' you would be left with about half of this space to decorate."

Suddenly, Christine was not in the mood to continue. Hearing that he had several women working for him did nothing to improve her mood. Speculating on the relationship between Tanya and Damian was irrational, she knew, but she couldn't stop herself. She saw them together for less than three minutes, yet, she couldn't deny the two seemed extremely friendly. Without much creative enthusiasm, Christine took a quick look around, jotted down a few meaningless notes and headed for the door. "I think I have all I need for now. I'll begin pulling samples for your review in the next couple of weeks."

As he followed her to the reception area, Damian made a quick stop in his office and grabbed his jacket and briefcase. When he returned to the lobby, Christine had already pushed the down button for the elevator and stood staring at the door, aimlessly tapping her pen against her portfolio.

"Is it necessary for you to rush off? I was hoping we could have dinner together."

Just then, they heard a clash of thunder.

Relieved at having an excuse, Christine replied, "I think it's best if I get home, Mr. Ware. I don't want to be caught in the storm."

They stepped into the elevator together. The doors closed and they descended in an uncomfortable silence. Passing the sixth floor, they felt a jerk that caused them both to lose their balance. Bumping into each other, Damian wrapped his arms around Christine's waist to prevent her from falling. The elevator came to an abrupt stop.

"What happened?" Christine asked, with a slight tremor in her voice.

"Don't worry," Damian answered, reluctantly releasing her. "It looks like we're stuck, but I'll call for help." Pulling his cell phone out of his pocket, he dialed the number posted on the elevator wall.

Damian spoke to the building engineer who informed him that it shouldn't take long to get the elevator moving again, but to remain calm.

"It may be a power outage," Damian said. When he didn't get a response, Damian looked over at Christine as his eyes adjusted to the soft emergency lighting. He watched as she slowly began to move backwards, stopping only when she bumped up against the elevator wall. Her hands began to reach about wildly. When she finally found the railing, he watched her grip become deathlike around it and her breathing become erratic.

"Christine, what is it?"

Her eyes darted back and forth wildly and she shook her head from side to side. Seeing the expression of sheer panic on her face, Damian quickly moved into action. Grabbing her, he began to try and pry her hands off of the railing.

"It's OK," he started in a soft, soothing voice. "I'm right here with you. I just want you to relax. Take a deep breath."

Seeing no change, he stepped directly in front of her. "Look at me, Christine. Breathe." When he saw her eyes focus in on him, he was encouraged. "That's it, breathe with me." Taking deep breaths, her breathing rhythm fell in with his. Inhale. Exhale. Inhale. Exhale. "Good, that's it. I'm right here with you."

Damian had never been in a situation like this before, but he understood that he had just found out that Christine was claustrophobic. He swore under his breath when he realized he had to keep her calm. Easing his arms around her, Damian continued to speak encouraging words to her. "Why don't we sit down and get comfortable?"

Looking lost for a moment, Christine shook her head "yes," and he eased her down to the floor. Damian leaned back against the wall and opening his legs, he sat Christine in between them. She rested her head against his chest. Feeling the tenseness in her body, Damian searched his mind for a way to take her mind off their current situation.

"Have you ever been to Jamaica?"

When he did not get a response, he continued. "I haven't been, but Michael, one of my field supervisors, has been. He said it was beautiful. He stayed in Montego Bay and said there was nothing but wide open space, warm beaches, beautiful sunrises and breathtaking sunsets. I think the resort where he stayed was featured in *Travel & Leisure Magazine*."

Feeling her body relax a little, he sighed with relief and continued, "Now, I have been to the Bahamas. Talk about the best snorkeling. I swam with colorful fish, stingrays, dolphins, sharks, seals . . ." Her soft laugh was music to his ears.

"Dolphins and sharks?" she asked in disbelief.

"Why Christine Davenport," he said with a bad southern accent, "I do believe I hear doubt in your voice."

As she slowly relaxed, they began to talk about the places they had traveled to and the places they still wanted to go.

Damian, fighting the reaction his body was having to her closeness, knew this was not the time to allow his hormones to take control. What she needed was comfort. He ignored the fact that the faint smell of her fragrance was driving him crazy with desire. Wrapping his arms around her, he focused on his objective which was to help her through this ordeal.

Just then, they heard the elevator motor and a split second later, they started to drop. The only thing he heard was Christine's scream.

Immediately, the elevator came to another stop, and Christine began to struggle out of Damian's arms in an effort to stand up. "Oh my God, oh my God, I've got to get out of here!"

Standing as well, Damian reached for her just as they heard a male voice. "Are you folks all right in there?"

"Yes, yes!" Christine yelled.

"We'll have the elevator moving in a few minutes."

Watching her rock from one foot to the other, Damian knew she was petrified. He wasn't sure how much longer she would hold up. "It will just be a minute," he whispered in her ear.

"You don't understand, I have to get out of here," she said with more pleading in her voice than fear. "I'm afraid."

Overrun with emotion, Damian's heart went out to her. Pulling her closely into him, he continued to rub her back as he whispered calming words into her ear. "I would never let anything happen to you. I'm right here to protect you."

A few moments later, the lights came on and the elevator began moving again, stopping on the lobby floor. The doors opened and they were greeted by several engineers and maintenance men.

After assuring everyone that they were all right, Damian led Christine to the stairwell and down to the garage. Damian led a quiet Christine to his car.

"Get in, I'm taking you home," he said.

Damian was unsure of what to do as they rode in complete silence. She hadn't spoken any words since they left his office building, and he wondered if she was in some sort of trance from the trauma she had just endured. Pulling into her driveway, he cut off the car engine. Holding out his hand, she reached into her purse and handed him her house keys.

Once inside the foyer, he said, "I'll make you some tea. Where's the kitchen?"

As she lead him down the hallway, the only noise came from her heels clicking against the polished hardwood floors. Entering the kitchen on the left, she then headed for the pantry.

"Since neither one of us has eaten, I'll just fix us something."

Relief flooded into him at her words. He wasn't sure what he expected her to say, but he was glad she had said something. "That sounds great. Let me help."

They worked together in comfortable silence as she broiled two steaks and baked potatoes. He fixed a salad and set the table. Noticing how comfortably he worked in her kitchen, Christine found it hard to believe it was Damian's first time there. She smiled and quickly realized she could get used to having him around.

After they had eaten most of their meal in silence, Christine asked, "I guess you want to know what happened back in that elevator?"

"Actually, I was wondering something . . . can I ask you a question?" he said, wanting to take advantage of the personal time they had.

"No."

Surprised at her response, Damian was silent for several moments. "Why not?"

Taking a deep breath, she said, "The last time you said that, we got onto subjects I don't care to discuss."

Staring into her big, brown eyes, he smiled. "I promise, no questions on love."

Pausing a moment, Damian continued. "Why did you cut your hair?"

She was startled. Knowing his efforts were to take her mind off the experience she just had, he had just stumbled upon the very reason for her panic attack in the elevator. It had been years since she had experienced one that severe and she rationalized that it was due to dealing with the death of both her parents in such a short period of time, her new business, and the stir of emotions caused by the man sitting directly across from her.

Most of Christine's friends and colleagues accepted her new look as just a change in her outer appearance. Only

Stephanie truly understood the significance of the new hairstyle. Taking her time, Christine debated whether she could open herself up to Damian and reveal a very personal part of her life.

Seeing the struggle play across her face, Damian remained silent. Hoping she would trust him with her answer, he waited patiently.

"The day you saw me in the park was the day my mother died," Christine calmly began. "About a year before her death, Henry died." Seeing the confusion on his face, she answered his unasked question. "Henry was my father, whose sole purpose in life was to make my mother's life hell." She paused a moment, swallowing hard to keep the tears at bay.

"This is becoming a terrible habit for me . . . crying on your shoulder," she said, trying to lighten the mood with a joke.

Smiling, Damian replied, "I actually think you were made for my shoulder. You're a perfect fit."

Looking up, Christine smiled, and his heart soared. He hated her tears, but adored her smile.

Seeing that he had drudged up painful memories, he said, "If you don't want to continue. . . ."

Christine placed her fork down and pushed back from the table. "No, I'm OK. Henry was abusive to my mother and it nearly drove me crazy. Nothing my mother did was ever good enough. His food was too cold, the temperature in the room was too hot. His clothes weren't pressed properly and the house was never cleaned the way he liked it. There were times when he directed his anger toward me, but for the most part, he spewed his venom at my mom."

"Growing up, Henry had this image of what a woman's appearance was supposed to be. He was extremely meticulous about how he wanted us to behave, dress and look. One thing that he despised was short hair and he never allowed my mother to cut my hair. When I was seven years old, my mother began receiving *Ebony* magazine. I became intrigued by the fashion section. All the glamorous women and the colorful clothes began my interest in design. I found myself sketching my own designs and creating outfits I hoped would be worn by top fashion models one day.

"One day, an issue arrived with a spread on the 'natural look.' This article featured women who had natural hairstyles, braids, cornrows and afros. I saw Deanna Bishop, a top fashion model, wearing a small bush, and I wanted that hair." She paused a moment and reached for a napkin. She hated that she was crying, but she felt tears were finally going to set her free.

"By this time, my hair had grown down to the center of my back. I begged my mother for weeks to let me cut my hair. I had been wearing it in ponytails all my life, but I was determined to do something different. Finally, my mother gave in, even though she knew she was going against her husband for the first time. She ripped the photo out of the magazine and took me to the salon. After my hair was cut, I gazed in the mirror at my reflection and loved what I saw. I believed I was the most beautiful person in the world. That all changed the minute Henry arrived home from work."

"One look at me and his face grew dark with anger. He called my mother a stupid, ignorant fool for allowing me do it. Then, he turned to me and said 'you are the ugliest thing I ever laid eyes on. Who would ever want someone as ugly as you?' He told me he couldn't stand the sight of me and grabbed my arm and threw me into the basement storage room which was about half the size of that elevator. He left me there for two days. He told my mother if she let me out, he would send me away . . . and I guess she believed him, because she only came to give me food." She dried her eyes and looked up at Damian.

"He took the one thing that made me feel good about myself and turned it into something ugly. From that day forward, I stopped calling him Daddy and started calling him

Henry. You know what? I don't even think he cared." Standing up, she began clearing the table. "It's funny though, but I never cut my hair again. I hated him, but in some sick, twisted way, I wanted to please him."

Damian followed her into the kitchen with his dishes, but did not say anything. She relished the quiet strength he was giving her.

"After he died, I thought about my hair constantly. A few weeks before my mom died, she told me I had to forgive him and move on with my life and not let him steal happiness from me. She told me that it was OK to not be angry anymore. Those words stayed with me, and the day of her funeral, I did it. I cut it all off."

Turning around to face him, her face was dry and the corners of her mouth began to curve into a smile. "Of course, it's not quite an Afro, but I have never felt so free in my entire life."

Stepping in front of her, Damian's gaze lowered and so did his voice. "I think, Christine Davenport, that you are the most beautiful woman in the world." Leaning forward, he hesitated in order to give her a chance to pull away. She didn't. The kiss was surprisingly gentle, as if he didn't want to hurt her. His soft touch sent shockwaves throughout her entire body, and Christine found herself leaning into him, demanding more. Feeling reckless, she latched her hands behind his neck and allowed him full access to her hungry desire. Drinking in the sweetness of his taste, she was lost to everything around her.

The ringing of the telephone caused her to jump out of his arms. This time, Damian was relieved when he saw no anger reflected in her eyes.

Pulling herself together, she picked up the phone. "Christine, I'm glad I finally got you. I've been trying to reach you all afternoon."

"Mr. Murphy? What can I do for you?"

"I got a letter today from Jackson, Stewart & Taylor," the attorney answered. "A law firm."

"I've never heard of them. What's this about?"

"It's about your mother's estate. There's a chance it might be contested."

Christine turned to Damian with a shocked look on her face. He rushed to her side, knowing whatever she was being told was not good news.

"By whom? Both sets of my grandparents are gone. My mother was an only child, and Henry's sister passed away five years ago."

"It's coming from a Margaret Donovan . . ." his voice trailed off as he tried to find the right words.

"I don't know a Margaret Donovan," Christine said, quickly scanning her memory for a distant relative. "No one in my family has the last name Donovan."

"It's not a family member . . . I mean, she's not related."

"What are you trying to tell me, Mr. Murphy? Just please, spit it out."

Hearing a heavy sigh on the other end, Christine's worry level increased.

"Margaret Donovan claims to be your father's mistress. She is also the mother of one daughter . . . she says that Henry is the father."

"Daughter . . ." Christine said softly.

"Christine, it's only a claim. I have yet to see any proof."

"Henry had another daughter . . ." she said again with wonder.

"I've already requested official documentation that supports this claim."

Feeling overwhelmed, Christine remained quiet as she digested the information.

"Christine, are you still there?"

"Yes, I'm here."

"I know this is a shock. If you want, I can come by and we can talk further. I don't want you to have to deal with this alone." He hesitated a moment and then continued, "And neither would your mother."

"That's not necessary," she said, attempting to sound strong. "Besides, what is there to contest?" she asked bewildered. "Henry drank his money as fast as he could make it. His insurance money went to cover mom's medical bills. The only thing she had was the house."

"That's what I've been trying to meet with you about . . . your mother's estate."

Noticing the hesitation in his voice, Christine knew she was in store for some more unexpected news. She waited for the next bomb to drop.

"Christine, your mother has over a million dollars in stocks and cash."

# FOUR

Christine turned onto her side and punched her pillow. Glancing at the time on the night-stand clock, she pressed her lips together in frustration. It was just after three A.M. and she was no closer to sleep than she was when she got into bed four hours earlier. She recalled Damian being puzzled by her abrupt change of attitude when she asked him to leave shortly after she got off the phone with Mr. Murphy. His eyes had searched her face, trying to reach into her thoughts and wondering what happened to the closeness they had just shared. But for Christine, the news of Henry's betrayal brought to the surface her feelings of distrust toward men.

Sitting up, Christine stared blankly into the darkness for several moments. She turned on the small Tiffany lamp beside the bed, and the bedroom, decorated in soft shades of blue, suddenly became encased in a light glow. Usually, the room decor soothed her after a stressful day, but this time, it wasn't working. Closing her eyes, she cringed and felt a chill as she remembered the tension that filled the house she grew up in. Her mother worked relentlessly to keep the house spotless, not knowing what small thing would set Henry off. A hot tear rolled down her cheek as she recalled her mother reprimanding her for making too much noise when Henry was trying to rest.

She recalled the times she had quietly stood at the entrance to her mother's room, listening to her pray for strength and patience, until the day when her love and adoration would overtake his mean and evil streak. But her prayers were never answered. Henry died a mean and spiteful man. And now, Christine was left to deal with his ultimate betrayal. A mistress. A daughter. A half sister. She knew that Mr. Murphy had said the claim could be false, but deep inside, Christine knew Henry Davenport was capable of all the charges levied against him.

She slipped on her silk robe and walked slowly down the stairs to the kitchen. Combating the strain of the emotional ride she had taken today, she popped two aspirins to deter the onset of a major headache. Recalling the panic attack in the elevator, the kiss she had shared with Damian, and finally, the call informing her of Henry's deception and her mother's money, she hurriedly emptied the remainder of her water in the sink and headed back upstairs. How in the world did Ruth Davenport manage to hide a million dollars from her? What had been going on in her mother's life during the years they had been estranged? Christine's eyebrows furrowed in a frown and she realized she had absolutely no idea.

When she left for college, she had severed the fragile ties she had with her mother. She had rarely come home, and when she had, she'd stayed with friends. Christine couldn't understand why her mother continued to subject herself to Henry's verbal and physical abuse.

As a child, Christine sought refuge from the screaming and yelling matches between her parents. Huddling in the corner of her room, she held tightly to her stuffed bear and waited for the drama to end. Time and time again, she listened to Henry tell her mother that she was nothing without him. Hearing this, Christine made a promise to herself, that no man would ever control her.

After he died, Ruth had attempted to repair their severely damaged mother-daughter relationship. Wanting the same, Christine had responded positively to her mother's attempts and their relationship began to prosper. Then, nine months later, her mother was diagnosed with inoperable cancer. Christine fought to control the gamut of emotions as she recalled sitting in the doctor's office hearing the news. Three months later, her mother was dead.

Christine had felt her heart being ripped apart when she got the call from the hospital to come immediately. She drove like a maniac and made it to the hospital in record time, and it was an act of God that she didn't get pulled over and charged with reckless endangerment. Once inside deep sobs racked her body as she held her dead mother's hand. Ten minutes. She had missed saying good-bye by ten minutes. She was too late; too late to continue building their relationship, too late for more laughs, and too late for that cruise they had talked about taking. But mostly, it was too late to tell her mother she was sorry. Still, the guilt of those ten minutes weighed heavily on Christine's heart.

Shaking off the memories, Christine turned out the light. *One million dollars. Where did her mother get that kind of money?* Slipping back under the covers, Christine had no answers. However, she was sure of one thing, and that was that the money belonged to her mother, and no ex-mistress of Henry's or his daughter were going to get their hands on one red cent. Feeling empowered by that declaration, Christine closed her eyes and prayed for a few hours sleep.

Christine opened her eyes slowly, hearing the distant sounds of a ringing phone. *Who was calling her in the middle of the night?* Reaching wildly for the phone on her nightstand, she missed and moaned as she heard the phone crashing against the hardwood floors.

"Hel . . . lo," she panted in a broken whisper.

"Christine? Is that you?"

"Damian?" she asked. "Why are you calling me in the middle of the night?"

Damian drew a deep breath. The low, sultry voice wrapped

him in an invisible warmth. He had spent a restless night, tossing and turning, with visions of Christine dancing through his mind.

"Christine, I was calling because your car is at my office and I didn't know your schedule."

She took a quick peek at the nightstand and gasped. Her clock read 7:03. She shuddered inwardly. Ms. Vanderpool! How was she ever going to make her appointment? It was logistically impossible for her to go to her office to retrieve the fabrics and get to Ms. Vanderpool's by 8:00 A.M.

"What is it Christine?"

Sitting up, she flung the covers off. "Damian, I gotta go. I'm late . . . I need to . . ." she began breathlessly.

"Christine, calm down. That's why I'm calling. You're not going anywhere. Your car is at my office."

Christine stopped what she was doing and sat down on the bed. "I'm never going to make it now," she moaned.

"Slow down, Christine. What's going on?"

Christine quickly explained her dilemma.

"No problem. I'm at a job site not ten minutes from your office. I can pick up the fabrics for you. Just call a car service and go straight to your client's home. I'll meet you there. Is there someone at your office who knows what fabrics to give me?"

Christine made quick work of giving Damian her assistant's name and Ms. Vanderpool's address. She was grateful that her assistant lived just ten minutes from the office and agreed to meet Damian. Dressing quickly in a plum DKNY pantsuit, she was out the door in twenty-five minutes. If traffic was on her side, she would only be about five minutes late.

Unfortunately, traffic was heavy and the black Lincoln town car turned into the gated driveway at eight twenty, parking just behind a dark blue pickup truck. Her mouth curled into a smile upon seeing the emblem on the door introducing Ware Construction Company. At least the fabrics were here.

If she was lucky, the tongue lashing regarding unprofessional behavior would be short and Ms. Vanderpool would have already made her selection.

Christine's steps slowed the closer she got to the front door of the century old mansion in Northwest Washington DC. Christine had learned early in their professional relationship that there were few things Ms. Vanderpool tolerated, and tardiness was not one of them. Squaring her shoulders and reaching the large wooden double door, she raised her hand to ring the bell, when the door suddenly swung open. Startled, Christine prepared herself for Cynthia Vanderpool's wrath.

"Good morning, Ms. Davenport," Sarah, the housekeeper, said as she stepped aside to allow Christine to enter.

"Good morning, Sarah," Christine answered calmly. She had spoken to Sarah on several occasions since starting this project, and decided to take advantage of their friendly exchanges. "How is your boss doing this morning?"

Sarah gave Christine an encouraging smile before she turned and walked through the marble foyer. Christine took a deep breath and followed, rehearsing her excuse for her late arrival. She only hoped that Damian had not been too inconvenienced by this unplanned stop and the rude reception he more than likely was receiving from Ms. Vanderpool.

Stepping aside, Sarah motioned for Christine to enter the library. Lifting her chin and pasting on a smile she hoped looked sincere, Christine stepped in, only to be abruptly stopped by a strange sound: laughter. Ms. Vanderpool was laughing. Christine racked her brain trying to recall if at any time during their meetings, she had ever heard that sound. Taking a step further into the room, she cleared her throat with emphasis, alerting the occupants of her arrival.

"Christine, darling. Come in, come in," Ms. Vanderpool drawled sweetly.

*Darling?*

"I understand you had some unforeseen circumstances

that delayed your arrival. I do hope that everything is all right," she added with a look of sincere concern.

Christine wondered if she had just entered the twilight zone. All of her dealings with Ms. Vanderpool had been polite, but never friendly. Ms. Vanderpool never engaged in idle chatter. Cynthia Vanderpool's only concern had been making sure the job was finished and letting Christine know that she was in charge.

From the outset, it looked as if everything was the same. Ms. Vanderpool's completely gray hair was pulled back into its normal, tight bun. Her reading glasses hung on a gold chain around her neck. The blue, double-breasted St. John's suit was accented with a triple strand pearl necklace and matching bracelet. She looked ready for a board meeting. No one would have ever guessed by her outward appearance that she hadn't been to an office in more than ten years.

"We were just about to enjoy some coffee and pastries," she continued, as Sarah entered with a silver tray filled with hot coffee and warm, fruit-filled croissants. "Would you care to join us?"

Now Christine knew she was having an out of body experience. Not once, in the seven meetings she'd had with her wealthy client had she ever been offered food or drink. What had happened to this woman? Could she actually be a part of the human race?

"Damian has been sharing such wonderful stories with me about his business," Ms. Vanderpool stated, turning her attention to the man standing near the window.

For the first time, Christine noticed Damian standing by the bay window overlooking the pool and garden. Christine realized it wasn't a "what" that had taken over the stiff Ms. Vanderpool, but an obviously very charming "who." Dressed for work on a construction site, his well-worn jeans and flannel shirt gave him a rugged, sexy look. The clothes could not hide the rich outlines of his muscular physique. He stared back at Christine boldly, assessing everything about her. She didn't miss his obvious examination and the approval reflected back in his eyes. Fighting to deny the magnetic connection between them, she forced a smile and gave a hesitant nod of acknowledgment.

Turning his attention back to their host, Damian said, "I just hope I didn't bore you, too much, Cynthia."

*Cynthia!* Ms. Vanderpool had never extended an invitation to Christine to call her anything but her formal name. Fighting the desire to challenge the sudden change in her client's attitude, Christine took a deep breath and focused her attention on the matter at hand—choosing drape patterns. Now was not the time to debate how this woman, who seemed so cold and unfeeling in all of their previous exchanges, had become a sweet, accommodating human being after being in the presence of Damian Ware for less than an hour.

As if reading her mind, Ms. Vanderpool said, "I have to admit, Christine, I was quite put off when Mr. Ware was escorted in here with my fabrics, especially after the mix up with the delivery yesterday." She filled her own cup and took a seat on the sixteenth century sofa. "I trusted your company to handle my affairs with the utmost professionalism, given Robert's recommendation, and was gravely disappointed when your word was not honored yesterday and it seemed as though your word would not be honored this morning."

Christine opened her mouth to object, but caught Damian out of the corner of her eyes, wrinkling his nose and quickly shaking his head from side to side. She picked up his silent signal to remain quiet.

"But after speaking with this fine young man," Ms. Vanderpool said, glancing back at Damian and giving him a nod of approval, "who explained that you were detained for reasons beyond your control, my disappointment waned. I must admit that I was not pleased with this information, but he convinced me to be sympathetic and trust that your delay could not be avoided."

Momentarily stunned beyond words, she turned to Damian,

who used his fingers to pull the edges of his mouth up, urging Christine to smile. Feeling relieved and agitated at the same time, Christine took the hint and returned her attention to her client.

"Come dear," Ms. Vanderpool said, patting the empty seat beside her, "let's talk about these fabulous fabrics you've ordered for me."

Damian, taking a bite out of his third muffin, stared at Christine and wondered why his reaction to her was so strong. Physically, he could understand. Her wavy, short hair served as a crowning glory for her delicate face, highlighted by exotic cheekbones. Her body was shapely with fine hips and beautiful legs. He never imagined her walking back into his life after their silent meeting in the park three months ago, but now, she sat less than twenty feet away from him looking as adoring and enchanting as ever. Realizing that she had less than thirty minutes to get dressed, he thought she looked the consummate professional in a plum pantsuit, with matching pumps, pearl earrings and matching bracelet. He observed Christine's body beginning to relax and her attitude becoming more animated, as she described draperies that would put the final touches on the project. Her earlier stress and agitation were seemingly dissipated. Refilling his coffee cup, Damian realized that never before had a woman caused such a shiver of wanting to course through him.

The first time they met, she looked vulnerable and insecure. At the reception, she was radiant and confident. Today, she was the ultimate businesswoman. Adding cream to his coffee, Damian's jaw began to clench and his eyes slightly narrowed. Although he was deeply attracted to Christine, he had no intention of permitting himself to fall under a woman's spell. Danielle had proven how a woman could steer a man off track. His business was doing better than ever and he was preparing to bid on his biggest contract yet. Did he really need the complications of developing a meaningful relationship right now? But using the excuse of Danielle to stay away from Christine was beginning to sound weak to him. Danielle was a long time ago. Maybe he was giving her too much power and control over his life . . . and it was time to take it back. Glancing at Christine, he smiled. Yes, he had definitely given Danielle too much control and at that moment he decided he was going to do something about it.

Thirty minutes later, Christine and Damian said good-bye to Ms. Vanderpool. As soon as they stepped outside, Christine walked ahead of Damian, heading straight for his truck. She settled into the seat and stared straight ahead, her agitation very apparent. Damian was confused. Even though her morning had gotten off to a rocky start, everything had turned out well. Cynthia was extremely satisfied with her final selection, and had informed Christine that a member of her garden club was looking for someone to redecorate her summer home and she would be sure to recommend Davenport & Associates.

Shutting her door, Damian noticed her arms folded across her chest and her refusal to look at him. He headed around to the driver's side and buckled himself in. *What the hell was her problem? She should be thanking me for my help.*

Christine leaned back against the headrest. No words had passed between the two of them the entire time they were in Ms. Vanderpool's house. Christine was relieved that Ms. Vanderpool was pleased with her project and would refer her to Mrs. Angeline Darby. But she couldn't help but feel a little put out that her client took to Damian so quickly.

"I think everything worked out just fine," Damian said, seemingly pleased with the role he had played.

Irked by his cool, aloof manner, Christine replied, "Yes, everything is just peachy."

Watching her lean against the door and peer out the window, Damian had no idea what could have caused her sour mood. He decided on the friendly approach.

"Would you like to stop for breakfast? I noticed you didn't eat anything at Cynthia's house."

Turning to him, Christine's eyes narrowed and she curtly replied, "No, thank you."

Baffled by her attitude, Damian decided to ditch the friendly approach and try the direct approach. He was about to ask for an explanation when a ringing sound from his pocket prevented him.

"Yes," he spat out as he answered the phone, hating the interruption. Listening intently, he rolled his eyes heavenward. This day was full of surprises. "I'm about fifteen minutes from the site, I can . . ." Remembering his companion, he put the caller on hold and told Christine that a building inspector had showed up unexpectedly at one of his sites. "Do you have time to stop?"

Not turning her head, she answered, "Fine."

The sarcasm in that remark grated on his nerves, but he held his tongue, quickly finished his call and headed to the job site.

Damian parked the truck in the makeshift gravel lot, reached in the back for his hard hat and opened the door.

"Are you staying in the truck?" When she nodded, he jumped out and headed toward the half built structure.

When he reached the small, temporary trailer, Damian stepped inside and warmly greeted Alicia Jones, the office assistant. Sitting behind a corner steel desk, she fit right in wearing comfortable jeans, a thick button down shirt and work boots. At nineteen, Alicia had been through some rough times. Growing up in a tough part of town, she got into trouble when she was fifteen and spent one year in a juvenile detention center. But it was during that year she realized that if she didn't turn her life around, she would end up spending the rest of her life behind bars. That was when she decided to make something of herself. She was grateful to Damian for giving her this opportunity.

Glancing up, Alicia offered a friendly smile.

"Good morning, Damian. It's nice to see you."

"I got a call from Tanya. She said she spoke with you this

morning and you mentioned an inspection today. I thought it was understood that anytime county inspectors were going to be on site, I was to be notified, especially after that mix up with the lumber order last week. Why didn't you let me know?" he asked, his face full of concern.

Alicia looked stricken, as her duties were called into question. "I did know it was an inspection today, but Justin told me not to worry about notifying you. He said he would take care of it. I'm sorry Damian. If I had known he hadn't done it, I would have told you." She stood up and seemed upset at the mishap. "I should have followed up with Justin, but he's the foreman on the job and I just didn't think he would forget."

Realizing the sincerity in her apology, Damian responded, "Don't worry about it, Alicia. Next time, let Justin know it's your job to notify me of inspections."

Nodding her head "yes," Alicia sat back down tentatively. "It won't happen again."

"Thanks, Alicia," he said with a forgiving smile. "I'm going to head back out. The inspector is already here."

As he walked back into the work area, Damian spotted the county inspector, but still no sign of Justin.

"Good morning," Damian yelled loudly above the noisy machines. Stretching out his hand, he continued, "Damian Ware, owner of the construction company."

The men shook hands. "Carl Mitchells. Nice to meet you."

"If Justin is around, we can go ahead and get started," Damian said, glancing around the work area.

"Actually, we were just about finished," the inspector replied, removing his hard hat. "Everything looks good."

"Glad to hear it." They shook hands again and Damian watched the inspector head for his government issued vehicle.

"Damian, I heard you were on the site."

Turning toward the approaching voice, Damian arched his eyebrows in slight irritation. Justin stopped a few feet from him dressed in normal construction garb. Standing almost six feet tall with a buffed body, he could easily have been mistaken for a professional wrestler. His skin, deeply tanned from years of working in the sun, was a stark contrast to his light gray eyes. The dreadlocks, his trademark, hung down to his shoulders, under his bright, yellow hard hat.

An employee of the company for five years, Damian was impressed with Justin's knowledge and attention to details. Construction was a tedious business, and skilled workers and managers were sometimes hard to come by. In an era where technology was the industry of choice, finding and retaining people who work with their hands had been a challenge. Damian was glad to have Justin on board, but incidents like this would not be tolerated.

Always one to be straight with his men, Damian took the direct approach. "Justin, you want to tell me why I had no idea about the inspection today?"

"I apologize, Damian. I told Alicia I would call it in to the office, but with the mix up in lumber last week, it just slipped my mind," he answered, his face laced with concern. "It won't happen again."

"I know that you have a lot of responsibility as foreman, but inspections must always be a top priority. I don't expect this to happen again."

When Justin nodded agreement, Damian continued. "Why don't you come with me to the trailer. I just want to go over the next section of the plans."

Christine stayed in the truck and watched as Damian strode confidently back to the trailer. Irritated at his ability to appeal to Ms. Vanderpool, she had stayed in the truck to pout. But Christine also acknowledged that something in him soothed her and she couldn't deny the spark of pleasure and awareness she felt every time he was near. She recalled the promise she made to herself after Henry had locked her in the storage closet and that was to never allow herself to fall in love. The price of love was too high. Until that moment, that promise had been easy to keep. No one had ever enticed her the way Damian Ware had.

In college, she had focused her attention on finishing at the top of her class. Her small circle of friends, who refused to accept her limited social life, coaxed and prodded her to lighten up and enjoy life more. Continuously trying to set her up with blind dates, they eventually gave up after their efforts never panned out. The only one who didn't give up on her was Stephanie. Refusing to give in to Christine's philosophy of not needing a man, she set Christine up on one date after another. She recruited all types for the cause. From lower classmen to football players, to the highly intellectual types, and even one or two professors. Stephanie, determined not to see her best friend alone, took it as a personal challenge to show Christine that she was wrong about men and relationships.

Luckily, Christine had always managed to rid herself of her suitors in three dates or less. It usually didn't take much. Informing them up front regarding her feelings on men, love and marriage, either caused them to run away scared or be unwilling to expend the energy to show her anything different. There were a few who saw her as a challenge, but they quickly faded away, tired of working against the demons that haunted her.

A thoughtful smile curved Christine's mouth as she remembered Stephanie's dramatics at the reception, making certain the night ended with her and Damian together. While her heart was grateful for his support the past few days, her mind reminded her of the high price to be paid for loving someone.

Turning to face Damian again, warning spasms of alarm erupted within her. Damian was going to be one of those guys who would challenge her philosophy. Licking her lips nervously, she watched him shake hands with a large man with dreadlocks and head back toward the truck. He was successful, handsome, charming and available. A combination that even the most celibate person couldn't resist. A few feet from the truck, Damian's eyes locked with hers, seemingly reaching right into her thoughts. Fighting an overwhelming need to jump out and run to him, she looked away. *How in the world was she going to be able to resist him?*

Damian smiled after watching Christine quickly avert her eyes. She may try to fight it, but the eyes don't lie. That flash of desire she tried so desperately to hide, shone through. However, he understood that after witnessing the destructive relationship of her parents, the last thing she would admit to herself is that she wanted to develop a personal relationship with him.

Last night, after hanging up with the lawyer, Christine quickly thanked him for seeing her home and escorted him to the door. He felt her rebuild the wall of defense he so desperately tried to tear down. Understanding she could possibly be in shock from the news about her father, as well as recovering from the panic attack in the elevator, Damian reached his hand to hers, trying to recapture the feelings that embodied their first kiss. However, she gently pulled away and opened the front door.

Standing on her porch alone, he wondered if he had imagined the entire scene in the kitchen. Was it possible that he hadn't broken through to her soul? Was it possible that her actions were based on the emotion of the moment, and not for a desire to get close to him? He knew she was attracted to him. Her eyes were filled with a curious, deep longing, but she was fighting it all the way.

Opening the car door, Damian dropped his hard hat in the back seat and smoothly slid into the driver's seat. She could deny it all she wanted, but he knew there was something special between them. He knew it that day in the park, he felt it when they embraced after the reception, and he confirmed it when they kissed. Christine Davenport was the one for him. He just needed to make her see it.

"Sorry about this," he said. "We just completed another

phase of this building and the inspector wanted to check our work."

"It doesn't seem fair that an inspector could just show up like that. Don't they have to make appointments?"

"Well, actually, my foreman knew, but didn't notify me. Tanya tried to call me earlier this morning, but by that time, I was already at Cynthia's. Seeing how livid she was when I arrived instead of you, I turned off my cell phone so that I could give her my undivided attention."

At the mention of Ms. Vanderpool's name, Christine felt her anger rising all over again. She had worked hard on that account and didn't get one ounce of respect from that woman. Damian, with his twenty minutes of charm, gained not only respect, but an open invitation to her home. Christine folded her arms in her lap. "If you're looking for a 'thank you', you can forget it. I could have explained the situation to her, probably better than you, and she would have been fine."

Damian chuckled, finally understanding what had Christine in such a foul mood. "I don't think so. That woman bad mouthed you and your company the first five minutes I was there. I don't know how you've put up with her."

Christine had asked herself that same question many times, and the answer was always the same. "When you're just starting out, you can't be choosy."

"Well," Damian said, as he turned into the garage of his building, "At least you won't have her saying nasty things about your company anymore. I politely explained to her how unbecoming her negative attitude was on a woman of her beauty, stature and importance. It would be advantageous of her to recognize that Davenport & Associates is a company moving in important circles and it wouldn't be wise to alienate herself from that growing group."

Seething with anger and humiliation, Christine jumped out of the truck as soon as he parked and headed straight to her car. Running to catch up with her, Damian took hold of her hand and pulled her back. "What is your problem?"

Jerking her hand away, Christine answered him in a cold, flat tone. "Don't ever grab me again."

A sudden, thin chill hung on the edge of her words.

Taken aback by the venom in her voice, he slowly took a step back. In a calm manner, he said, "I'm not like that Christine. I was just trying to prevent you from leaving like this. If I frightened you, I'm sorry, but you have to believe that I would never physically hurt a woman."

She leaned her head back and gazed into his eyes and Christine realized she had overreacted and relaxed her stance. However, that didn't change the fact that he was a man. A man who just showed what a manipulator he could be. "I believe you, but let's get one thing straight. You may have charmed Ms. Vanderpool with your deep voice, your sexy smile and your sincere demeanor, but it won't work on me. Henry had those same qualities. That's part of the reason why my mother stayed. He always knew the right thing to say and when to say it. And you know what, he was a dog. He hurt people, and now," she continued in a harsh, raw tone, "I find out that he had an affair . . . and another child! Men are manipulators and you just proved that." Grabbing her keys out of her purse, she turned to walk to her car. "Now, if you'll excuse me, I have an appointment."

As he watched her drive out of the garage, Damian stood motionless for several minutes, contemplating all that she had revealed. The good news was that she found him sexy and charming. The bad news was that those were the very reasons she was not going to allow them to move beyond a business relationship. Never one to back down from a challenge, he began to whistle an upbeat tune. There was an undeniable magnetism building between them, and he was determined to help her release the past so they could forge a future together. *I'll show you, Christine Davenport. Every man is not like your father.*

* * *

Later that afternoon, Christine checked the address on the building against the business card in her hand and confirmed that she had the correct location. Entering through the revolving doors, she was impressed with the marble floors and high, arched ceilings. She had never been to Douglas Murphy's law office before, but it was located in one of the newest office buildings in Arlington, VA, just a few blocks away from the Pentagon. Signing in at the security desk, she was then directed to the elevator. When the doors opened, Christine hesitated a moment and then drew a deep breath and stepped inside.

From the moment that Mr. Murphy had approached her at the funeral, Christine had dreaded this meeting. After explaining that he possessed information to settle her mother's financial affairs, Mr. Murphy had tried unsuccessfully to meet with Christine on several occasions.

Since their initial meeting, Christine had learned that her father was an adulterer, and that her mother had more money than she ever thought possible. Feeling confused and betrayed, she wondered what other secrets would come to light about her family. Why was she one who had to deal with this mess? Her memories of her childhood were finally beginning to subside and she just wanted to get this part of her life settled so that she could move on. Everything had become so complicated lately. All she wanted to do was return to her simple dream of building the best interior design firm in the area. Making a silent resolution to herself, she affirmed that after she settled her mother's estate and finished the project for Damian, she would return to the life she had: simple.

As she stepped off the elevator, Christine was caught off guard by what she saw. She hadn't known what to expect, but it was definitely not the plush burgundy carpet, the expensive paintings on the wall, and the bronze, shiny reception desk with the words Murphy, Carter & Delaney hanging above it.

"May I help you?" asked the perky blonde woman behind the desk.

Christine took a glance at the name plate before she answered. "Um, yes . . . Nancy . . . I'm here to see Douglas Murphy. My name is . . ."

"Christine Davenport," she interrupted. Noticing Christine's confused look, she continued. "He's been expecting you . . . several times now," she added with a smile.

Christine blushed slightly from embarrassment. This was the fifth appointment she had set and the first one she had shown up for. She hadn't even bothered to call and cancel three of the previous appointments.

"Just go through those double glass doors," Nancy said, pointing to the left. "His secretary, Elise, is on the left. She'll announce you."

"Thanks."

Elise was on the phone when Christine reached her desk and Christine took the opportunity to take a closer look at her surroundings. The furnishings reaped of success. Elise's desk, solid oak with hand-crafted designs, sat atop a multi-colored Persian rug. Noticing the framed works on the wall, she was genuinely impressed. She had attended enough art functions to know that the two paintings were originals and cost well into five figures.

Suddenly, her eyebrows slanted into a frown, and questions began to surface in her mind. How would her mother have known Douglas Murphy? Her parents moved in very limited circles. This office spoke of money, power and success, three things that had eluded her parents their entire lives. Exactly what was the relationship between Douglas Murphy and her mom?

"I'm sorry to keep you waiting," Elise said, ending her call. "Mr. Murphy is expecting you. You can go right in."

Entering the office through the wooden door, the first

thing Christine noticed was the understatement of the decor. After walking through the lobby and the secretary's station, Christine thought this office would mirror the exhibition of wealth. While the rich wallpaper and strategically placed artifacts were exquisite and expensive, the total ensemble was understated.

Mr. Murphy stood and walked around his desk to greet Christine and offer his hand.

"I'm glad to see you finally made it in," he said with a friendly smile. He motioned to a small conference table in the corner. "Why don't we sit over here. Can I offer you something to drink?"

Christine stared at the older gentleman and tried to picture him with her mother. While he and Henry were about the same height, her father had let himself go over the years and it had been reflected in his receding hairline and pot belly. But Mr. Murphy seemed to have taken good care of himself over the years. Christine knew he had to be at least fifty years old but he could have easily passed for someone younger.

"No, thank you. I just want to get down to business." Christine knew she was being curt, but her thoughts were running a hundred miles an hour. Her life had been filled with one surprise after another the past few days, and she wasn't sure how much more she could handle. Seeing Damian at her reception, allowing an intimate moment between them at the gazebo, the fear she felt being stuck in the elevator, the comfort she received from him during the ordeal, the kiss they shared, and their exchange this morning had her emotions on the verge of exploding. And now she was forced to deal with her mother's death, her unknown wealth, a cheating father, a possible half sister, and a mistress out for revenge. Now was not the time for small talk and pleasantries. She wanted answers and she wanted them now.

Watching the gamut of emotions play across her face, Mr. Murphy felt sympathy. She had been through so much, not only because of recent events, but because of the challenges she had endured growing up. He wanted to help, to offer her his friendship, but he doubted that she was ready to accept it.

"Christine, I'm not here to make your life complicated. Ruth shared a great deal with me over the years, and I would hope that, as she and I were friends, you and I could become friends. That would be something I know she would have wanted."

"Well, Mr. Murphy," Christine started, in a tone void of emotion, "you seem to know an awful lot about my mother and my family, but I don't know anything about you. My mother never mentioned you, and now you show up with stories of your friendship, information about Henry and access to a million dollars you claim to be my mother's money. So, while I'm not quite interested in being your friend, I would like to know exactly what kind of relationship you had with my mother. My mother didn't move in the circle of high powered attorneys with plush offices that display artwork more expensive than her house." Christine continued. "She was a simple woman with simple tastes. She knew nothing of fine clothes." Christine paused as her gaze traveled the length of his suit, indicating she recognized a three thousand dollar suit when she saw one. "Or expensive jewelry," she continued, staring pointedly at the gold and diamond ring on his right hand. "So, tell me Mr. Murphy, how did someone like that come into one million dollars?"

Douglas stared at Christine with understanding eyes. He knew the childhood she had endured and the strained relationship that had existed between her and her mother after she had left for college. Christine had forgiven her mother after Henry died, and they were close before Ruth's death. He understood Christine's desire to succeed alone, declaring herself satisfied to live her life without loving or being loved. He also believed that declaration was a bunch of crock. Ruth told him how Christine believed that men did nothing but manipulate and strip women of their dreams. Ruth had been excited that they had formed a meaningful relationship the past year, but also knew that Christine believed that she had wasted her life and her talents on Henry. But while he understood, he would not silently stand by and allow Christine to continue with these untrue thoughts of Ruth.

"If I recall, you had not been a part of your mother's life for the past ten years, while I had been a part of her life on almost a daily basis for the past twenty years. What makes you think you have the right to tell me what kind of woman Ruth was?" he asked, in a calm, but emotion-filled voice. "Your mother loved you dearly, but she was not the woman you just described."

Rising from his chair, he walked over to the window and watched a 727 fly over the Fourteenth Street bridge to make its landing at Ronald Reagan National Airport.

Christine sat silently, thinking about what Mr. Murphy had said. Suddenly, Christine felt both sad and overwhelmed. Every word he had said was true. Because she had allowed her anger to keep her away, she had no idea what kind of person her mother had become. She didn't want to think of how she may have misjudged her mother and that it was too late to change it. She only wanted to concentrate on her mother's legacy and the impending challenge. There was no way that Margaret Donovan was going to see any of her mother's money. Speaking in a quiet, but firm tone, Christine said, "Tell me about the money."

# FIVE

Stephanie glanced at the grandfather clock in the corner of the living room. Six-thirty. Christine should have been here an hour ago. She took a quick peek out the window, but there wasn't one car in sight on her quiet suburban street. The appointment with Mr. Murphy should have ended an hour ago and Stephanie wondered what was keeping Christine.

She had spoken to Christine after her appointment with Ms. Vanderpool, and got a quick synopsis of the events of the past two days. If Christine hadn't been so upset, she would have sworn she made the entire story up. She wondered how the news of her father's affair affected Christine's feelings for Damian.

Christine harbored ill feelings toward her father and men, but had made tremendous progress in moving forward with her life when she bridged the gap between herself and Ruth. She seemed to be finally coming into her own, especially after meeting Damian. Stephanie had watched Christine with enough men to know that Damian sparked a fire in her that she had never felt before. There was a sparkle in her eyes when Christine spoke about their strange encounter in the park, and it was divine intervention that he was invited to their reception. Stephanie believed that Damian Ware could help Christine let go of the past and embrace a future.

Startled out of her thoughts by the ringing phone, she

went to answer it and hoped it was Christine with news of her delay.

"Stephanie, it's Nathan."

She tried to speak, but her voice wavered. This was the last person she wanted to talk to.

"Stephanie?" he asked, waiting patiently for a response.

"Yes, Nathan, I'm here, but I can't talk," she said, hoping her voice sounded strong and nonchalant. "I'm expecting Christine any minute."

"We need to talk, and you know it," he said in a compassionate tone.

"Look, Nathan, you're right, we do. But now is not a good time. Work is really busy and my friend is going through a tough time right now," she answered, hoping to end the call before she reneged on her promise to herself to let him go.

Nathan Hollister was the sweetest, sexiest, and most persistent man she knew. They had met a year ago at a CPA conference in Atlanta when they were assigned to the same dinner table the first night. She was immediately drawn to his eyes—light and sexy, and surrounded by thick brows and long lashes. She thought she would lose herself in their depth. The attraction was mutual and they spent the remaining two days of the conference ducking out of seminars early, enjoying leisurely lunches and taking tours, as Nathan was anxious to show off his city. At the airport, Stephanie said good-bye to Nathan, explaining that she didn't believe in long distance relationships.

But Nathan had other plans. Within two weeks of her return home, he had sent flowers, candy, and an airline ticket. She flew down the next weekend and was treated like a queen. He reserved a suite for her at the best hotel, and left her at the door each night with a chaste kiss. And they'd been together ever since. Showering her with gifts, visits to DC, and theater tickets, Nathan Hollister was too good to be true. And that was the problem.

Stephanie had dated many men over the years and they

all had flaws. Some small and some large, but flaws none-theless. There was the drinking flaw, the I-don't-want-to-work flaw, the social drug use flaw, and the infamous "meet my four kids" flaw. Throughout all of her time with Nathan, she could not find one real flaw. He had a great career, no hidden wives, a genuine respect for women, and a desire to settle down with that special someone.

When he had come to visit last month and confessed his love, Stephanie had panicked. People always viewed her as outgoing, but Nathan was able to break through her outer shell, and touch her inner soul. Through all the outrageous clothes, the parties and the men, he knew she was just a woman who was looking for that one special man to spend the rest of her life with.

Nathan's words of love scared her. Over the course of her life, all of the people that had loved her eventually left her. Afraid that this relationship would end the same, Stephanie began withdrawing from him by avoiding his calls, ignoring his gifts and deleting all of his e-mails without reading them.

"I know what you're trying to do," Nathan said, breaking through her thoughts. "But it's not going to work."

"I don't know what you're talking about," she answered, trying unsuccessfully to sound agitated.

"I know you've been disappointed in the past by those who have loved you, but deep down I know you believe that I love you and would never hurt you."

"I have to go. I'm expecting someone any minute," she said, trying to keep the tears from falling. She wanted to believe in him, but her will to protect herself was stronger. She didn't think she could survive it when he decided to leave her . . . and she knew that someday he would.

Hearing the strain in her voice, Nathan sighed. He had to find a way to break through her wall. "I'm a very patient man, Stephanie, and I know you are worth the wait."

A lone tear fell down her cheek.

"I'll give you some time, but I called to tell you I have a

job interview in two weeks at a firm in DC. I want to see you, but you'll have to want to see me." He paused, hoping to get a word of encouragement. When he did not get one, he continued. "I know we can work this out. Good-bye, Stephanie."

Stephanie held the phone for several minutes, listening to the dial tone until the loud voice of the operator asked her to make a call or hang up. She returned the phone to the cradle and sat stoically for several minutes. Deep in her heart, she knew Nathan meant everything he said, including the fact that he would not contact her again. He had placed the ball in her court. While he would fight to make their relationship work, she would have to make the next move. Hearing a car pull into the driveway, she rushed to the bathroom to destroy all evidence of her tears.

"Where the hell have you been?"

"Well, hello to you, too," Christine answered sarcastically, entering the foyer and hanging her coat in the closet.

"You should have been here an hour ago," Stephanie replied, her voice laced with agitation.

"I got here as soon as I could."

Christine walked into the living room and took a seat on the sofa. She was glad to see that Stephanie had finally hung up above the fireplace the scenic picture of the mountains she had purchased over six months ago.

They had both shopped for houses almost two years ago. Six months, five real estate agents and hundreds of road miles later, Christine had settled on a four-bedroom colonial with a large sun room surrounded by Palladian windows, and Stephanie had chosen a sophisticated two bedroom, one story that featured a spacious living room with a fireplace, built-in bookshelves and a rear window wall that stretched into the morning room.

What sealed the deal for both Stephanie and Christine were the master suites. Both were twice the size of their other bedrooms, featuring huge walk-in closets with built in shoe racks. The master bath played host to an oversized sunken tub with spa. They both felt content and comfortable with their selections. The interesting thing was that Christine furnished and decorated her house in about four months, while Stephanie had yet to complete one room.

Christine watched Stephanie pace the floor and instantly knew something was wrong. Very few things got Stephanie worked up, and she was definitely chomping at the bit about something. One name came to mind.

"What did Nathan do to put you in such a foul mood?"

Shooting her a cold look, Stephanie replied, "Who?"

"What did he do this time?" Christine asked, amusement reflected in her voice. "Did he offer to take you on a fabulous vacation? Send you another airline ticket to come visit him? Oh, I know, maybe he asked you to marry him." Ignoring Stephanie's tightened jaw, she continued. "I don't know why you continue to give that man such a hard time."

"Look, Christine, you did not come over here to talk about me. What did the attorney say?"

Growing serious, Christine stared at Stephanie for several seconds. "Stephanie, you have to talk about it at some point. I've seen you two together and I see it in both your eyes. Why won't you give the two of you a chance?"

"Mind your own business, Chris," Stephanie warned, before she stood and headed for the kitchen.

As she followed behind her, Christine wasn't going to let Stephanie off the hook that easily. For the past year, Christine watched Stephanie get closer to Nathan, only to pull back. This passive-aggressive behavior had to stop. She either had to fish or cut bait.

"You really have some nerve telling me to mind my own business," Christine said, watching her friend pull two coffee mugs out of the cabinet. "I seem to recall a certain someone who had herself in my business for as long as I can remember. Setting me up on dates, telling me how to handle my boyfriends, and not to mention that stunt you pulled with

Damian. But you know what I've just realized?" she asked, her voice reflecting the tension that was beginning to fill the air. "You were so busy running my life, that you forgot to have one of your own. Why is that? What are you so afraid of? Why are you running from Nathan?"

Stephanie slammed the mugs onto the table. "You don't know what you're talking about. I'm not running from anybody."

"Yes, you are," Christine countered. "From what I see, you have a man who adores you and I think you adore him too. So what is the problem?"

Stephanie turned to face her friend and a lone tear trickled down her cheek. "He does love me, and everyone who's loved me has left me."

Christine outstretched her arms and embraced Stephanie. "I love you and I'm still here. You have to talk to him. Let him know what you're feeling. Don't let fear prevent you from finding happiness."

Pulling away from her embrace, Stephanie looked at her friend and asked, "Does that mean you are going to follow your own advice?"

Stephanie saw the questioning gaze in Christine's eyes. "I know you're interested in Damian, so let's make a deal. I won't let my fear prevent me from developing my relationship with Nathan, and you won't let your past prevent you from pursuing a relationship with Damian. Deal?"

As Stephanie stretched out her hand for a shake, Christine wondered how she got herself backed into this corner. "Deal?"

Forcing an expression of indifference, Christine took her hand and shook. "Deal."

Setting the coffee on the kitchen table, Stephanie grabbed a cherry cheesecake from the refrigerator and set two plates down. "Now, tell me about this million dollars."

* * *

"No," Natalie Donovan yelled, putting on her wool coat and heading for the door. "I told you I will not take part in your revenge."

As she walked from her bedroom to the living room in her high-rise apartment, Natalie hoped to avoid having this conversation, yet one more time. She was running late for work and she couldn't afford to be late for her first meeting of the day. Pulling her shoulder length, jet black hair out of her collar, she picked up her briefcase and grabbed her keys.

When she moved out of her mother's house last year at twenty-seven, she had hoped to avoid having these scenes with her. It was always something with Margaret. A complaint about this, a problem with that. It was never ending. Whenever she got a new job, it was always the boss or a co-worker who had it out for her, therefore leading to her termination. Not happy with any part of her life, Margaret constantly laid blame elsewhere. Now here she was, standing in her living room at seven o'clock in the morning, trying, once again, to convince Natalie to place herself right in the middle of her latest drama.

"Look," Margaret replied, following Natalie down the hallway. "You don't understand. I deserve some of this money and so do you."

"You are missing my point, Mother," Natalie replied, stopping at the door. She was meeting with a high profile client that day, and she wanted to arrive early. She had a goal of making partner at the CPA firm she worked for in the next three years, before stepping out on her own. However, if she didn't get her mother out of here soon, there was no way she would arrive before nine o'clock and she didn't want that negative mark on her record. "I don't want any of that money."

"Well, I do, and the only person who has a legitimate claim is you," Margaret said, stepping in front of her to block her exit.

Natalie stared at her mother and her eyes reflected pity.

Margaret's long brown hair was laced with gray and was unruly to her shoulders. Her wool pants and cardigan sweater hung loosely on her body and Natalie couldn't help but notice she looked like she was losing weight. "Suing the estate was your idea. You want this, not me."

Leaning back against the front door, Margaret sighed heavily. Running her fingers through her graying hair, she looked older than her forty-seven years. "I have done everything for you. I worked two jobs to put you through that private school. I took out a loan to help with your college education. I struggled to buy you that car so that you could intern at that fancy accounting firm, and this is the thanks I get?"

Margaret lowered her voice to almost a whisper. "It took me two months to convince your Uncle Paul to represent me. Now he tells me that I probably don't have a claim as his mistress, but as his daughter, you do. Can't you do this one little thing for your mama?"

"Cut the drama, Mother," Natalie said, resentful of the situation her mother was trying to put her in. "You know I appreciate all you've done for me, but let's not forget the contributions I've made. I worked the last two years of high school and paid over half of the tuition bill to that private school. My scholarship covered most of my college expenses, and that amount surpassed the loans you took out to help me. By the way, I am now paying back those loans. And as for the car, well, since you wrecked yours, you've been using it more than me. But do you hear me complain? No, because you're my mother and I don't mind helping you. Now," Natalie continued, gently grabbing her mother's arm and pushing her to one side, "if you will please move out of my way, I can go to work."

Stepping aside, Margaret sniffled loudly, and covered her face with her hands. "He never sent us money. It was so hard for me. Raising you with low paying jobs, always having to ask Paul for help." The tears soon followed and Natalie took a deep breath. This was what she wanted to avoid. A dramatic scene that ended with her mother in tears. She loved her mother dearly, but wished she would stop feeling sorry for herself and take control of her life.

Margaret wiped her face and continued, "Now I find out that he had a million dollars. . . . A MILLION DOLLARS! Don't tell me it doesn't bother you that all those times we struggled, trying to make ends meet, that he had this kind of money."

Natalie set her briefcase on the floor and walked over to her mother. "I know it was hard for you, raising me by yourself, and yes, it would have been better if he had given us more support. But he didn't." Reaching out, she pulled her mother close and gave her a hug. "Besides, the money that was left to his daughter, wasn't even his, it was his wife's."

"Exactly," Margaret replied, extracting herself from the embrace and looking her daughter straight in the eye. "That's why the claim has to come from you. My name was on the initial letter, but there's nothing I can do. Because it's all in his wife's name, I have no claim, but because she probably used money from their relationship, you have a claim as his daughter."

Natalie sighed. She had been hearing this argument for a week now. Her mother was trying desperately to get her to sue the estate of Ruth Davenport and lay claim to the money Ruth had accumulated during the years of marriage. Natalie had to admit that she did harbor anger at Henry Davenport for not accepting her and for not being a father to her. Even though they lived less than an hour away, she only saw him four times in her entire life, and the fourth time was when he was lying in his coffin. The monetary support would have come in handy. She remembered the time when her mother had worked days as an administrative assistant and nights in a fast food restaurant and left Natalie with neighbors.

But Natalie learned a long time ago that regret, bitterness and anger could eat a person alive if they let it. Glancing at her mother, she knew where she learned that lesson from because those three things had practically destroyed her mother. Natalie knew that her mother didn't regret having her, but she knew she regretted being sweet talked by the smooth talking Henry Davenport. Not knowing he was married, Margaret had quickly and willingly given herself to him. When she turned up pregnant, he turned up married, and it nearly destroyed Margaret. Only a sophomore in college, she had no choice but to drop out of school and move in with her brother, Paul, because Margaret's parents were too ashamed to take her in.

Hard times followed for Margaret. Paul was finishing law school and money was tight. For Margaret, jobs were hard to find and the arguments between the siblings continued to grow. A year after Natalie was born, Margaret got a job as a secretary and moved out. She tried contacting Henry several times after she had moved out in an attempt to steal him away from his wife. When that didn't work, she hoped to settle for an affair and a father for her child. Henry laughed in her face, telling her that he hardly wanted the family he had. He definitely didn't want another.

Over the next few years, Natalie saw her father a total of three times. And as time went on, the bitterness in her mother grew. Now, Margaret was consumed with anger. Anger at Henry, anger at Ruth, and anger at the hand that life had dealt her. And now, she was angry that this million dollars existed and that she may not be able to get any of it.

Natalie desperately wanted to help her mother and had tried to ease her pain, but nothing worked. Not even straight A's in school, nor being accepted to American University on an academic scholarship, nor receiving an internship at the biggest accounting firm in the state seemed to make Margaret any happier. Looking at her mother, Natalie saw the desperation in her eyes. She knew at that moment what would ease her mother's pain, and while her mind told her not to, her heart reached out to give Margaret Donovan the one thing she wanted.

"OK, Mom. Call Uncle Paul. I'll file the claim and contest the will of Ruth Davenport."

"Somebody better explain to me why the Wilson Medical Center project is almost one month behind schedule," Damian said, glaring at four pairs of eyes sitting around the conference table. Not waiting for an answer, he began pacing the room before continuing. "I thought I made it very clear that every project was to come in on time."

"But, Damian, we discussed . . ."

"I don't want to hear it," he said, cutting off Jason Lewis, one of his top engineers. "Ware Construction always brings their projects in on time and under budget. Now you guys figure out how we are going to do that with this project."

"Damian, you're not being . . ."

"This meeting is over," Damian barked, closing the files in front of him.

As the group gathered their notes and began exiting the conference room, Damian took a seat at the head of long oak table and exhaled a breath. Turning his chair to face the wall, he stared blankly ahead. He didn't see Tanya walk in.

"What the hell is your problem?"

"Not now, Tanya," he scowled, a shadow of annoyance crossing his face.

"Yes, now, Damian," she replied, turning his chair to face her. "You have been walking around here for a week, barking orders and yelling at staff. You need a serious attitude adjustment."

"I don't need you to tell me about my attitude. My attitude is about running this company. If people would just do their jobs, there would be nothing for me to say," he replied, through clenched teeth.

"Bull," she answered.

Raising a brow, he said, "What do you mean 'bull'?"

"Just call her."

"I don't know what you're talking about."

"The hell you don't. You must have forgotten that I know you very well. And I can tell your problem has nothing to do with deadlines, suppliers or budgets, but with a young woman who has turned over your redecorating project to one of her associates."

"Christine Davenport has nothing to do with me or my so-called attitude."

Tanya laughed. Damian hadn't seen Christine since the day they met at Ms. Vanderpool's, almost two weeks ago. "Call her."

Damian stood up and went over to the small table set up with coffee and bagels for the meeting and filled a cup with the steaming stimulant. He sighed. He hated to admit to himself that Tanya was right. Christine had not returned any of his calls, and he was livid when she had assigned his project to one of her associates. What was it about her that drove him crazy? He could not get her out of his mind. Every time the phone rang, he hoped it was her. But he'd heard nothing. Not one word.

"If she wants to talk to me, she'll call."

"I always admired your tenacity. Why aren't you using it in this situation?"

He turned to face the woman who had been his friend through thick and thin. "I'm not calling her anymore . . . period," he sternly said.

Moving toward him with a smug grin, Tanya looked directly into his eyes and placed a comforting hand on his shoulder. "Who said anything about calling?"


"What do you mean we lost the deal?" Christine said through clenched teeth, causing the three people around the table to physically cringe.

"They decided to go with another firm," William Marshall, an associate designer, answered.

"What do you mean they decided to go with another firm. Why?"

"Well. I—umm . . . didn't ask why," he replied, looking around the table for support. Watching the other two designers suddenly find something very interesting on their notepads, he knew he was on his own.

"Well," Christine started sarcastically, "perhaps you should find out, so that we can determine if we need to make some adjustments in the way we do business. Do I make myself clear?"

Not waiting for a response, Christine gathered her notes and announced, "this meeting is adjourned."

Not wanting to spend any unnecessary time in her presence, her associates quickly left the room, almost running Stephanie over in the process.

"You better be careful, there's rumor of mutiny," Stephanie said.

"Very funny, Stephanie. Is there anything wrong with wanting to run an effective business?"

"No," Stephanie said, "but there is something wrong with treating people badly, especially when they don't deserve it."

Christine pinched her nose in an attempt to combat an oncoming headache. "Look, maybe I haven't been the best employer lately, but between dealing with the will, a possible half sister and running this business . . ."

"And Damian."

"Damian has nothing to do with me," she answered defensively. "He's a client and that's it. And now that William is handling his project, there is no reason to discuss him."

"Why haven't you returned his calls?"

"William provides regular updates to me regarding his project," she said, heading for the door.

Stephanie stepped in front of her to block her exit. "We had a deal. I've contacted Nathan . . . now it's your turn."

Christine exhaled deeply before replying. "I agreed to not let fear rule my relationship, but in this case, there is no relationship."

"Because you haven't called him back," Stephanie countered.

"Look, Stephanie, I have been busy. I have this issue with the will and I am running a new business. Our schedules just have not been conducive to talking with each other."

"So, you haven't been purposely avoiding him? It's just that you guys haven't caught up with each other?" she asked with sarcasm.

"Exactly. Now, if you'll excuse me, I'm going to head back to my office to see if I can get some work done before the weekend."

"That's wonderful because Damian is in your office."

Shock flew through her body. "What do you mean he's in my office?"

"Like you said, I figured it was more of a scheduling issue that prevented you from returning his call," Stephanie said heading for the door. "So, when he arrived while you were in this meeting, I just escorted him to your office and told him to sit tight. You'd be in right after your meeting ended."

Grunting in frustration, Christine tried to gather her thoughts as she headed down the hall. The last image she wanted to portray to Damian was that she missed him. Standing outside her office door, Christine forced her lips apart in a curved, stiff smile and stepped inside. "I understand you wanted to see me," she said.

"You haven't returned any of my calls."

His voice stopped Christine dead in her tracks as all her senses came to life. The sight of him casually leaning against her desk looking devilishly handsome in black slacks and a black turtleneck caused sweat to form at the top of her brow. His voice, deep and sensual, sent a ripple of awareness through her. She squeezed the files she carried in an effort to squelch the overwhelming desire to reach out and touch him. Somehow, she found the strength to respond.

"I've been busy," she replied, making a beeline for the chair behind her desk. The large steel object served as a shield. She felt comfortable when she had something between them.

"And I've been missing you."

Startled by his admission, Christine sat and searched her mind for a proper response that would not reveal that she had missed him, too.

"Christine, I'm too old for games. I want to spend time with you and get to know you. I don't know where it will lead, but I want to find out. If you're not interested, tell me now and I'll be gone."

His gaze traveled over her face and searched her eyes. What he saw encouraged him to continue. "Come away with me this weekend."

Christine was startled by his suggestion and felt the pink rise to her cheeks. "How dare you think I would just jump into bed with you."

Seeing that she had completely misunderstood him, Damian quickly answered. "Sleeping arrangements were not on my mind when I made this offer. Stephanie told me you've been worried and busy with the contesting of the will, and that you've been a bear to your staff. Well," he continued, leaning forward, "I hate to admit it, but I've been pretty rotten to be around myself these last two weeks." He watched for her reaction before he continued. "I think we both know why."

Admitting to herself that her bad attitude was directly related to her time away from him, Christine lowered her gaze.

"I have a beach house on the eastern shore of Maryland. I know it's November, but it's a wonderful getaway. We could both relax, take our minds off our business and get to know each other. And it has three bedrooms, so you would have total privacy."

Christine looked past him at the woman standing in the doorway and realized Stephanie had overheard the request. Mouthing the words "don't forget out deal," she turned and left. Christine turned her attention back to the tall, handsome man standing before her. Avoiding relationships all her life had been easy, because the men were never that interesting. But this time was different. He was different. And she knew it.

He would be the one to challenge her, to break down the barrier she had erected long ago. Many had tried over the years, but they all eventually gave up. She shuddered slightly as his eyes narrowed expectantly. It wasn't a weekend away that made her nervous, but the feeling that he would be the one. The one who would not give up, not until he got exactly what he wanted.

Pushing down her nerves and clearing her throat, Christine raised her head confidently and said, "What time do we leave?"

Few words were spoken as Damian loaded Christine's overnight bag into the back of his Ford Expedition. They had decided to leave right after the evening rush hour ended, just after seven, and hoped to arrive at the beach house around ten. Within thirty minutes, the city lights gave way to the quiet hum of the engine as it moved down the dark highway.

Damian cut his eye over to Christine and smiled. He could tell that she was tense earlier that day at her office, but he hoped that a relaxing getaway would help take her mind off her business and give them a chance to get to know one another. Highlighted from the glow of the moon, Damian silently admired her beauty. She had changed from the power suit that she had worn at the office into an old faded pair of jeans that fit her body like a glove. The oversized college sweatshirt portrayed a look of youth and innocence. She glanced at him, curving her lips into a timid smile. He hoped the clothes were just the first step in taking all her stress away.

"You want to talk about it?"

Christine stared at him for a moment, as if debating an answer, then exhaled deeply before leaning her head back against the headrest. As she rested with her eyes closed for several minutes, Damian said nothing. He wanted her to open up to him, but he also understood the baggage she carried around with her ran deep. More than he realized, he wanted to be the one to help her unload, but he knew he couldn't push her. She had to learn to trust him, and only then would she open herself up to him. The scene in his office building's garage a few weeks ago only confirmed what he already knew: she trusted no man.

"If Stephanie hadn't overheard your request, I may not have come. She seems to think I need to loosen up and enjoy life."

"Do you want to go back?" Damian held his breath. There was no way he wanted to turn around and drop her off at her house . . . alone. Danielle's deception ran so deep and hurt so bad, that he never thought that he would be able to pull himself out of the lonely hole he wallowed in and allow himself the possibility of beginning a relationship with someone else. Yet, here he was, with a woman who confused him and set him on fire at the same time. A woman, who at this very moment, could tell him that she didn't want to give them a chance. He didn't want to take her back, but he re-signed himself to the fact that he would if she asked. All she had to do was say the word.

"You must be feeling pretty sure of yourself since you got me to agree to come?"

Damian rolled his eyes. He decided to take her head-on and find out exactly what was going on in that pretty head of hers. "Are you always difficult, or do you reserve that funky attitude for me?"

"Excuse me?" Christine said, raising her voice and eyebrows.

"Every time we get together, you end up getting an attitude and leaving. I just want to know if that's your normal m.o. or if you reserve that behavior just for me."

"I don't know what you're talking about."

"Well, I am sure that you were present all the times you were difficult, but if you need a recap, here it is. First meeting . . . you left me standing at the park without a word. I was worried about you and you wouldn't even tell me your name. Difficult."

"Second meeting . . . Davenport & Associates' reception. We were enjoying each other's company in the gazebo and then you left me standing there, only to end up giving me the silent treatment the entire ride to your house."

Christine's eyes widened in amazement. "Excuse me, Mr. Ware, but as I recall, that was right after you informed me that there was no way you wanted to pursue a personal relationship with me. So the way I see it, you were the one being difficult."

"Ahhh," Damian replied with a smile, "but I apologized and you didn't accept my apology. That qualifies you as being the difficult one."

"Meeting three . . . my office. I comfort you in the elevator, I see you safely home, you get some disturbing news, I offer my help, and you kick me out of your house."

Christine was starting to lose patience and if the car had not been dark, Damian would have seen the veins begin to pulse in her neck. "You call finding out my father cheated on my mother and had an illegitimate child, and my mother had one million dollars hidden away 'disturbing'? Well, I call it shocking and I don't think calling it a night to digest what I just learned being difficult."

"You weren't digesting," he said, mocking her. "You were shutting me out. Being difficult."

"Finally, Ms. Vanderpool. I still haven't completely figured that one out. All I know is that it ended with you storming away from me, assigning a new designer to my account, and not returning my phone calls. I rest my case. Now, answer my question, are you this difficult with everyone or is it just me?"

Christine stared out the window as the surrounding cars began to slow down to pay the toll to cross the Bay Bridge. Sighing loudly, she struggled internally with her emotions. She wanted so desperately to relax, to let her guard down and enjoy life. All her life, her friends had told her that she was uptight, conservative, afraid to let her hair down, and scared of living life. For many years, she was able to ignore that analysis and concentrate on her career. But now, she couldn't ignore it anymore. It had begun to eat away at her after her mother died, and had been magnified by the man sitting beside her. It was decision time. She wanted to release the weight of mistrust that she carried around like an iron ball and chain, but she wasn't sure she knew how. She figured the first step would be an apology.

"I'm sorry," she stated simply, without turning away from the window.

Damian smiled. Something in her voice told him they had reached a turning point.

Picking up speed, Damian merged carefully into traffic to begin the trek across the steel bridge.

"I always get nervous crossing this bridge. I know it probably sounds silly, but in the back of mind, I wonder if the bridge can handle all the cars and trucks."

Damian chuckled. "It is pretty amazing that structures like this are built. But knowing a little something about construction, I'll let you in on a little secret."

Christine blushed slightly. She should have known better than to make comments like that to a construction company owner.

Damian leaned over slightly and continued in a low, sultry voice. "The secret is in the foundation."

"The foundation?"

"The key to building something strong and lasting is to go down deep, to the root of it. In the case of this bridge, I would say that before one beam was put where you see it, the workers were underwater, working on the foundation. They probably spent a significant amount of time building the part of the bridge we can't see. It's a tedious and pains-taking project, as well as an engineer's challenge, but when the winds blow, a storm comes, or the weight of trucks and cars traveling over the bridge grows, it doesn't matter. The foundation is so strong, nothing can destroy it." Pausing a moment, Damian suddenly had a revelation. Cutting his eyes quickly at Christine, he confidently continued. "It's like love. If you spend the time to build a strong foundation, when the winds blow and the storm comes, it can't be destroyed . . . because it was built on a solid foundation."

Christine stared intently at Damian as he put his attention back on the road. His words spoke directly to her heart. She was struggling to let go of the pain and mistrust she harbored for men, and Damian just gave her the recipe for doing that. She began to relax for the first time since they began this trip. She decided to build a foundation with Damian, and suddenly a small portion of the weight of the world that sat so heavily on her shoulders evaporated.

Pulling into a gravel driveway, Damian stopped the car under the carport and cut off the engine. Looking over at Christine, he smiled. She looked peaceful and serene leaning back in her seat. She had fallen asleep an hour ago and Damian hated to wake her up. Leaning toward her, he watched the rise and fall of her chest and listened to the even tone of her breathing. Even in her sleep, she was exquisite. He reached his hand out to shake her gently, and at the last moment, decided on another tactic.

His lips touched her like a gentle breeze. At first, they were small butterfly kisses, aimed at just waking her up. But without opening her eyes, Christine began to respond. She pressed her lips forward and lifted her arm to pull him closer. Damian continued to tease her with light kisses, but then began to probe deeper when he heard the moan from deep in her throat. Rising up to meet him, Christine opened her mouth, allowing him full access. As they continued their exploration, their breathing became labored and the windows began to fog. When the moans came again, neither could tell who they belonged to.

As his lips continued their exploration, so did his hands, and when he brushed against her breast, Christine pulled away. Pulling back as well, Damian gave a tentative smile and said, "We're here!"

She turned to open her door, feeling slightly embarrassed.

"Christine, please don't shut me out again," Damian pleaded, hoping that the intimate exchange between them would not drive them further apart.

"I'm not. Believe me, I enjoyed every minute of it. It's just that it's pretty cold and we should get inside." She smiled and added, "For goodness sakes, the windows are fogged up!"

Damian laughed, "I know. I haven't fogged up windows like this since high school."

Christine looked at him pointedly, and he saw the look of confusion reflected.

"What is it, Christine?"

She turned and managed a small shrug. "It's just amazing to me when I realize how sheltered I've lived my life."

"What do you mean?"

She stepped completely out of the truck and turned to Damian. "I've never fogged up windows." She firmly shut the door.

Christine followed Damian up the steps leading to the porch. Even though it was dark, she made out the chairs and rocker on the porch and smiled at the homey feeling she got. Damian opened the door and then at the sound of the alarm, quickly punched in the alarm code.

"Hungry?" he asked, setting the two suitcases on the floor at the foot of the steps.

Shaking her head from side to side, Christine tried unsuccessfully to stifle a yawn.

"It is pretty late and I can see you're tired. Why don't I just show you to your room, and tomorrow I'll give you the grand tour."

"Good idea," she answered, turning toward the staircase. "I think I'll turn in."

Christine felt her muscles relax as she eased into the sunken tub. She was pleasantly surprised at her accommodations. The large bedroom had a small sitting area in the front, a comfortable, cushioned window seat and a queen size four poster bed with thick, soft covers. She was relieved when she was able to shut the door on Damian. He followed behind her closely as they walked down the hallway before stopping at the second door on the right. Watching her intently, she could feel the heat radiating from his body as he stood directly in front of her. She sighed with relief as he gave her a chaste kiss on the cheek and headed to his own room next door.

Leaning back and resting her head on the cool tile, Christine smiled as she remembered the sweet kisses they had shared earlier. Her response was immediate and filled with passion. Just moments before his lips touched hers, she was dreaming of the two of them, exploring each other's bodies and joining together as one. She let herself get carried away as she felt fantasy mix with reality. When his hand touched her lightly on her breast, she had snapped back to reality, realizing that she was no longer dreaming, but was in fact locked in the arms of the man of her dreams. She gently washed her body as she recalled the tenderness of his kisses. Could she have actually found a man that she could trust? Someone she could open up her heart to? Someone that would cherish and love her, not as Henry loved Ruth, but as a true friend and companion?

Stepping out of the tepid water, she dried her body with a fluffy terry cloth towel. As she dried the last drops of water from her body, she watched the bubbles flow smoothly down the drain. If only all her doubts and fears could go away as easily. She then slipped on her silk pajamas and slid underneath the covers. Suddenly, she remembered a conversation she had had with her mother after she was diagnosed with cancer.

They had been sharing a light dinner when her mother turned to her. *"I pray that you find forgiveness in your heart. Not for your father's sake and most definitely not for mine, but for the sake of the young man that God has put on this earth for you. If you fail to forgive, you will miss the opportunity to share your life with someone special."*

Closing her eyes, Christine thought about her father's mistress's claim, about her half sister, and the mysterious million dollars, but the confusion and anger that usually accompanied those thoughts seemed less than before. The hurt and disappointment she felt was still there, just not as prevalent. Was she finally on the road to true forgiveness? She wondered why now. And then she understood. She had to let go of the past before she could embrace her future. A future she wanted with Damian. Turning over, she fluffed her pillow and closed her eyes for a peaceful night of sleep.

# SIX

Christine stretched and opened her eyes slightly as the sun peered in through the mini blinds. She sat up and glanced over at the clock on the nightstand. Startled, she couldn't believe her eyes. It was eleven-thirty. She couldn't remember the last time she had slept so late. Jumping out of bed with an extra spring in her step, she dressed in a pair of black stretch pants and an oversized green sweater, and then went in search of Damian.

She stepped into the hallway and smelled fresh brewed coffee. Following the scent, she turned left at the bottom of the steps and passed what looked like a great room and an office. At the end of the hall, she entered the kitchen.

She stopped short of entering when she noticed Damian bent over at the stove. Going unnoticed, she took advantage of the opportunity to study him. At 6'3, one would have thought he would move a little awkwardly, but he moved with the grace of a swan. Opting for a pair of jeans, his muscular thighs stretched the material just enough to entice. The black turtleneck was covered by a long sleeve polo shirt which hung loosely over his broad shoulders and muscular arms. Catching herself fanning her face, this picture confirmed what she thought the first day she met him. He was one fine specimen.

She stepped forward and said, "Good morning."

"More like good afternoon," he answered, pulling a pan

of fresh biscuits out of the oven. "Have a seat. You're just in time for my world famous buttery, fluffy, flaky biscuits."

Turning down her offer to help, Damian pulled out a chair for Christine and began placing dishes in all shapes and sizes on the wooden dinette table. Eggs, bacon, pancakes, fruit salad, fried potatoes, grits, and fluffy biscuits. Christine laughed and asked, "Who else is coming to breakfast? Did we invite kids from the local high school to join us?"

Seating himself, Damian looked over the spread and grinned. "I guess I did go a little overboard. I wasn't quite sure what you would like, so I just made a little of everything. So, dig in."

After sampling everything on the table, Christine put her fork down and pushed back from the table. "I can't believe I ate all that food. Everything was delicious. Who taught you how to cook like that?"

Reaching for his fourth biscuit, Damian smiled warmly. "My mom used to drag my brother and me into the kitchen to help her with not just the cooking, but the cleaning as well. Her philosophy was that we should be able to care for ourselves and not depend on a woman to do it for us."

"Your mother sounds like a very smart woman."

After working together to clean the kitchen, they grabbed their heavy jackets and headed out for a walk around the island. Over the next few hours, they talked comfortably about many topics, including their views on politics, racism, music, movies and even the best vacation spots.

Christine learned Damian exercised daily, loved Chinese food, adored his job, never missed an action movie, and volunteered at a youth foundation. Originally from San Francisco, his family moved to the east coast when he was twelve after his father accepted a position as a professor at Georgetown University. His parents had returned to California three years ago in order to be closer to family and friends. After their father retired, Damian and his brother, Brandon, chose to remain on the east coast.

Damian learned that Christine also loved Chinese food, hated scary movies, collected abstract art by black artists, adored white roses, and worked in the nursery of her church. She attended Florida A & M University and came back to DC to complete her design studies. She admitted to having one real weakness . . . chocolate.

Walking along the main street, the late afternoon sun shone brightly through the clouds. Neither had spoken for several minutes, and Damian gently led his hand to hers and grasped it. He held his breath, hoping that she wouldn't pull away. She didn't and the relief rushed through him.

Christine was the first to break the silence. "She did it all for me."

Damian kept looking straight ahead, not responding. He knew she was referring to her mother and the money. Christine had not mentioned anything about her mother's wealth or the pending claim, but he knew it was never far from her mind. He hoped that she would open up to him and trust him to help her through this. Giving her hand an encouraging squeeze, he waited for her to continue. He didn't have to wait long. He listened patiently as she began her monologue.

"I'm beginning to doubt if I ever really knew my mother. During the time I was growing up, I spent all of my time judging her, but never trying to understand her. Mr. Murphy talked about my mother with admiration, respect and love. They grew up in the same neighborhood in North Carolina and went to high school together. Ruth Davis was something back then. One of the most popular girls in school, she participated in student government and cheerleading.

"During their senior year, a young man from New York moved to town. His name was Henry Davenport, and he was sent to live with a great aunt after his parents felt they couldn't handle him anymore. He was a rebel, a bad boy, and all the girls were drawn to this city boy who seemed to live life on the edge. But Henry Davenport only had eyes for my mom. And even though Mr. Murphy continuously warned her about getting involved with him, she found herself unable to resist him.

"Mr. Murphy and my mom were accepted to Howard University, but a week before the deadline to register for classes, Henry convinced my mom not to go, telling her he wanted to marry her, and that he had big plans for them. She bought his load of crock hook, line and sinker and convinced herself that she didn't need an education and that all she needed was him. Mr. Murphy said he pleaded, begged and even cried to try to convince my mom to go. But it was to no avail. She was helpless to go against the wishes of the man she loved.

"They married a week after graduation and I came along about a year later. For the next two years, they struggled as Henry couldn't find steady work in North Carolina. After losing his fourth job, he convinced her to move to DC where the opportunities were better. He eventually got a job at the gas company, where he worked until the day he died.

"During that time, Mr. Murphy, who was home on school break from Howard, learned from his mother that my folks were now living in the Washington DC area. Anxious to see his old friend, he looked her up and planned a surprise visit. He wasn't thrilled at seeing Henry again, but he couldn't wait to reunite with an old friend.

"Mr. Murphy said my mom's eyes lit up when she opened the door and they hugged each other warmly. However, in an instant, her entire demeanor changed. She looked up and down the street nervously, fear reflected in her eyes. She said that while she was glad to see him, it probably wasn't a good idea if they visited with each other. Henry would be home soon and she didn't think he would appreciate her having a male visitor. She asked that he not contact her again. He tried to talk to her, to find out what she was afraid of, but she asked him to leave. Regretfully, he left. He didn't try to contact her again until he graduated.

"This time he was more clever. He waited across the street

until he saw Henry leave for work, and then ringing the doorbell, he pushed his way into the house before Ruth had a
chance to stop him. He was determined to visit with Ruth
and get some answers regarding her strange behavior the last
time he had seen her. The fear on her face stayed with him
and Mr. Murphy was convinced that he knew what had put
it there: domestic violence. He had to make sure she was
OK and wanted to offer his help, and maybe even help her
to leave."

*"What are you doing here? I thought I asked you not to
come around here anymore."*

*"Ruth, I'm just here visiting an old friend," he said, look-
ing at her intently. "Surely no one would object to that."*

*"Look, my daughter is upstairs and I don't want her to
come down and see you. I think it would be best if you
leave . . . and don't come back."*

She backed up slightly as he moved toward her, crossing
her arms protectively across her chest. *"What are you afraid
of Ruth . . . or better yet, who are you afraid of?"*

Tears formed in the corner of her eyes as she turned toward the door. *"If you don't leave now, I'll call the police."*

*"Is that what we have become Ruth? Enemies? I thought
we were friends." He sighed then continued. "We shared Sunday school classes, you cheered while I played football, we
attended the junior prom together. I thought that counted for
something. Tell me, is he beating you?"*

Appalled by the blunt question, the slight hesitation in her
answer told him all he needed to know. *"Let me help you.
Pack your bags, get your daughter and come with me."*

*"Are you crazy?" she asked in shock. "I can't leave him.
Besides, you're wrong. He doesn't beat me. He just wouldn't
like me having a male friend." Opening the door, she looked
at him with pleading eyes. "Please, just go and don't come
back. I don't ever want to see you again."*

He walked slowly to the door, but stopped, quickly jotted
down his phone number, and handed it to her. *"If you ever*

*need anything, anything at all, please call me. I'll always be there for you."*

"It had taken Ruth a couple of years to finally make the call. When she did, it was not because she was ready to leave Henry, but because she wanted to create something for me. She wanted to give me a chance at life. The day after that disastrous scene regarding my haircut, she called Mr. Murphy. That's when they put together a plan.

"My mom began working part-time as a seamstress, much to Henry's dismay. She was making about seventy-five dollars a week, but told Henry she was making fifty dollars. She hid the extra twenty-five to give to Mr. Murphy. In addition, she began skimming money from the allowance Henry gave her to buy groceries, clothes and shoes. She also gave this money to Mr. Murphy and he began investing it for her.

"As the years went by, she began working full-time and altering clothes for her own clients. What started out as a hundred and fifty dollar a month investment, became upwards of one thousand dollars a month prior to Henry's death."

"That still doesn't sound like enough to have a million dollars, even if you're talking twenty years," Damian interrupted for the first time.

"That's what I said, but Mr. Murphy went on to explain that ten years ago, Henry's great aunt passed, and she had an insurance policy worth two hundred fifty thousand dollars. She named my mother as the sole beneficiary. The check came with a letter begging my mother not to tell Henry about the money and to take it and run as far away from him as possible. She knew the hell that Henry was putting her through and she wanted to help. Well, instead of taking the money and running, my mom gave it to Mr. Murphy who invested it all in a startup tech company. The money tripled in value. That's where the rest of her wealth comes from."

"Wow," Damian said, amazed by what he had just heard. "It's an amazing story. She did all of that for you."

Christine stopped abruptly and stared at Damian, a tear forming in the corner of her eye. "That's right, and if the two women from Henry's past think they can get their hands on any of it, they are in for the fight of their lives."

After returning from their walk, Christine went upstairs to lie down, while Damian took care of some business in his office. As Christine stared up at the ceiling, the words played over and over in her mind. *"She did all that for you."*

Tossing and turning, Christine thought of all the years she had wasted being angry at her mother. Those same years her mother had been working to leave something behind for her daughter. Even after Henry's death, when they had started to repair their damaged relationship, she had still refused to go to Ruth's house. Christine remembered a conversation between her and her mother, soon after Ruth's diagnosis. They had been walking along the waterfront at Haines Point Park, and stopped to watch a group of ducks playing in the water. They stood in silence for several minutes.

*"I know you hated your father,"* Ruth said. *"I know you hated him for how he treated you and me."*

*Christine didn't answer. It was true she hated him from the core of her being. But how could she voice that to the woman that had been married to him for thirty years.*

*"I know you hated me, too,"* she continued, *still looking out over the water.*

*Christine started to object.*

*"It's OK. I let him do things to you that I am ashamed of. I let him treat me badly in front of you. I know you wanted me to stand up to him in order to stop the abuse and force him to leave."* She paused, wiping the tears forming in her eyes. *"But I was afraid to stand up to him. I didn't know how*

*to make him stop and took a vow that made it difficult for
me to leave. And for that, I know you hated me."*

"Mama," Christine said as she searched for the right
words. *"I just didn't understand. I couldn't comprehend how
you could allow him to behave that way."*

Ruth shook her head regretfully. *"I carried a lot of guilt.
From the first time he yelled at you, until the day you left
for college, I cried almost daily from the guilt. But I took a
vow of marriage before God and I harbored hope that someday soon, he would change. He wasn't always mean, and I
kept looking for the old Henry. The one with a zest for life
and dreams for a bright future."*

"I never knew him to be any of those things," Christine
whispered.

"Well," she continued, turning to look into her daughter's
eyes, *"the day after you left for college, I had a long talk
with myself. I had to either let go of the guilt for the past or
it was going to eat me alive."* She grabbed her daughter's
hands. *"So I let go. I just told myself that I could not change
the past. I had made my bed, so to speak."* She squeezed
Christine's hands and smiled. *"Things changed after that
day. Not because your father changed, but because I
changed. I began to stand up to Henry, and over a period
of time, he began to change. He never became the man he
was, but before he died, he apologized."* She reached over to
wipe the tears from Christine's eyes. *"He wanted me to tell
you he was sorry."*

Ruth continued, speaking with passion. *"Don't ever let
guilt consume you. Deal with it and move on. Otherwise, it
will eat you alive."*

Christine sniffled as the tears slid unobstructed down her
face to her neck. She hadn't realized until that very moment
the guilt that had been consuming her. She had isolated her
mother for ten years, and all the while her mother was thinking of her, loving her, and preparing a legacy for her. She
could not change the past, but she could release her guilt.

Speaking aloud to the empty room, Christine said, "I'm sorry, Mom. I'm sorry for the years I wasted, but I am grateful for the time we had. I wanted to punish myself by carrying the guilt. But I won't. I can't. You taught me that, and I am forever grateful. I'm letting go and moving on. Thank you, Mom. I love you." Closing her eyes, Christine felt a little more weight being lifted from her shoulders.

Stephanie sipped her glass of water and nervously glanced around the restaurant. She had agreed to meet Nathan at one of his favorite DC restaurants, Georgia Brown's. The southern cuisine was the best around and the atmosphere was intimate. She took the chicken's way out when she called him, waiting until she knew he was at work and then leaving a message on his answering machine to meet her here.

Sitting at a small table by the window, she watched him step out of his rental car and hand the keys to the valet. As he held the door for two women exiting the restaurant, Stephanie observed their look of admiration for Nathan before they continued on their way. Stephanie was sure it was the same scene no matter where he was. He was everything a woman could hope for in a man. Standing six feet tall with a solid body that reflected his commitment to physical fitness, Nathan was smart, successful and handsome. On the inside, he had a peace about him that allowed him not to worry or let things get to him. She had yet to meet anyone like him.

Life had been challenging for Stephanie. She had lost both her parents at a very young age and had had to endure her teenage years with an overbearing, but loving, grandmother. She missed her parents immensely, and losing them had taught her how precious life could be. She was only ten when a drunk driver, ignoring a friend's advice to take a cab, crossed the yellow line, slamming into her parents' car head on, killing her father instantly. Her mother hung on for four days, before the pain overcame her.

The ironic thing about the night her parents died was that Stephanie was supposed to be in the car with them. Her parents had stopped off at her grandmother's house after dining out, and when Stephanie found out that her grandma was making peach cobbler for her church bake sale, Stephanie had begged her parents to let her stay and help. It was the first time her parents had let her stay over on a school night.

After the funeral, Stephanie had moved in with her maternal grandmother. The older woman held a tight reign on Stephanie, fearful that Stephanie would meet an untimely death just as her daughter and son-in-law had. So, when Stephanie got a full scholarship to a college five states away, she jumped at the opportunity, committing herself to live life to the fullest.

At first, she thought that meant not missing one party. And for the first two years, she had just about met that goal. But reality set in at the end of her sophomore year when she was in danger of losing her scholarship and her grandmother told her that she just didn't have the money for tuition. Stephanie quickly settled down, found a summer job, and got serious about school. She was able to keep her scholarship and graduated at the top of her class. She returned home to DC after graduation and built a successful career.

"Care to let me in on your thoughts?"

Stephanie startled, and looked up at Nathan who was standing at her table with smile on his face.

"I'm sorry, what did you say?"

Nathan sat down and accepted a menu from the waiter. "That must have been some place you were at. I've been calling your name for almost a minute. What were you thinking about anyway?"

With a wave of her hand, she dismissed his inquiry. "It was nothing. How was your flight?"

"Why do you do that?" he asked, slightly irritated.

"Do what?" she replied innocently.

"Every time I ask you to share a part of you with me, you change the subject."

They were interrupted by the waiter who took their wine order. Stephanie hoped Nathan would drop the subject.

"I love their fried green tomatoes. Are you going to have an appetizer?"

"I might have some soup," Nathan replied, as he watched her look over the menu as if it held the secrets to the building of the pyramids. They had eaten here enough times that she probably knew the menu by heart. But he wasn't surprised at her avoidance tactic. Every time he asked her to share a little of herself with him, she clammed up. Tonight, he was determined to change that scenario. If there was going to be any conversation during dinner, it was going to come from her.

Watching the candlelight dance across her face, her beauty never failed to set his insides on fire. She was kind, compassionate, funny, smart and sincere. But he could tell she had been hurt before, and that caused her to put her guard up. The first time he had come to visit her from Atlanta, he shared dinner with her and Christine. His initial impression was that they were complete opposites, and after hearing Stephanie tell him about the challenges Christine was facing, first in trying to have a relationship, he was convinced more than ever that they were different.

Stephanie possessed an outward appearance of confidence, vibrancy and spirit that attracted people to her. Christine was competent, but reserved. She was a fabulous designer and businesswoman, but she purposely held back socially to keep people from getting too close to her.

But ever since he had confessed his love to Stephanie, he began to wonder if his initial assessment was incorrect. Based on her reaction to his declaration, he would say that she had some of the same hang-ups as Christine, and this weekend, he was determined to break through to her.

Deep inside, he knew she was the one for him. He would get her to open up to him no matter what. Without realizing, he touched the inside pocket of his jacket and felt for the box. A two-carat, pear-shaped solitaire diamond increased his confidence in completing his mission. This weekend, she would accept his proposal.

Stephanie declined another glass of wine as the waiter cleared away their entree dishes. Sneaking a glance at Nathan, she wondered what was on his mind. He was uncharacteristically quiet and she felt a need to fill in the silence. She updated him on Christine's legal issues, the goings-on at the design firm, and engaged him in a brief conversation about his upcoming interview. But she felt the conversation was extremely one-sided. Never one to be short on words, Nathan loved talking about a variety of topics. However, when she brought up politics, the economy and some hot news items, he just nodded, not offering more than a few words. The one topic she didn't want to bring up was his family.

Nathan's parents, three brothers and two sisters were at the top of his conversation list, but Stephanie hesitated on inquiring about them. It wasn't that she didn't want to hear about them, it was just hard for her because her family were all dead. After her parents died, her grandmother was the only living relative she knew. When she passed a year after Stephanie graduated from college, Stephanie became truly all alone.

As the waiter brought over the assortment of fresh desserts for the day, she knew that she couldn't take it anymore. His silence was killing her. After their orders were placed, Stephanie took a deep breath and asked, "So how are your folks doing. I think you said that they went to Spain. Did they enjoy themselves?"

Nathan, about to take a sip of wine, placed his glass back onto the table and stared at her, a smile beginning to form on his face.

"What?" she asked, a little confused by his behavior.

"Do you know in the year that we've been together, this is the first time you've asked me about my family."

Stephanie laughed. "What are you talking about. You talk about your family all the time."

"Yes," he answered as he reached across the table for her hand. "I do talk about my family, but you've never *asked* me about my family. Why is that?"

Pulling her hands away from his, she placed them into her lap. "Stop analyzing me."

The waiter returned with dessert, but neither ate.

"I'm not analyzing. I'm just asking a question," Nathan finally said.

"You are analyzing and I don't appreciate it one bit. For the past month, every time we talk or get together, you tell me I never open up and that I've put up a barrier. Well, you know what?" she said, her voice level rising. "You're wrong. There is nothing wrong with me. I'm sorry if I don't measure up to whatever vision you have of me, but this is what you get. You can take it or leave it."

Breathing deeply, she glanced around consciously, as a few people at nearby tables stopped eating to stare at her. Turning her attention back to Nathan, she said, "I'm ready to go."

"Stephanie . . ." he started.

She placed her purse onto the table and pulled out her wallet. "I said I'm ready to go."

Not wanting to cause a bigger scene, Nathan signaled the waiter for the check and handed him his platinum visa. "Put your money away. This one's on me," he said.

They exited the restaurant and were silent while they waited for the valets to get their cars. Stephanie's black 750 BMW arrived first. She took her keys and handed the valet a tip before she hurried toward the open door. Before she got in, Nathan reached out and gently grabbed her arm.

"I'm not sure what happened in there, but it doesn't have to end like this. I want to work this out."

She got inside and attempted to shut the car door, but he blocked her way.

"Is everything OK, ma'am?" the valet asked, with a concerned look on his face. "Should I call security?"

"I'm staying at the Park Hyatt on Twenty-fourth Street, room 742," he said, stepping away from the car.

Not responding, Stephanie slammed the car door and drove off. Nathan didn't move until he could no longer see her taillights.

Christine watched Damian add more logs to the fire. They were relaxing in the great room after finishing a fabulous dinner of fresh grilled salmon, homemade mashed potatoes and lightly grilled asparagus with butter. It was the best meal Christine had eaten in weeks, and she complemented the chef on his culinary skills. She was curious about the groceries. They hadn't been apart since they had arrived, and she hadn't noticed him unloading any bags. When she finally questioned Damian about the groceries, he admitted that Mrs. Watson, the caretaker, had stocked the refrigerator yesterday at his request.

Feeling completely relaxed, she pulled her left foot under her right leg, and basked in the comfort of the room. The entire house radiated coziness. With its wraparound porch and soaring windows, it was ideal for beach living. The great room was the focal point for relaxation. It was located in the center of the house and had oak hardwood floors which were covered with several area rugs.

The rest of the room was decorated in hunter green and black and definitely reflected a man's taste. The large entertainment center, consisting of a big screen TV, a very expensive stereo system, and more videos than Blockbuster, gave off a comfortable feel. The oak floor to ceiling shelves on each side of the fireplace were filled with books on just about every subject. She even saw a section housing paperback romance novels. She made a mental note to ask Damian to whom they belonged. Leaning back against the overstuffed pillows, Christine felt light and happy. Looking at the pictures on the coffee table, she picked up a picture of Damian with another young man. He was a younger version of Damian, only his eyes were brighter and his smile a little more devious.

"Is this your brother?"

Glancing at the photograph, Damian smiled warmly. "Yes, that is the infamous Brandon Ware."

"What makes him infamous?"

He moved to sit beside her and took the picture out her hand to look at it. "Let's just say he has a reputation of living life on the edge."

"Is that such a bad thing? I think it would be good to be carefree and not to get bogged down with issues, problems . . . life."

"I think there's a difference between carefree and my brother. He has a habit of doing things without thinking or considering the consequences. That type of behavior can be destructive."

"You sound like you don't approve."

"Brandon has a tendency to only think of himself . . . and let's just say that can leave a trail of hurt people behind."

"Has he hurt you?"

"Not me, so much, as the people I care about. But enough about Brandon Ware," he said, placing the photograph back on the table. "I'd rather talk about Christine. What's on your mind?"

"Actually, I was just admiring this room. I'm trying to remember the last time I've been this relaxed," she answered. "It's been a while."

"Well, if you want the ultimate in relaxation, we could try out the hot tub. It's in a heated enclosed deck."

Christine laughed, "Are you serious! I may not get out much, but I know a lame line when I hear one."

"Me, give you a line?" Damian asked in mocked amusement. "Never! It even has a glass ceiling so we can gaze up at the stars."

"Gaze up at the stars," she repeated with a smirk. "Now I know you're feeding me a line. Besides, it's the first week of November. I didn't exactly think I would be needing a bathing suit."

"No problem. There are new suits hanging in the closet in the bedroom across from you. You can pick any one you like, or," he said with a look of mischievousness, "you can not wear one at all."

Christine's smile faltered. "Do you keep suits on hand for all the women you wine and dine at your beach house?"

Seeing where this conversation was headed, Damian quickly back tracked. "You've got the wrong idea. My brother is what you could call a playboy. We both own this house and while I use it as a getaway, a place to think and regroup, he uses it as his own personal vacation spot to enjoy with his many girlfriends. He actually bought those suits himself, just in case."

Christine wondered if he was telling the truth. Deciding to put her suspicions aside, her smile returned and she agreed. "I'll meet you on the deck in fifteen minutes."

Damian followed her up the stairs and watched as she entered the bedroom. Quickly, he changed into loose swim trunks. He returned downstairs and started the hot tub jets before he ran to the kitchen to get a bottle of champagne, two flutes, and a bowl of strawberries and grapes. He placed the items on the hot tub ledge and eased himself into the water.

Christine stood in front of the open closet door. She couldn't believe her eyes as they roamed over twenty bathing suits in a variety of sizes. She searched for a size ten and found three, but didn't know if any were her style. Immediately, she began to smile. Throwing caution to the wind, and refusing to think of the consequences, she made a quick decision. She pulled off her clothes, working quickly, before she changed her mind.

She then walked briskly down the hall and was relieved when she realized Damian was already downstairs. When she reached the bottom of the staircase, she paused for a moment, almost losing her nerve. She glanced from left to right making sure the coast was clear. If she was going to pull this off, she had to get herself together. She took a deep breath and walked confidently through the great room to the sliding doors that led out to the patio. Opening the door, she stepped outside and was glad to see it was just as warm on deck as it was inside the house. Damian, struggling to uncork the champagne, looked up as he worked the edge of the cork out. Just as the cork popped off, his mouth dropped open. He didn't notice as most of the bubbly gushed out of the bottle and into the water.

# SEVEN

Damian's reaction excited her and increased her confidence in her appearance. Feeling both giddy and beautiful, she turned around with the grace of a runway model.

"You like?" she asked, with a satisfied grin. She had never felt such power and freedom in her life. "It's from the Adam and Eve collection."

"I . . . I . . ." he started, not quite knowing what to say.

Laughing, she said, "Close your mouth, dear. We already have a tub full of champagne. Let's not add your drool to the mix."

"Damn!" Damian yelled, realizing for the first time that half of the bottle was now mixed in with the warm, steamy water. He placed the bottle back onto the ledge, but couldn't take his eyes off of her.

She took a step and swirled one foot around the edge of the water. "How is it? It seems to be hot and steamy." She stepped in and eased her body down. After a few moments of silence, Christine smiled. "You were absolutely right, Damian. This is total relaxation. Why don't you pass me a glass of champagne?"

Damian turned and began to fill the glasses with what remained in the bottle. You could have knocked him over with a feather when he saw her standing at the door. The Adam and Eve collection! Never in a million years would he have expected her to choose a suit that was made only of strings and three small leaves placed in very strategic places.

Handing her a glass, he finally became able to form a complete sentence. "For someone who has never fogged up car windows, you sure do know how to make an entrance, Miss Eve."

"Well then, I propose a toast," she replied, raising her glass, "To fogging up windows."

He stared intently at her and smiled. "I don't know what's going on, but it looks like you passed a milestone."

"What do you mean?"

"It's in your eyes. When I saw you at the park, they were filled with sadness. When we met at the reception, they were filled with fear. When you work, they're filled with excitement. But tonight, they seemed to reflect something else . . . peace."

As she moved closer to Damian, she noticed the fruit on the ledge. "Feed me."

Christine enjoyed the attention as Damian peeled grapes for her before placing them in her mouth. Reacting with a boldness she didn't know she possessed, Christine pulled his finger into her mouth and sucked it lightly. The game continued in silence as he fed her grapes and she reciprocated with strawberries. When it was once again Damian's turn, he left the grapes alone and leaned forward. The electricity flowed between them the moment their lips touched.

What started out as a soft, featherlike kiss quickly escalated into something more. As he traced the outline of her lips with his warm tongue, Christine felt her entire body react, from the tingling in her toes, to the lightness in her head.

Christine answered his silent question and opened her mouth to welcome him. The faint taste of strawberries and champagne was intoxicating and Christine found herself in an exploration of his mouth. Never had she felt such excitement. Moving away from her mouth, Damian began branding her with his hot kisses down her cheek, across her neck and behind her ears. Simultaneously, his hands were conducting a deep exploration of their own. While one hand gently massaged behind her neck, the other hand began a trail down her arm and around her waist. Moving upward, the tips of his fingers traced a circular motion around her breast, never quite touching its core.

She moaned at the torture, wanting so desperately to feel his touch. He continued his teasing until she couldn't take it anymore.

"Please, Damian, touch me."

Moving his lips back to hers, he continued his exploration of her mouth as his hand cupped her breast and gave her the pleasure she had been seeking. The touch sent currents of desire through her body and settled in the center of her being. Her eager response only served to excite him more.

"Let's move this upstairs," he said between breaths.

He felt her body become tense and opened his eyes. Moving back a little, he stared at her.

"Christine?"

A flicker of apprehension coursed through her and a pregnant silence enveloped the room. The freedom and excitement she had felt moments ago had suddenly turned to doubt and fear. She knew from the very beginning that there was something special about him. He was honest, successful, kind and sincere. No one had ever touched her the way he had. She sucked in a short breath as she realized she was falling in love with him. Wanting to let go of herself for one night, she smiled slowly.

"I'm sorry," she said, shaking her head from side to side. "It must be the champagne. Cupping her hands on each side of his face, she kissed him. "Let's move our party upstairs."

"Are you sure?" he asked, not wanting her to regret it in the morning.

"I'm sure."

Stepping out of the hot tub, he wrapped her in a thick, terry cloth towel, and as his lips captured hers, they made a silent promise of the passion yet to come. Moving back into the great room, he walked behind her, gently rubbing her shoulders. As they began to climb the stairs, Christine jumped at the sound of a ringing telephone.

"Who could that be at this hour?" Christine asked.

"The only person who knows I'm here," he said through clenched teeth. "And it better be a matter of life or death."

She followed him into his office and listened as he answered the call.

"Hello, Tanya," he barked. "This had better be good."


Twenty minutes later, they were packed and on the road. Christine drove while Damian held various conversations on his cell phone. In the time since they had left the beach house, he had spoken to his head engineer three times, Tanya twice, and the authorities once. He didn't have all the details, but evidently, one of his almost-completed buildings had caught fire.

The fire had spread quickly and part of the structure had collapsed. It had started about two hours ago, long after the crews had gone home. It was located on a busy downtown street, and the authorities had yet to determine whether anyone had been trapped by falling debris.

"Damn," Damian said, disconnecting his call with Justin, the foreman, who was assigned to that job. He had only arrived at the scene moments before. He could provide Damian with only a very limited amount of information.

"They're still searching the rubble with dogs, but so far, they haven't found any indication that people are trapped. But they don't deny that it's still a possibility."

Christine watched Damian lean his head back on the headrest and close his eyes. She didn't know what to say.

"The media arrived fifteen minutes ago. I've got to find out what happened before they make up their own story."

Christine felt helpless to offer any comfort. She knew that until she got him to the site, where he could assess the damage for himself and find out if anyone was hurt, there was nothing she could say. So she settled for, "we should be there in about an hour."

The street was barricaded when they arrived, and they were only let through when Damian's identity was confirmed. It didn't take long for the microphones to be shoved into his face. He kept walking, with Christine following close behind.

"Could you tell us what happened?"

"Do you know if anyone was trapped inside?"

"Is this a result of faulty work?"

The last question stopped Damian dead in his tracks. Turning, he had to squint at the bright lights illuminating from at least four different cameras.

"Ware Construction Company does not do faulty work. Please wait for an official report before you begin reporting information you can't back up with facts," he said, trying to contain his aggravation at their line of questioning.

Moving beyond the yellow police rope, Christine and Damian were met by an anxious Tanya.

"Damian, I'm glad you made it safely," Tanya said, giving him a warm hug.

Christine felt that little twinge of jealously she felt at their first meeting.

Turning to Christine, Tanya took her hand and squeezed it. "It's good to see you again. I'm glad you came with him."

Christine listened for a tone of anger or agitation, but didn't hear any. Could Tanya be sincere in her friendliness toward her? She returned the smile. "No problem."

For the next two hours, Christine stood around in near-freezing weather drinking coffee provided to her by the fire department, while the building was inspected by the authorities with Damian following close behind them. The media and crowd that had gathered breathed a sigh of relief when the news was announced that no one was trapped inside.

Christine watched as Damian talked with city officials,

the fire department and his own men. She knew he was tired and upset, but his professional demeanor never wavered. He had told Christine several times that she didn't have to stay and could take the Ford Expedition while he caught a ride with Tanya, but she had refused to leave. She wanted to be there for him because he had been so supportive of her and the challenges she had been facing. She wanted to give some of that support back. She didn't know what she could do, but she hoped just being there would be worth something.

Damian looked around and found little comfort at the number of employees who were there to offer help. Even though the fire had been extinguished, there were still many unanswered questions. Did someone start the fire? Could it have been prevented? What was this going to do to his business?

"I don't know if there is much more we can do here."

Damian turned and came face-to-face with Justin and one of his laborers, Alex Smith.

"I know, Justin, but I'm not leaving here until somebody tells me what the hell happened. I have cameras in my face, reporters on my back, and the authorities breathing down my neck, all looking for answers."

"Let's just wait to see what the cause of the fire is," Justin said, hearing the anger and frustration in his boss' voice. "It probably has nothing to do with our work."

Blowing on his hands to keep them warm, Damian said with deadly force, "It better not, because if we are at fault in anyway, heads are going to roll. And you can count on that." Turning away from him, he headed toward the fire chief to check the status of the investigation.

"You want some more coffee?"

Turning toward the female voice, Christine laughed. "No, thank you. I might not be able to go to sleep for the next several days as it is. I'll just have to take my chances with the cold weather."

After standing together for several minutes in silence, Tanya said, "Damian and I are just friends."

"I don't recall asking anything about you and Damian," Christine answered, looking out toward the half-demolished building.

"You can probably see that we are close. But I want you to know that we are just friends. Always have been and hopefully always will be."

"You don't owe me an explanation."

"I know, but if I were you, I would be curious."

Once again, hearing the sincerity in her voice, Christine smiled and turned back toward her. "Well, just a little."

"You're good for him, Christine. I don't think I've ever seen him this happy, and I've known him for more than fifteen years."

Christine gave Tanya a genuine smile. "It's good that he has you as a friend."

"I came as soon as I heard."

The two women turned to the male voice, and Christine recognized him right away. Brandon.

Tanya shivered and pulled her coat tighter around herself. "Hi, Brandon. I know Damian appreciates your coming, but I'm freezing. I'm going to see if they need me. If not, I'm heading home."

Brandon stared after her for a moment, then turned his attention back to Christine. Giving her a charming smile, he said, "You don't look like a construction worker."

"I'll let that chauvinistic comment slide since you are Damian's brother."

"Have we met?" he asked.

"No," she said, stretching out her hand. "Christine Davenport."

"Ahh," he answered, cupping her hand in his. "I see everything my brother said about you is true . . . beautiful and sassy."

Damian walked over, looking tired. He gave his brother a hug and they spoke briefly before Damian said, "There's nothing more we can do tonight. Let's go home."

A short while later, Damian pulled into Christine's driveway and rubbed his eyes. It was after four A.M. and he hadn't slept in more than twenty hours.

"I know you only live about twenty minutes away, but I don't think you're in any position to drive. Get out. You're staying here," Christine said.

Damian grabbed their bags out the back of the truck and followed Christine into the house.

She showed him to the guest room. "You're lucky I'm too tired to object to these sleeping arrangements."

"I'll take that as a compliment."

Growing serious, Damian pulled her into his arms. "I just wanted to thank you for hanging in there with me tonight. I can't believe this happened. I just don't know what could have gone wrong."

Hearing the weariness in his voice, she answered, "I'm sure everything will work out. I'm here for you . . . whenever you need me." She kissed him sweetly on the lips, said goodnight and headed to her own room.

The next morning, Christine awoke to an incessant knocking at her front door. Going to bed only a few hours ago, she was hoping to sleep in. Slowly sitting up, she waited to see if her uninvited visitor would go away. Hearing the doorbell ring again, she sighed loudly, and moved to the window to see if she recognized a car. Pulling back the drapes, she smiled. She should have known.

Opening the front door, she said, "You better come bearing gifts of coffee and bagels at this hour."

Pulling the bag from behind her back, Stephanie said, "Of course I did. I didn't want to get all the juicy details of your weekend on an empty stomach."

Settling in the kitchen, Christine relayed the events of her weekend, from the moment Damian picked her up, until the phone call came that sent them scrambling to get back home.

"That man has definitely changed you," Stephanie said. "You have a certain glow about you that I've never seen before. You look truly happy."

Christine rose to refill their coffee cups. "Oh, Stephanie, I can't explain to you how being with him has affected me. It's almost too good to be true."

"I'm thrilled for you. No one deserves it more than you," Stephanie exclaimed.

"It's scary," Christine said, resuming her seat at the table, "After seeing the disastrous relationship of my parents, I never thought I would allow myself to make room for something in my life other than my business, but I have and it feels wonderful."

Stephanie raised her coffee cup in the air and smiled. "I want to wear something simple in the wedding. Please don't put me in fuscia taffeta."

Slowly placing her mug on the table, Christine stared at her friend. "I'm not getting married."

"If Damian has the same look on him, as you have on you, it won't be long before he pops the question."

"He can pop anything he wants, but there is no way I'm going to marry him."

Hearing the seriousness in her tone, Stephanie stared at her. "What's going on? Didn't you just say he makes you feel things you never thought were possible?"

Placing her hands in her lap, she played with her napkin. "Yes, but that will have to be enough for him. My mother once told me that Henry changed after they married, and it nearly destroyed her. I won't let that happen to me."

"You can't be serious?" Stephanie asked. "Have you discussed this with Damian?"

"Not in so many words."

Stephanie raised her brow in confusion.

"He knows about my childhood and the sorry state of my parents' marriage. He has to understand that marriage is not for me."

"And what if he doesn't? Are you going to be willing to give him up? To let him walk out of your life?"

Christine pondered her questions with concern. She wanted to believe that she could have love without the marriage. Her hope was that Damian would understand. "It'll work out Stephanie, you'll see. Now," she said, changing the subject, "Tell me about your dinner with Nathan. What happened?"

Stephanie shifted uncomfortably in her chair. "Nothing happened. It's over."

Looking closely at her friend, Christine asked, "What did you do?"

Stephanie rolled her eyes heavenward. "Look, I didn't do anything. Nathan and I. . . . we just weren't meant to be."

"You know what I think?"

"I'm not interested in what you think."

"I think you finally found the one person who touched your soul. All your life you lived superficially. Except for me, you've never allowed anyone to get close to you. Maybe it's because you lost your parents so young. I don't know, but I do know that Nathan is the first one who sees the person on the inside and refuses to go away until you let her out."

"Why is everybody trying to analyze me?" she spat. "Did you and Nathan take the same Psych 101 class?"

"Maybe the only reason what we're saying bothers you is because it's true. And you, my dear, don't want to admit it."

"Well, it doesn't matter now. Nathan Hollister will have his job interview tomorrow and he will fly back to Atlanta and out of my life. I know him," she said sadly. "He won't contact me again."

"Then I guess it's up to you to contact him. But I wouldn't wait too long," Christine said, filling up the coffee cups.

"You never know . . . a man like that is a great catch . . . and the women in DC are fierce," she added with a smile.


Later that day, Stephanie made a right turn onto Twenty-Fourth Street and pulled into a metered parking space. Second thoughts ran through her mind as she got out of the car. Nodding to the doorman as he held open the door for her, she stopped at the mirrored wall and checked herself. Blue was Nathan's favorite color, so she had opted for a pair of navy blue pants with a matching velour sweater. Stepping onto the elevator, she secretly hoped that he wasn't here. She had purposely not called. In that way, if she missed him, she could never claim that she hadn't tried.

Stepping off the elevator, she slowed her step as she approached room 724. Christine had touched a nerve with her earlier and made her rethink her position on their relationship. She understood Nathan's concerns, and deep inside, Stephanie knew he was right. It had always been difficult for her to completely give her all, for fear that it would only end in pain. But knowing that he had reached the point of cutting bait, she visualized him with another woman. That's when it registered. He needed her to trust him . . . with herself. And that's exactly what she planned to do. Knocking on the door, she barely had time to lower her hand when it swung open.

Stephanie had a moment of panic as she saw that he was dressed as if he was going out. Could he have found someone already? It hadn't been twenty-four hours. But there he was in a smoke gray pair of slacks, with a black turtleneck and multicolored blazer. The scent of his cologne, carried by the wind created from the door being opened, nearly made her drunk with awareness.

"Stephanie?" he said, not able to hide his surprise.

She felt foolish for not calling. "I was in the neighborhood and thought I would stop by. But it looks like you're going out."

Not wanting to make this easy for her, he simply replied, "Yes."

"Who is she?" she asked flatly.

"Who said it was a she?"

"I don't have time for games, Nathan. I'm outta here." Turning, she started down the hall, expecting Nathan to call out to her to wait. This was the part where he would tell her that he wasn't seeing another woman and to come back so they could sit and talk and work things out. But she didn't hear a word. She knew he was still standing there because she didn't hear his door shut. *Please, Nathan, say something. Stop me.*

When she reached the elevator, she paused several seconds before she pushed the button. She still had not heard the door shut. *Please stop me, Nathan. I love you.* The elevator came and the doors opened. An elderly couple stood inside holding hands. They smiled warmly at her and took a step back to make room for her. Taking a step forward, she entered, and the doors slid closed.

Nathan heard the elevator doors close and a permanent sorrow engulfed him. He had just gambled and lost the love of his life. Last night, when he had returned to his hotel room, he immediately reached for the phone. He had punched the first three numbers, when he realized the role he played in their predicament. Every time they argued, he was the one to make the reconnection. She would run scared and he would coax her back to him. It was then that he realized that if Stephanie was ever going to freely love and trust him, he had to allow her to come willingly, on her own, with no help from him.

His heart nearly stopped when he heard the bell on the elevator door, and heard the doors slide shut. He couldn't reach her because she didn't want to be reached. Taking one last look down the hall, he turned to go back inside.

"Wait!"

Nathan glanced up and couldn't believe his eyes. She looked delicate and ethereal as she took tentative steps toward him. The smile in his eyes contained a sensuous flame as they drank in the most beautiful sight. She was coming back to him.

Shutting the door behind them, he calmly walked to the phone and dialed. He watched with interest as she moved to the desk, picking up tourist brochures and putting them down. Next, she walked over to the window and looked out onto the busy streets of DC.

"Hey, Dennis, I'm going to have to cancel our dinner plans tonight. I'll call you tomorrow."

He hung up and calmly placed his hands into his pockets, and waited.

Stephanie sat in the chair next to the window, rigidly holding her tears in check.

Moving toward her, he stopped in front of her and kneeled down. Gently wiping a lone tear from her cheek, he watched her solemnly. "What do you want, Stephanie?"

"I don't want to get hurt," she answered in a broken whisper.

"I would never do anything with the intention of hurting you."

"I know," she said, nervously fingering the pearls around her neck. "But I'm afraid."

"Why?"

"Because all the people I've loved have left me, and I don't know if I could survive if you left me, too."

"I would never intentionally cause you pain," he said with quiet emphasis.

"Promise?"

"Listen to me, sweetheart. I stopped seeing other women the first time you came to Atlanta. I have a great career and no hidden vices. I'm in good health and I'm looking to settle down with one woman for the rest of my life. I'm sorry to disappoint you by being a devoted, successful man madly in love with you."

"I love you, too," she said, relieved that the words had finally been set free.

"Don't move." He rose in one fluid motion and retrieved the jacket he had worn the previous night. Kneeling again, Stephanie's eyes widened in anticipation.

"Stephanie Renee Jackson, will you marry me?"


Stepping out of the shower, Christine began to pat herself dry as she hummed one of her favorite songs. Leaving work early that day, Christine had decided to jump start the weekend and give herself a little extra time to prepare for the evening. She hadn't seen Damian all week, as he had spent every day trying to piece together what had happened to his building. With all the media attention being given about the accident, as well as Ware Construction Company, Christine's interest was peaked and she spent a little time at the library to find out all she could about Damian Ware and Ware Construction Company.

His construction company was one of the largest in the area and had given back to the community by refurbishing an old building into a shelter for the homeless and by helping local churches make much needed repairs to their buildings. Named Entrepreneur of the Year his second year in business, he was on the fast track to being part of the Washington, DC business elite. The last article Christine read stuck with her the most. It was from the society page of the *Washington Post*. An engagement announcement.

*Damian Ware, owner of one of the largest privately owned construction companies in the area, announced his engagement to Danielle Olivia. The famous runway model, who is beginning a career in acting, has graced the runways of Paris, Milan, and New York. The couple have been seen around the world together, as the construction company owner travels frequently with his fiancé on assignment. They have been spotted in Spain, Cannes, Los Angeles, and New York. They've set a date in the near future and the couple plan to begin a family right away. They'll make their home in Potomac, MD.*

Christine studied the picture above the short article. Danielle Olivia was no stranger to her. She had seen her in many print ads and in several commercials. Just recently, she was one of the presenters on a music award show. She thought back to when she and Damian had their conversation about love, and he admitted to loving someone who was deceitful. She wondered if this was the person to whom he was referring. Remembering how happy the couple looked in the photo, she wondered what could have happened to end it all. Whatever the reason, Christine had to admit that Danielle Olivia was an extremely attractive woman.

Pushing thoughts of Danielle out of her mind, she sat on the bed and reached for her favorite scented body oil. Rubbing every part of her body, she anxiously anticipated spending time with Damian. Not in the mood for going out, Christine agreed to dinner at his home. Moving to the entrance of her closet, she wanted to select something to impress and entice. Then she saw the outfit, with the tags still hanging from it. Bought on one of her shopping trips with Stephanie last year, she never had the nerve, or the occasion to wear it. Pulling if off the rack, she looked it over. It was short, black and tight. She smiled. If she could wear the Adam and Eve collection bathing suit, she could definitely pull this one off. She continued to prepare for her date.

Damian put the finishing touches on his salad and set it on the table. The week had been treacherous. The investigation revealed that the fire was caused by the wiring in the walls. The wires were of a low, thin grade and the insulation in some of the wires were crushed. So when the electric company had turned power on in the building, three weeks prior to the tenants moving in, it was too hot for the wires to handle.

Damian was able to prove through his purchase orders that he had ordered the thicker, durable wires, but something happened between the order and the installation. He had to find out how and why the switch happened.

But tonight, he wanted to put all of that business out of his mind. He didn't realize how much Christine had become a part of his life until he was forced to go a week without seeing her. Heading out of the kitchen, he went into the family room to turn on some soft jazz. This was the room that had sold him on this house. Shaped like an octagon, the room was warm and inviting with a fireplace and two bay windows with cozy window seats.

He remembered the first time he had seen the house. Many thought he would build his own home, but the minute the real estate agent drove up the circular driveway, he knew he had found the right home. The multi-level home was spectacular. With a two-story high entry way leading to an open railed stairway, it possessed an understated elegance. The sunken formal living and dining rooms were defined by oval archways and cathedral ceilings. His master suite came with its own fireplace, a huge walk-in closet, separate dressing areas and a bathroom with double sinks and a Jacuzzi tub with a separate shower. The basement featured a recreation room, an exercise room and two extra bedrooms. His family, unaware of his intentions to marry Danielle, wondered why he wanted to live in such a big house all by himself.

When he found this house, he was disappointed when Danielle didn't want to see it. She said she trusted his judgment and whatever he wanted was fine. He thought the house would be a stepping stone to being together as they prepared to marry, but after they moved in, she never stayed more than one or two nights a week, always traveling in and out of town. She never bought one thing for the house and never moved any of her things in. The day their entire relationship fell apart, he didn't think he would be able to live in this house with the memories. But he realized that Danielle never made this place her own. So he had decided to stay, and now, thinking of Christine, he was glad he had.

Hearing the doorbell, he took one last look at the setting and headed to the front door. Opening the door, complete shock flew through his entire body.

"Hi honey, I'm home."

"What the hell are you doing here?"

Not waiting to be asked in, she breezed past him and walked into the foyer, swinging her fur coat in the process. "Now, is that any way to greet an old friend?"

"No, but then I don't consider you a friend," he said with cold sarcasm.

"Testy, testy."

"What are you doing here, Danielle. What do you want?"

She removed her coat. "Be a sweetheart and hang this up for me please."

"I don't think you'll be staying that long."

"Where is this all hostility coming from?" she asked innocently. "I fly all the way from Paris to offer my support and this is the welcome I get."

Slamming the door shut, he said, "I thought I made it clear that I never wanted to see you again."

The phone began to ring and Damian hesitated. He wanted to get this woman out of his house.

"Aren't you going to get that?" she asked with a sneaky grin. "Or should I?"

Thinking it could be Christine, he walked down the hall to his study.

"Hi, Tanya. . . . You're a little late on the heads up. She got here about five minutes ago . . . Yeah, well, she's being her normal self . . . I'll call you later."

Hanging up, he saw Danielle standing at the door. "Let

me guess. That was my dear sister, Tanya, calling to warn you that I was on my way over."

Damian stared at her and wondered what he had seen in her all those years ago. After he was named Entrepreneur of the Year, he quickly became the toast of the town. He had met Danielle at the awards ceremony, and was totally mesmerized. Tanya warned him that Danielle had a one-track mind: career. But he didn't listen.

Over the next six months, he fell completely under her spell. Living the glamorous life, he accompanied her to movie premieres, commercial shoots, and even spent a month at her Santa Monica home. Tanya warned him repeatedly that his business was suffering, but he told her that he had everything under control. Less than a year after their meeting, he proposed and she accepted. He spoke to her about moving to the east coast permanently and beginning a family. She agreed wholeheartedly and they began to make plans for a lavish wedding.

Three months later, it was over. The deceit and lies hidden in the darkness came to light and he let her go once and for all. Danielle immediately returned to California then accepted a modeling assignment in Paris.

Immersing himself in business after that, he realized how much had gotten away from him in the time he had spent traveling around with Danielle. His profits decreased, his payments to suppliers were behind, and two high profile projects were behind schedule and over budget. It took him a year to put it all back together. He promised himself that he would never allow a woman to sidetrack him from his construction company again. That was, until he met Christine. *Christine!* She was going to be here any minute. Walking past Danielle, he went straight to the front door. She reluctantly followed.

"Good night, Danielle."

"It's Friday night and I know you've had a rough week. Why don't you let me cook dinner for you?"

Before he could respond, she walked past him toward the kitchen.

Stopping abruptly, her eyes roamed the room and took in the fresh flowers, the wine chilling on ice and the pots simmering on the stove. She turned around and took a good look at Damian. Dressed in navy slacks, a designer sweater and loafers, her look quickly changed to anger.

"Well, it looks like you have plans for this evening. Who is she, Damian?"

"You lost the right to ask that question many years ago. Now," he said, taking a step toward her and gently grabbing her elbow, "I've tried to be polite, but it hasn't worked." Leading her back out to the foyer, he handed her the fur coat she had lain across the staircase railing. "Leave."

Putting on her coat, the rage in her eyes was reflected in her tone. "I know you haven't been seriously seeing anyone since I left you. I'm sure whoever she is she won't measure up to me."

Not responding, he opened the door. Christine stood in front of him, about to knock.

Christine's eyes moved from him to the woman standing in the door. She recognized her right away. Danielle. Her eyes moved back to Damian filled with questions.

"She was just leaving," Damian said through clenched teeth.

Stepping forward, Danielle stopped directly in front of Christine and examined her slowly from head to toe. Glancing back at Damian, she smiled, "Like I thought, not even close. Talk to you later." Turning, she leaned in to him, placing her lips firmly on his. She then gave Christine another insignificant look and walked confidently down the steps and jumped into her Porsche and sped off.

Holding her anger in check, Christine balled her fingers into a fist. Danielle's look of disgust and insignificance reminded her of the way Henry had treated her. She promised herself she would never accept that behavior from anyone.

Turning on her heels, she walked briskly to her car, ignoring Damian who called her name. Slamming the car door shut, her hands shook and her breathing was heavy as she attempted to put the keys in the ignition. The banging on her window caused her to jump. Damian was standing there, shivering in the cold air.

Ignoring him, she started the car and shifted the gear into drive. He stepped in front of the car. She rolled down her window. "Are you crazy! Get out of my way!" she yelled.

"Not unless you agree to come back into the house and talk to me. I'm not sure what you think happened back there, but I can tell by your reaction that it's not correct. That was just somebody I used to know."

"Don't you mean someone you were planning to marry?"

Damian, shocked that Christine knew already, replied, "Can we please go back inside? If we don't talk this out, she wins."

"Move out of my way," Christine screamed, revving the engine for emphasis.

Defeated, Damian stepped aside and watched her drive off.

# $\mathcal{EIGHT}$

Shutting the door with enough force to shatter the glass, Damian seethed with mounting rage. With a purposeful stride, he entered the dining room and blew out the candles. Moving through the swinging doors, he shut off the oven. Pacing back and forth, he forced himself to calm down. Never in his life had he felt such raw anger toward a person. Not even when Danielle confessed to the ultimate betrayal did he feel such scalding fury coursing through his entire body. He paced the floor for almost an hour before he calmed down enough to speak.

Grabbing the phone, he punched in Christine's number and slammed it down when her answering machine picked up. Checking his watch, he wondered where she was. If she was going straight home, she should have been there already. Hearing the ringing of the phone, he picked it up on the first ring.

"Christine?" he asked, hopefully.

"Man, you must have it bad. You sound desperate," Brandon said, trying unsuccessfully to stifle a chuckle.

"Not now, Brandon." Damian barked. Tonight was not the time for the playful antics of his brother.

"What's up?" Brandon asked, all signs of jokes gone from his voice.

Damian conveyed the night's activities, feeling his agitation increase with each word.

Brandon released a slow whistle. "Danielle is a definite

piece of work. I knew she was trouble the first time I met her," Brandon said.

"Yeah, right," Damian said sarcastically, "Weren't you the one trying to finagle free tickets from her to her photo shoots in order to meet her model friends."

"That's my point," he said laughing. "She never gave me a ticket."

Hearing Damian join in the laughter caused Brandon to relax. It felt good to be there when his brother needed him.

Growing up, Damian played the role of big brother, getting Brandon out of one jam, only to see him get into another. Most of those situations involved Brandon's latest girlfriend. While Brandon had sworn off "til death do you part" and "happily ever after," Damian knew that Brandon longed to share his life with that one special person.

Brandon had a front row seat for the devastation Damian felt when Danielle showed her true colors. Watching him walk around in a fog for weeks, Brandon refused to let his brother sulk. Recruiting the help of Tanya, the two of them reminded Damian that he had a business to run and pushed him back into the game of life. And it worked. His company bounced back and flourished, and now it looked as if he had a second chance at love.

According to Damian, his attraction to Christine was immediate. From the moment he sat beside her on that park bench, he knew he wanted to be a part of her life. After spending the weekend at his beach house, Damian confessed his growing attraction for Christine was becoming something deeper. While Brandon balked at all that love and commitment stuff, he was pulling for his big brother to find true love.

Brandon prided himself on being a confirmed bachelor. Believing settling down was not for him, he never allowed himself to get emotionally close to any one woman. The idea of spending his entire life with one person didn't appeal to any part of him. It felt limiting. Whenever he thought a woman was getting too attached, he quickly broke it off. He'd never regretted his decision, except once.

Shaking thoughts of her out of his mind, he asked, "So what are you going to do big brother? I can't imagine you letting Danielle win this one."

"You're right about that. I just have to figure out a way to get Christine to listen to me. I'll call you later."

Brandon hung up with his brother and headed to his bedroom. Lying horizontally across his king-size bed, he stared up at the ceiling. It was Friday night, and he was home alone . . . by choice. It was the beginning of the holiday season and on his dresser were invitations to various high profile events, where the who's who of Washington DC came out in force. Besides those invitations, there were messages from several women looking to be his escort for the evening. But he wasn't in the mood.

Who would have thought that the man known in his circles for having more women than Hugh Hefner, would consciously choose to spend an evening at home, by himself. At thirty-three, he had established a career in his field that most people only dared to dream about. Graduating in the top five percent of his law class at Georgetown University, he was wooed by some of the biggest firms in the country. Not only were they looking to add a brilliant attorney to their staff, but the fact the he was African-American was an added plus, as companies began to diversify their workplace to meet the changing needs of their clients.

Deciding to stay in the DC area, he began working for Morgan, Rock, Stanton & Mills, one of the biggest corporate law firms in the world. And in the seven years that he'd been there, he'd billed more hours, brought in more clients, and earned more money than most people make in a lifetime. And this week, he just found out his name was being added to the stationary and stenciled on the door.

Passionate about his work, he enjoyed every minute of the ride to the top and all it afforded him. His business circle included CEOs from the top companies in the world, politicians, and bank presidents. And in his arms were sexy, successful women, including supermodels, business owners, and even a princess. The results of these relationships were usually the same. They would spend three or four months wining and dining each other and enjoying the high life. But when the relationship began to turn serious, he cut the rope.

When his success was growing, as well as his bank account, this lifestyle was perfect for him. Riding the wave in style, he had no qualms moving from one relationship to another. But ever since she had come into his life, he began questioning whether he was truly happy living a life filled with one meaningless relationship after another.

She was beautiful, intelligent, successful and he disliked her on the spot. It wasn't because she was rude or arrogant, it was because she ignored him. Used to getting his way with people of the female persuasion, he was highly irritated when he approached her with his charm and wit, and she turned him down cold.

Always up for a challenge, he pursued her with a vengeance. Claiming she knew his type and wasn't interested in a temporary, meaningless affair, she politely told him to get lost, over and over again. The chase went on for months, but he eventually wore her down and won her over, convincing her that he had changed and that he was now looking for the same things in life that she was.

But the joke was on him. After six months of dating, his feelings for her grew deeper and it scared him. He had never been in this place before and he wasn't sure if he was ready. When she confessed her love, he couldn't reply in kind, and he saw the disappointment on her face. However, she never gave up. She believed in him and told him so, letting him know that she understood that he needed time. It was as if she was too good to be true, and instead of embracing her and allowing her to love him and show him how to love, he retreated to his comfort zone, and betrayed her trust and destroyed her love. Embarrassed and hurt by his behavior, she let him go completely and never looked back.

Relieved that he was free from the pressure of a serious relationship and all the things that came with it, he began to go back to his lifestyle as a confirmed bachelor. Unfortunately, it was not as fun as he had remembered. He found himself comparing every woman to her, and no one could measure up. She was feisty, spirited and committed to her friends, family and him, and he threw it all away, out of fear; the fear of commitment.

Now, here he sat, miserable. If only he had not given in to his fears, and allowed himself to give into the love he now knew he had for her. But it was too late. The times he tried to make contact, she had refused to talk to him. The last time he called, she told him quite clearly that he made his choice when he betrayed her trust, and he would have to live with that choice. And that was the hardest thing he had ever had to do. Live without the love of Tanya Kennedy.


The next morning, Christine laid in bed staring up at the ceiling. She had spent that night ignoring the ringing phone and the constant messages Damian left on her answering machine. Finally, his last message just asked for her to ring his phone once to alert him that she was home and safe. Hearing the desperation in his voice, she reluctantly dialed his number, let it ring once and immediately hung up. Unplugging the phone from the wall, she went to bed.

Turning over, she stared at the clock. Eleven forty-five A.M. She normally didn't allow herself the luxury of sleeping in. Her schedule was always tight and she hated to have her days unplanned. Every night before she went to bed, she reviewed a list of things to do the next day. On the weekends, they included picking up dry cleaning, working out for two hours at the gym, grocery shopping for the week, going through the mail and paying bills.

But this Saturday was different. She promised Mr. Murphy that she would meet him at Ruth's house by one o'clock. After all that had been revealed to her about her mom these past few weeks, she felt a strange anxiousness to visit the place she swore she would never set foot in again.

Dressing warmly in black corduroy pants, a black turtleneck and gray cardigan sweater, Christine parked along the curb outside Ruth's house at about twelve-thirty. Arriving a little early, she wanted to spend a few minutes alone in the house.

The small, three-story frame house was located in an older, quieter, neighborhood of Washington, DC, lined with mature trees, bare during the winter months. Getting out of the car, she stared at the structure. It still looked the same as the day she left. Stepping slowly up the concrete walkway and steps, she noticed the cracks and loose pieces of concrete, results of harsh winter weather and lack of upkeep over the years. Stopping on the small porch, she absorbed all that was around her. The paint was chipped, the shutters were loose and the screen door had a slight tear in it, and as she absorbed it all, she felt an unexpected swell of emotion fill her. Refusing to give into the tears, she turned and rested her eyes on the wooden rocker and picnic bench. Slowly, she traced her hands along the arm of the chair. She closed her eyes and envisioned a little girl, alone and crying, sitting on the chair, waiting for the yelling inside to stop.

Examining her key ring, she picked the one key she hadn't used in ten years. She felt a strange sense of confusion as she realized that while she promised herself she would never return to the place that held such painful memories, she held on to the one thing that would allow her complete and total access.

Pushing the door open slowly, she mentally prepared herself for the smell, dust and maybe cobwebs, of a house that had been closed up for almost six months. After her mother was diagnosed, she usually stayed with Christine a few nights each week. Christine couldn't bring herself to visit when her mother was home. As she stepped inside, she knew she would need to hire a cleaning team to go through the house before she put it on the market.

To her surprise, the hardwood floors in the entryway were free from dust and the air exuded the scent of fresh pine. Looking to the right, she took a few tentative steps forward and looked into the dining room. The same wood table, four chairs, and china closet stood stately, polished to a shine. She smiled at the set of dishes and serving trays displayed through the glass cabinet. Those place settings and serving dishes were some of the few things Ruth brought with her when she left her home in North Carolina. On special occasions, she would set the table with the china dishes laced with blue and gold, and tell Christine how one day, she would be honored to eat at her home, with her family on these dishes. Feeling a lump begin to develop in her throat, she quickly retreated out of that room and headed for the kitchen.

Entering the small, but functional kitchen, she was startled to see a shine on the appliances and the dishes stacked neatly on the open shelves, with the pots and pans hanging on hooks above the small center island. Seeing the door beside the refrigerator prompted a frown from Christine. The basement. She had not stepped foot in that area of the house since that fateful day when she was banished to the small room. Turning abruptly on her heels, she headed upstairs.

The wooden stairs creaked loudly as she worked her way to the top. Switching on the light in the hall bathroom, she noticed the clean floor, the fresh towels and the smell of potpourri. She glanced in the master bedroom for a moment, saw the neatly made bed, the lazy boy chair, and the small dresser. Who had been taking care of this house?

Walking to the opposite end of the hall, she saw the door to her old room. She wondered what her mother did with the room once she left for college. Ruth had frequently spoken about sewing for some of the people in the neighborhood, and she teased Christine that as soon as she left, it would be her private workshop. Christine's breath caught as she realized she never asked her mother what she had done the years that she was away.

Did she ever take that sewing class she talked about? Had she ever perfected her crocheting techniques, as her grandmother had taught her? Did she ever take a vacation, tour a museum, or take in an award winning play? She knew her mother loved Tina Turner. Did she ever attend one of her concerts? Christine swallowed back the tears as she realized how her selfishness had prevented her from truly knowing her mother. When they began to repair their relationship, Christine didn't want to talk about the past. They only spoke of the present and the future. She now understood that her self-centered behavior had caused her to waste precious time, time with her mother that she would never get back.

Stepping into her room, she held onto the door for support. Everything was as she had left it the day she went to college. The lavender print curtains still hung at the window. The matching comforter neatly covered her twin bed and all the stuffed animals she left behind were propped against her pillow. Stepping over to the window, she touched the arm of the chair they had bought at a yard sale, and then sat down on the bed. Exhaling deeply, she felt surrounded by serenity, a feeling she so desperately searched out during her teenage years. Why had her mother kept everything the same?

"Christine, Christine, are you here?"

Exiting the room, she firmly shut the door behind her. "I'll be right down."

Stopping in the bathroom, she fixed her face. She found Mr. Murphy on the sofa in the living room, arranging various papers on the coffee table. Sitting across from him in a high back chair, neither said anything. Proudly displayed on the end table were various school pictures she had taken over the years. There was the one with her hair parted down the middle with a ponytail on each side, ending right below her shoulders, and then there was the one with her hair in a short afro. She smiled at that picture. Henry had forbidden that picture to be displayed in his house, but Ruth held her own and this was one time Christine recalled her mother winning a battle.

Reaching over, she picked up the yellow photo album on the coffee table. Flipping through the pages, she took a ride down memory lane, recognizing snapshots of past Halloweens, Christmases and birthdays. Even though she never had a birthday party, Ruth always made sure that Christine had a cake, ice cream and a special present. Gently touching the face of her mother in a picture taken at her high school graduation, she saw pride reflected in her eyes.

An outsider looking at these memories would only see a mother who adored her child. They would have no idea of the constant fights, the loud arguments, the pushes, the shoves or the fists. They would only see a woman who adored her child, documenting the events of her childhood. That was how Christine was viewing these pictures now: as an outsider. Having been away for so many years, the abuse that swirled around her on a daily basis seemed a distant memory, and the good times her mother created for her were now in the forefront of her mind. She felt appreciation, love and respect for her mother, but she would never be able to tell her mother 'thank you'. And that made her angry . . . at herself.

Shutting the album, she placed it back on the table. "Who's been taking care of the house?"

"I made arrangements to have someone come in once a week since Ruth died," Mr. Murphy answered without looking up.

"Why?" she asked, surprised.

"Because there was no one else to do it," he said, staring at her intently. He knew it sounded harsh, but being back in this house had aroused memories for him he wasn't prepared to deal with. He had spent many nights in this house after

Henry died, comforting Ruth through her time of grief. It was hard to believe that a woman could grieve for a man that had disrespected her in every way possible, but she had given him thirty years of her life, and while it was hell a large portion of that time, there were good times, especially toward the end of his life. Ruth told Douglas that after Christine left for college, things did get better, and a few years before Henry died, life was actually good.

After Ruth was diagnosed with cancer, her main objective was to spend time with her daughter, and he could respect that. While he wanted to spend every moment with her, he had to settle for being with her when she wasn't staying at Christine's. Ruth requested that they not tell Christine about their relationship. She thought it would only complicate matters. She also wanted to give Christine her undivided attention. She felt she had not always been there for her daughter when she was growing up, so she was determined to be there for her during her last few months on earth. Christine had no idea how much her mother loved her.

Feeling chastised, Christine responded defensively. "Now listen Mr. Murphy . . ."

He interrupted, "Why don't you call me Doug."

"Mr. Murphy," she continued, "I don't like what you are insinuating. I cared deeply for my mother and for you to ascertain that I would not take care of her belongings is quite presumptuous of you."

"Is that so?" he asked, removing his glasses and crossing his arms across his chest. "Well, after you canceled five appointments with me, I thought you weren't interested in what happened with your mother's affairs or this house."

Knowing he had spoken the truth, feeling ashamed, Christine leaned her head back and closed her eyes. How had she allowed things to get so out of hand? She had no response for him. As much as she hated to admit it, he was right. She had avoided Ruth's affairs since her death, but it wasn't because she didn't care, it was because it was too painful.

Remembering Ruth in the months before she passed, she was a tower of strength. When Ruth was diagnosed, Christine broke down in front of the doctor, saying it was so unfair that as soon as they had begun to develop a meaningful relationship, something this devastating could happen. But her mother sat upright in that doctor's office, never changing her facial expression. Taking the doctor's advice, Ruth got a second and third opinion. When she met with the last doctor, she asked pointed questions about possible treatments, and when she realized there were none, she moved to acceptance, deciding to take whatever time she had left and make the best of it. Throughout the losing battle, she never complained.

Opening her eyes, Christine was suddenly hit with a revelation. She never recalled her mother whining or sulking about the life she had. She had always been a tower of strength and dignity, dealing with each situation the best way she could. Even in her final days, she had endured the pain, focusing her attention on spending time with her Christine.

Mr. Murphy stared intently at Christine, watching the emotions play across her face. He knew she was hurting, but he also knew that she had to face the past to move forward with her life. He hoped taking care of her mother's outstanding issues would be a step in that direction. He promised Ruth he wouldn't give her the letter until she had.

"I apologize, Mr. Murphy," she stated, with pure sincerity. "I know my behavior has not been conducive to someone who is concerned about her mother's affairs, but I can assure, I do care."

"I know you care, Christine," he said softly. "I know."

After a moment of silence, he put his glasses back on and continued. "Now, let's go over these papers."

They went through the bank accounts and her investment portfolio. Christine still couldn't believe that with a few signatures, she would have control of over one million dollars. Of course, it was untouchable with the pending litigation, but she didn't mind as she had no intention of spending that money. After witnessing the many financial highs and lows her parents went through, Christine had become paranoid about not being able to always support her needs. That's why she had begun working her first year in college, and saving every penny she could. While most of her classmates were spending their funds on the latest fashions and fancy spring break vacations, Christine continued to deposit her money into her savings account, only withdrawing money for absolute necessities.

When she began working full time at the design firm, she began to study investing and immediately maxed her contribution into her 401(k), adding that to her mutual fund contributions. By the time she began planning to open her own design company, she had enough money to purchase her house with a substantial down payment and pay cash for her late model Lexus.

"What have you decided to do with the house?" he asked, returning the signed papers to his briefcase.

"Sell it."

"I wish you would reconsider. Ruth loved this house," he said hopefully.

Rising, Christine picked up her purse and retrieved her keys. "Well, Mr. Murphy, I hate this house."

"I thought you were beginning to move beyond just thinking of only yourself," he said harshly.

After a moment of silence, he sighed, "I'm sorry, I had no right. It's just that after your father died, Ruth and I shared some special times in this house. I guess this house has come to mean something to me. But I do understand your wanting to sell. Your memories of your time here are very different from mine. If you're interested, I have the name of a very good real estate agent."

Tired and mentally drained, Christine nodded her head in agreement and headed for the front door.

Following her into the entryway, he said, "I heard from the Donovan's attorney."

Resting her head against the front door, she felt the tears begin to swell. "Please," she begged, "don't make me deal with that today, Mr. Murphy. I'll come to your office next week."

Feeling she was at her breaking point, he agreed. She left him standing alone.

"Why won't you listen to him?" Stephanie asked, sipping her Chardonnay at the crowded bar.

"Do you think our table is ready yet?" Christine answered, looking through the sea of people in search of the hostess. They had been waiting for almost an hour at the popular downtown DC restaurant. Opening less than a month ago, *Lenny's* had already established itself as one of the best up-scale restaurants in the city. Knowing they didn't take reservations still hadn't prepared them for the long line, the crowded bar, or the one hour wait.

She still couldn't believe she had allowed herself to be talked into a night on the town. Working fifteen hour days, she wasn't in the mood to spend her night standing shoulder to shoulder with people jockeying for a position that kept them in close range to the bar, but also allowed a birds eye view of the opposite sex. What she really wanted to do was go home, change into her most comfortable sweats, order a pizza, and finish it off with her two new best friends, Ben and Jerry.

But it was the Wednesday night before Thanksgiving and Stephanie was leaving for Atlanta in the morning to spend her holiday weekend with Nathan. One would think that the night before a major holiday, the restaurant would be empty. But not here. The young and single were out in full force.

Her week had been trying. Yesterday, she had met with Mr. Murphy and he had presented her with a settlement offer from Natalie Donovan. Her half sister was asking for half a million, on the premise that the money should be shared equally among Henry's children. Christine was astonished. The money was not Henry's, it was her mother's. There was no way she was giving any of it to a faceless woman from her father's past.

Mr. Murphy expressed empathy with Christine, but told her the law may have a different approach. The money was accumulated during her marriage to Henry with some of his funds and that made it possible for Ms. Donovan to stake a claim. He did agree that the amount was high, but he wanted her to think about a counter offer. Christine informed him that she needed no time to think about a counter offer. Henry betrayed Ruth with his extramarital affair and illegitimate child, and now they expected her to give up the legacy her mother had left her without a fight. They must be out of their minds. Mr. Murphy could tell them her offer was zero.

And on top of that, she still hadn't spoken with Damian since she zoomed out of his driveway. She had yet to return his calls or answer the door on the two occasions he had stopped by her house. Christine didn't want to admit that she was disappointed that he hadn't come by her office. That would have been the one place he knew he could catch her without causing a scene.

She convinced herself that she was justified in her behavior, and nothing he could say would change the fact that he let that shell of a woman speak to her that way. What kind of man could get engaged to a woman like that? Christine rationalized it was most likely a man who shared some of those same qualities. *He's nothing like her. He's kind, sweet, honest and hardworking.* Shaking that thought out of her mind, she reaffirmed that it was best to cut her losses before she got herself in too deep. But her conviction to leave him alone didn't change the fact that it was the week of Thanksgiving and her best friend was going to spend it in Atlanta, leaving her with nothing to do and no one to share the day with.

"Ladies, ladies, aren't we looking beautiful tonight?"

Christine and Stephanie turned to the two gentlemen who had approached them from behind. Dressed to the nines in Armani suits and Gucci shoes, they looked every part successful men. The taller of the two sported a short, cropped haircut with small glasses and a goatee. His friend, about a foot shorter, wore short dreadlocks and a diamond stud earring in one ear. Christine stifled a giggle. They reminded her of Shaquille O'Neil, a seven-foot center for the LA Lakers, standing next to Mugsy Bowes, one of the shortest to play in the NBA.

This was the exact kind of thing she wanted to avoid. A hot, new restaurant with a crowded bar was the perfect place for men on the prowl. She broke her promise to herself by allowing herself to get involved with Damian and she was not about to make the same mistake twice.

"I see you two have just about finished your wine," the one who looked like Shaq stated. "Please allow us to take care of the next round."

Stephanie smiled politely and waved her left hand in their faces, the glare of the diamond reflecting off his glasses. "Sorry, my friend, but we are not available."

Bowing gracefully, the men smiled and moved on to their next target, who just happened to be about three feet away.

"Thanks, Stephanie, I really am not in the mood to deal with any men right now."

"Of course, not. We're not available. You already have a man."

"I think the hostess is waving us over," she answered, heading toward the front of the restaurant.

As they maneuvered through the crowd of upwardly mobile African Americans flashing their platinum credit cards, Rolex watches, expensive suits and Italian shoes, Stephanie wasn't fooled by Christine's attempt to avoid responding to her last comment. That was OK. She had their entire dinner to talk some sense into her best friend.

"Your server will be right with you," the young, perky waitress said as she handed them menus.

After Stephanie placed an order for blackened catfish and Christine ordered jambalaya, Stephanie thought it was the perfect time to talk Christine into seeing Damian.

"You really should cut the guy some slack. You don't even know why Danielle was there in the first place. Besides, a good man like that deserves to be given the benefit of the doubt." Getting no response, Stephanie continued, "If you don't want him, I'm sure somebody will quickly snatch him up. You know the women in DC are fierce."

Christine glared at Stephanie, trying not to let her know that throwing her own words back in her face didn't bother her one bit. "If you are going to spend the evening talking about him, then I will leave now."

"Ok, ok," Stephanie replied, admitting defeat. "I'll drop it for now."

Reaching her hand out over the table, Stephanie squeezed her best friend's hand. "I am really going to miss you. I can't believe that in two months, I'll be moving to Atlanta. There's so much to do . . . putting my house on the market, finding a new job."

Squeezing her hand back, Christine said, "Please don't remind me. Why are you the one who has to move?"

"You know the deal. When Nathan's company found out he was about to jump ship, they offered him the world . . . and who can blame him. He accepted. So I agreed to move."

"I guess I can be mature about this whole thing," Christine said teasingly. "I really want to stomp my feet and cry and beg you to stay, but I know how happy you are with Nathan and I am happy for you. I just have to find myself an accounting wizard in less than two months."

"I hate to leave you in a bind, but I will be taking a little time off before finding another job. As soon as you hire someone, I'll be glad to help out in any way I can."

After a moment of silence, Stephanie said, "I wish you would reconsider and come to Atlanta. We would love to have you spend Thanksgiving with us."

"I appreciate the offer, but I won't be good company. With work, getting my mom's house ready to go on the market, and dealing with the will, I won't be any fun to be around."

"I'm used to your moody way," she answered lightly. "Come on, join us."

"Sorry, Steph, not this year."

As their food arrived, their conversation switched from Stephanie's impending departure to the issue of Ruth's will. Christine updated Stephanie, informing her that Henry's name was on Natalie's birth certificate and their offer for settlement at five-hundred thousand dollars.

"So what are you going to do?"

"Mr. Murphy thinks we have a strong case, but doesn't advise settling for half the money. It just seems strange that someone I have never met is after my mother's money."

"Maybe you should ask to meet them."

That wasn't the first time that thought had crossed her mind. "I don't know if I could stand to be in the same room with someone who would sleep with someone else's husband."

Taking a bite of her salad, Stephanie answered, "Maybe you could find out the whole story. Maybe she didn't know Henry was married."

"I don't know. Maybe I'll call Mr. Murphy and see what he thinks."

"Are you going to think about calling Damian, too?"

"Stephanie, Damian is a non-issue. It just wasn't meant to be."

"How can you say that. You let an outsider come in and dictate to you how you are going to live your life?" she asked, disbelief in her eyes.

"Whether Danielle showed up or not wouldn't have mattered. My objective is to build the best design firm I can. There was never a place in my life for love and the incident with Danielle just saved me from making a mistake."

"What are you talking about . . . a mistake? What I saw between you and Damian was no mistake. You said yourself that the time you spent at his beach house sparked feelings for him that you've never had for another person. Do you really want to spend the rest of your life alone? You can't curl up in a warm bed with wallpaper samples and fabric swatches."

"I didn't say I was going to spend the rest of my life alone. I just don't have time for a relationship now. Once my business is where I want it to be, I will find time for love. But I will not let a man take me away from what I want to do. I have my dreams, my goals and my life aspirations. I have a plan for me, and no man is going to stop me from fulfilling my dreams."

"Is that what you thought I would do? Stop you from achieving your dreams?"

The deep, timbre voice startled them both and she felt his presence embody her. They had been so deep in conversation that they failed to see Damian walk up to their table. Looking up, Christine swallowed deeply as she gazed into his questioning eyes. It couldn't be possible that he managed to get better looking in the time that they had been apart. Standing tall in a Hugo Boss suit and power tie, she felt her insides grow warm at the thought of removing each piece of clothing one by one.

"Damian, it's so good to see you," Stephanie squealed, rising and giving him a warm hug.

Suddenly, Christine broke her gaze at Damian and turned to Stephanie. The warmth she felt moments ago was quickly turning to anger. "You set me up!" she exclaimed, not caring who around her heard the outburst.

Momentarily stunned, Damian and Stephanie turned to her with perplexed looks.

"What are you talking about?" Stephanie asked, completely confused.

*"Oh, Christine, we have to try this new restaurant tonight,"* Christine said sarcastically. *"No, Christine, I'm leaving tomorrow for Atlanta, we have to go tonight. Ooohhh, Christine, why don't you wear something fun tonight?"* She cut her gaze from Stephanie to Damian and back to Stephanie. "It was all a ploy, just like the night of the reception. Now I suppose you'll have some emergency and Damian will be forced to take me home. Well, you can forget it, I'll take a cab."

Seeing how worked up she was getting, Stephanie sat down and stared directly into her eyes. "That is not true, Christine. I had no idea he would be here tonight. I just wanted you to get out and have some fun. Every night this week, the only thing you've done is work and sleep. I just wanted you to loosen up. You have to believe me. This was not my doing."

Standing, Christine gathered her belongings and reached into her purse and threw out a few large bills. "I don't believe you. I'm leaving."

"Damian, our table is ready."

Christine paused at the female voice coming from behind her. Turning around, she saw what could have been the twin of supermodel Tyra Banks. Long, straight, cinnamon hair, eyes the color of jade, and a body that fit the tight, black, Versace dress perfectly. Glancing from Stephanie, to Damian, and finally the Tyra look-alike, she realized what a grave mistake she had made. This was no pre-arranged meeting. Damian was here on a date. A date with someone else.

"Christine Davenport and Stephanie Jackson, I'd like you to meet Rachel Tyson," he said.

After strained hellos, Rachel repeated that their table was ready. Christine watched them retreat to an intimate table in the corner and held back the tears. Turning back to Stephanie she said, "I'm running to the ladies' room. When I return, I'll be ready to go."

Walking down the dimly lit hall, Christine held her tears in check. Seeing him with another woman was the last thing she expected. Could he have put her out of his mind . . . out of his heart . . . that fast? Splashing her face with cold water, Christine stared into the mirror. What a fool she had been. The time she spent convincing herself that she was doing the right thing by ignoring him, seemed silly now. Pulling powder, eyeliner and lipstick out of her evening bag, she attempted to make herself presentable again. Leaning forward into the mirror, she frowned. Could she have been so afraid of the feelings she was developing for Damian, that at the first chance to end it, she took advantage of it?

"You've really done it this time," she said to her reflection. "You let him get away."

Exiting the bathroom, she stopped when she saw him standing midway down the hall. Raising her chin, she refused to let him see how he had affected her.

Watching her move toward him, Damian stood motionless with his hands in his pockets. It was the only way he knew how to keep them from reaching out to her and wrapping her in his arms.

The time away from her had been torturous. After she failed to return his calls or answer her door, he contemplated going to her job. But he was a professional and he respected her career. He wanted her to want him and not put him in a situation where she had to deal with him. Dressed in tailored magenta pants and matching sweater, even in the recessed lighting, he could make out the subtle curve of her breasts. Inhaling deeply, he tried to get his emotions under control.

When she was just a few feet away, he stated, "I've been missing you."

Refusing to give in to his smooth voice, his intoxicating

cologne and his seductive smile, she countered, "Don't you have to get back to your date?"

"I want to talk to you . . . tonight. Can I come by your house?" he said, ignoring her question.

Her eyes widened at his audacity. "You're not coming to me after leaving another woman."

"Then I'll leave with you now," he said.

"You are that insensitive that you would leave your date stranded at the most popular restaurant in town? I thought I knew you better than that. I guess your true colors are really shining through. The way you let Danielle treat me and the way you are going to treat Ty . . . I mean Rachel . . . I can't believe I let myself fall in . . ." catching herself from making an admission, she swallowed back her words.

Stepping forward, Damian gently ran his fingers along her arm. "Rachel is just a friend. She would understand completely if I wanted to cut the evening short."

"How can you say that? I can't believe you would just . . ."

Damian covered her lips hungrily in an effort to shut her up. Temporarily paralyzed by the unexpected gesture, Christine felt the blood coursing through her veins like an awakened river. Initially, she held back, not wanting to give him the satisfaction of knowing just how much his touch and his kisses affected her. But as he continued his assault, her defenses began to completely break down. Prompting her with his tongue, she gave up the fight and opened her mouth and allowed him in. Having no regard that they were in a very public place, they reacquainted themselves after being apart.

Damian released her and said, "Rachel is my brother's latest heartbreak. Brandon said adios to her earlier this week. She was hoping that by having dinner with me, she could convince me to help her find a way back to him. The only problem is, my brother lives by his own golden rule. Never go back."

Taking a moment to let his words register, he watched her closely. Being next to her was wearing him out, but he had to find a way to get through to her. Overhearing her conversation with Stephanie, he realized how deep her doubts ran. He finally began to understand that she was a planner, calculating everything, leaving nothing to chance. She was on a methodical mission to live her life as she had already outlined it. He had to find a way to convince her their relationship could fit into her plans. She just needed to take a chance, to gamble on him . . . on them.

Relief flooded through her at his admission. She hated that she was jealous, but she was helpless to prevent it. "Don't miss your dinner with Rachel. I'll be home when you're finished," she said. "We can talk then."

Later that evening, Christine plopped on her bed in frustration. Wearing just her bra and panties, she had just discarded her fourth outfit. How hard could it be to dress for a male visitor? Looking at the mess she created that spread across the chair, the bed and the dresser, Christine smiled. She heard herself giggle. She leaned back on her bed and laughed hysterically. What a hypocrite she had been! She spent the last week convincing herself that the last thing she wanted or needed in her life was Damian Ware, and the minute he walked back into her life, it upset her entire balance. Standing, she wiped the tears of laughter that had escaped down her cheek. She hadn't felt this good in a long time.

Eeny-meeny-miny-mowing her four selections, she landed on a pair of aqua marine casual pants and a matching green and white v-neck sweater. Selecting her diamond earrings and matching pendant, she touched up her makeup and slipped on leather flat shoes. Entering the cozy family room, she quickly lit a fire. She knew he had eaten dinner, but she went to the kitchen and prepared a small fruit tray and chilled a bottle of wine. If she was going to eat crow, she might as well do it in style.

Hearing the doorbell ring, she checked herself in the oak-lined mirror in the foyer and opened the door.

Letting out a slow whistle, Damian took in the tight stretch pants and the low cut sweater.

"You look fabulous," he said, handing her a dozen white roses.

"Thank you, Damian," she smiled, ushering him into the family room.

After settling on the oversized loveseat, the room was engulfed in silence.

"Damian, I just wanted to . . ."

"Christine, let me explain . . ."

They laughed and visibly relaxed as they both tried to speak. "You first," Christine said.

"I just wanted to let you know that I had no idea that Danielle was going to show up on my doorstep. I hadn't spoken to her since the engagement was broken off and I thought she was still in Paris. She must have heard what happened with the fire. She claimed she came back to the States to offer her support."

"You sound as if you don't believe that?"

"I found out the hard way that Danielle never does anything out of the goodness of her heart. I'm positive she had an ulterior motive. I just wasn't interested in having her around long enough to find out what it was." Closing the space between them, he continued. "But enough about her, I came over to talk about us."

Rising, Christine walked over to the window overlooking the quiet suburban street. The air was cold and crisp and the weather was calling for snow.

"Damian, I won't deny that I'm attracted to you, but I'm not sure about getting involved in a relationship right now. I have so many things I want to accomplish. My business is very new and it demands an enormous amount of attention from me."

Stepping toward her, he answered, "I'm not here to stand between you and your dreams."

"That's what my mother thought. Henry convinced her to put off college and to hold off on her plans. She thought that she could do all the things she wanted to do after they were married. And you know how many goals she reached? None."

Praying for the right words to show her how she couldn't let her parents' lives dictate how she lived hers, he walked up behind her and wrapped his arms around her waist.

She inhaled deeply at the warmth that surrounded her and continued. "Ever since I was a child, I witnessed my mother's wants take second place to Henry's needs. All in the name of love. Well, I formulated a plan to dictate how my life would evolve so that I wouldn't have to fall victim to any man.

"I got a scholarship to a top college and graduated at the top of my class. I attended one of the best design schools and worked for a top design firm for a couple of years and then opened my own firm and became the top company in the area. I haven't finished that plan yet. I promised myself that I wouldn't let a man prevent me from completing my plan."

"I'm not trying to come between your life objectives," Damian started quietly. "I applaud what you want to accomplish. Believe me, I know what it's like to be driven. I started working with my hands during the summer of my sophomore year in high school and continued all the way through college. Knowing I wanted to own my own construction company, I worked during the day and completed my MBA at night. But I always knew that there were other things that were a part of my life. I took chances, risks and gambled. Sometimes I won, sometimes I lost, but I was always in the game. Don't take yourself out of the game. Give us a chance."

Leaning back into his arms, she wanted so desperately to let go and to not get bogged down with the past. "I don't know how to take chances."

"Let me show you how to take chances and be spontaneous."

Christine smiled. She knew he would be the one to challenge her.

Stepping in front of her, he kissed her forehead. "Trust me."

Contemplating all that he said, she was ready to try. She already felt more for him than she felt for any other man. What harm could it do to develop a relationship with him? It was actually appealing to her to begin the slow change of the way she approached life. "You have a deal."

"Good," he said, suddenly hit with the wildest idea of his life. "Now go upstairs and grab your toothbrush, we're about to be spontaneous."

"Excuse me?" she answered, stepping out of his embrace. "What do you mean?"

"You just said you would let me teach you how to be spontaneous. Well, it's the start of a long weekend, and if you don't have any plans for Thanksgiving, I'd like you to spend it with me."

Wondering what that glint in his eyes meant, Christine asked, "Why just a toothbrush? Won't I need other stuff? Am I going to be coming back tonight? What are we going to do?"

"You ask way too many questions. Remember . . . trust, risk, spontaneity? Well this is what it's all about. Are you in the game or not?"

Christine chewed nervously on her bottom lip as she debated her options. She could take the safe route and refuse to participate. She could take the middle of the road and agree to his plans, only if he shared them with her, or she could live a little and trust. Breaking into a huge grin, she nodded "yes." She decided to live a little. "I'll be right back."

As soon as she was out of sight, Damian moved into action. Grabbing his cell phone, he punched in the number of his good friend and accountant, Lester James. He knew he was pushing the limit by calling him at nine P.M. the night before a holiday. But if there was one person who could handle this request, it would be him.

When Lester answered, Damian explained his request and Lester literally dropped the phone.

"Did I hear you correctly?" Lester asked.

"You sure did. Can you take care of it?"

Even though Lester was skeptical of Damian's request, he agreed to take care of everything. "I'll ring you back in about fifteen," he told Damian.

Five minutes later, Christine returned with the excitement of a young child reflected in her eyes. "I have my toothbrush, now what?"

"Come with me, sweetheart."

Damian was purposely silent as they drove up Interstate 95 and the silence was driving Christine insane. She tried desperately not to ask any questions, but the planner in her was beginning to win the battle.

"Just tell me . . . " she started.

"Shhhh," he said, smiling at her.

The ensuing silence was interrupted by his ringing phone. The only words she heard from him were "number four, 10:45 P.M., and great." What was he planning? Pulling off the exit, Christine noticed they were following the signs for the Baltimore-Washington Airport. He couldn't seriously be planning a flight. Could he?

Valet parking the car, Damian led her to the area for chartered aircrafts. Christine's mind was racing. Was he crazy? They were actually going to take a flight. Where were they headed? Met at the door by an employee with the logo of

Maryland Aircrafts stenciled on his shirt, the couple was quickly escorted onto the airfield to a waiting plane. Flashing Damian a questioning gaze, he responded with a slow, secretive smile and slipped his fingers through hers as they approached the stairs to enter.

Stepping into the cabin, she noticed seating for at least nine people in oversized gray leather seats and a long sofa along the far wall. She took note of the bar at the far end, the large TV monitor, and the state-of-the-art music system.

The pilot stepped out of the cockpit and addressed Damian. "Welcome aboard, Mr. Ware. I'm Michael Randalson. I'll be your pilot this evening. My second in command is David White. He'll also attend to your needs during the flight. While this was very short notice, everything is in order. We've been cleared to take off in fifteen minutes. We should arrive in . . ."

"Ahh, thank you, sir," Damian interrupted, glancing over at Christine, who seemed to be paying very close attention to his conversation. "We'll just take our seats and buckle up."

Settling into their seats, Christine was torn. She was enjoying the adventure, but her inner self couldn't stand the not knowing. Leaning over, she whispered in Damian's ear, "Can I have just a little hint," she whispered in a soft, silky voice.

"All that breathy, sexy talk won't get you anywhere," he answered, trying, but failing miserably to sound stern.

Running her fingers up his thigh, she tried again, "All I want is a small clue."

Removing her hand and placing it firmly on her lap, he smiled. "In due time, my dear, in due time." Watching her playful pout, he smiled. Little did she know, if she touched him one more time, he would tell her anything she wanted to know.

After they were served drinks and light snacks, Christine

asked Damian if he had any more information about the fire at his job site.

"According to the investigator, the subcontractor we used to do all the electrical work skipped corners on the materials. It looks as though he invoiced us for the correct wire and ended up installing substandard wires with damaged insulation."

"Why would someone intentionally switch? Wouldn't they know that if they got too hot, it could cause a fire and people could get hurt?"

"I don't think they were thinking about the consequences, only the immediate gain."

Confused at his explanation, she asked, "Would it be worth it? It was just wires."

Damian smiled, understanding that Christine didn't know much, if anything, about the construction business. "That building cost around four million dollars to build. The wires that were supposed to be installed cost several hundred thousand dollars. The wires that were actually installed cost about half of that. Somebody at that electrical company put over a hundred grand into their own pocket."

"Wow," Christine said truly amazed, "I had no idea."

"The only thing that worries me is that I've used this company on three other projects and I wonder how they could have made a switch without any of my men knowing." Pausing a moment, he remembered his promise to not talk about work the entire weekend.

"Anyway, how did it go at your mother's house last Saturday?"

Christine brought him up-to-date on everything. Hearing her talk about Henry's mistress and daughter with hate and anger, Damian wondered if she ever thought about how tough it must have been for that woman to raise a daughter all by herself, without any financial help. Deciding it was best to keep his question to himself, he watched her fight a yawn. Suggesting she take a nap, she failed to put up much of a fight, and leaned into him, asleep in minutes. He watched her, noticing how her face looked so relaxed. He wanted to provide her that feeling all the time.

He chuckled quietly as he recalled Lester's reaction to his request. Lester, also a college friend of his father's, had been his accountant ever since he started his business. Advising him in all his financial matters, he knew Damian's spending habits and had educated him to be smart with his money. With his profits from his business, sound investments, and careful spending, Damian was a millionaire many times over. And even though he enjoyed a nice home, a luxury car and designer clothes, he never went overboard in his spending. Until now. The private jet was just the beginning. Before this weekend was over, Damian planned to risk more than he ever had in his entire life. Taking one last look at Christine before taking a nap himself, he understood the risk was not just a financial one, but a personal one. For the first time since Danielle, he was putting his heart on the line.

A few hours later, Damian was awakened by David. They would be landing in about fifteen minutes. Damian nudged Christine to wake her up. "We're almost there, honey."

Flickering her eyes, Christine took a moment to gather her thoughts. Remembering she was twenty-thousand feet in the air with no idea where she was going, she asked "Where is here?"

Lifting the shade covering the window, he answered, "Take a look out there, and tell me what you see."

Leaning over him to get a better view, Damian inhaled the distinctive fragrance of her perfume. He had been using every ounce of self control since he walked into her house four hours ago and he willed himself to hold onto what little control he had left. All he wanted to do was take her in his arms and show her what complete devotion and desire was all about.

"I see lights," she exclaimed. "Lots of lights . . . oh my

goodness . . . I don't believe it . . . it can't be." She squealed in delight and surprise. She never would have guessed.

"Welcome to The Land of Risk," he said, pleased at her obvious excitement.

Just then, the pilot made his announcement. "Mr. Ware, we have been cleared for landing. We should touch down in seven minutes. Welcome to Las Vegas."

# NINE

Stepping down the stairs onto the tarmac, Christine stopped short. A long, sleek, black, and shiny limousine awaited them. "Don't stop," Damian whispered into her ear. "Your chariot awaits."

Sliding into the soft, leather interior, Christine stared at the two dozen white roses, remembering how she shared with Damian that these were her favorites. The chauffeur, seemingly unfazed by the fact that they arrived with no luggage, settled into the front seat. Pushing a button that sent a private partition up between them, he pulled off of the airstrip and onto the airport roads.

"How about some champagne?" Damian asked as he lifted the bottle out of the ice bucket. Getting no response, he looked over at Christine and furrowed his brow in a frown. A lone tear slowly fell from her eye. "Christine, honey, what is it?"

"I can't believe this," she said, accepting the tissue he offered. "Why are you doing this for me?"

Seeing doubt reflected back at him, he knew she wasn't ready to hear that in the short time she has been a part of his life, he had become a changed man. No longer driven by the "business only" mentality, his heart had finally opened to give the love he thought no longer existed after Danielle. If he had his way, they would never be without each other. So, instead of declaring the undying love that flourished inside of him, he settled for, "I told you I would show you how to gamble, to live life free. What better place to let it all ride than in Las Vegas?"

Reaching out and wiping away the last remnants of her tears, he said, "Get ready to have the time of your life."

Christine rolled down the window as the glittering skyline came into view. She had seen the City of Lights on television and in photos on many occasions, but nothing prepared her for the influx of energy she got just gazing at the lights and sights. They decided to take a ride down the strip before going to their hotel. It was if she was traveling around the world without leaving her seat. She saw the Statue of Liberty, the pyramids, the Sphinx, a pirate ship, and a tenth century medieval castle. She was awed as they passed a circus and the city of Rome. All the glitzy lights had her head spinning in excitement. It was noisy, chaotic, crowded, energetic, colorful, bright, unique and alive. And Christine Davenport couldn't wait to become a part of it.

The limo finally came to a stop across from the city of New York, at four emerald green towers. Directly in front of them sat a giant, bronze one hundred thousand pound lion. Perched on a twenty-five foot pedestal, standing forty-five feet tall, the entrance to the MGM Grand Hotel stood majestic. Surrounded by water fountains and lush landscaping, the sight was breathtaking.

"Welcome to the MGM Grand Hotel, Mr. Ware. My name is Harold and I will be your host during your stay with us. I trust the flight and your ride here was adequate?" he asked.

Dressed in a dark suit, with an MGM emblem nameplate, he smiled sincerely as he stepped aside to let the couple enter. Bypassing the registration desk, they followed Harold to the VIP check-in area, in a private area of the hotel.

"The MGM Grand is the finest hotel in Las Vegas," he said. "And we are glad you chose to stay with us. We provide everything to satisfy your hearts desire. Sixteen restaurants, shopping for every occasion, including exquisite jewelry, designer clothes, and trinket souvenirs. We have the award winning show EFX, and the night life cranks it up with Studio 54. You can frolic in one of our five pools, get pampered in our state-of-the-art spa, visit with live lions living next to the lobby area, or get married in our tastefully decorated wedding chapel."

That last statement caused an immediate reaction from both Christine and Damian. Quickly averting their eyes from one another, they both laughed nervously, neither wanting to mention that the word wedding sent a warm feeling of affection through both of them.

"And of course," Harold said, stopping at the counter where only the rich or famous were allowed, "we have over one hundred and seventy thousand square feet of gaming. We offer slots, blackjack, craps, several types of poker, roulette and baccarat." Handing Damian a sheet of paper, the host continued, "Mr. James called ahead and completed all the necessary arrangements, all I need is your signature."

While Damian signed, Christine asked, "Who is Mr. James?"

"My accountant."

"What did he arrange?"

Handing the form back to the clerk behind the counter, they followed Harold to private elevators. Squeezing her hand, Damian smiled, "You ask too many questions"

Inserting a special key, the elevator doors closed and they began their ascent, stopping on the twenty-ninth floor. Walking down a tastefully decorated hall, they waited while Harold opened the door. Stepping inside, Christine thought she had entered a fantasy world. Trying not to appear too impressed, she glanced at Damian who gave her a 'go ahead' look, and she ran down the short hallway to look around the room . . . no suite . . . no apartment.

The two-story residence boasted over six-thousand square feet of elegant, luxury living space. The spiral staircase set the tone of the ultimate in indulgence, style and grace. She inventoried a full scale living and dining room, a sauna, gym, and kitchen. The wet bar, the grand piano, and the outdoor spa finished off the main floor. The ceiling to floor glass windows gave an awesome skyline view of the city. Climbing the stairs, she counted three bedrooms, with the master bath showing off an oversized spa tub, and an extensive vanity area, all resting on Italian green marble. Returning back downstairs, she was surprised to see that Damian and Harold had been joined by two others.

"Ah, here is the woman of the hour now," Damian said, holding out his hand for her to join him. "Christine, this is Charles, our butler, and Jacques, our personal chef." Suddenly stricken with a look of concern, he continued, "It has been a long trip, would you like something to eat?"

Completely speechless, Christine searched her mind to form one word that would not show her utter amazement that she had just been introduced to her personal chef and butler. "Ah, I . . ." she cleared her throat, "I'm not hungry at this time."

"Well," Harold said, heading for the door with the other two men. "We are but a phone call away if you require anything." Before closing the door behind him, he turned to Damian, "Mary Ann is ready when you are, sir. Just dial extension 3654."

Christine stared at Damian in confusion, "I'm almost afraid to ask who Mary Ann is."

Moving into the living room, he sat and pulled Christine with him. "Mary Ann is your personal shopper. Tonight, she can either escort you to some of the shops so that you can choose some personal items and sleepwear, or you can give her a list of those items and she can have them sent up. Tomorrow, you can shop for the rest of the clothes and accessories you'll need for this weekend."

Taking a deep breath, Christine said, "Damian, don't misunderstand me, I'm surprised and excited about my lesson in spontaneity, but a private jet, a limo and this suite has got to cost a pretty penny. I don't want you to think I can be bought."

"Is that what you think? That I would try to buy you? Listen, you're right," he said, as his lips curved in a seductive smile, "it is costing me a pretty penny, but it's my penny and it's what I wanted to do. Let's not forget the objective here. To gamble, to take risks, to let it all ride. For the next couple of days, the only thing we are going to do is enjoy. No thinking about budgets, fires, wills, trials, or business. Deal?"

"Deal," Christine said, with a smile. She agreed, but there was no way she was going to allow him to buy her clothes. She would just make sure that she went shopping without him.

"Now, unless you plan on sleeping in the buff . . . which I might add, I have no objection to, you better get Mary Ann on the phone. And," he continued, looking at his watch, "it is after 3:00 A.M. east coast time, so I suggest we get some sleep."

"What about you, don't you need something to sleep in?"

"Nope," he answered with a wicked grin.

Realizing the implications of his answer, Christine's cheeks grew warm with embarrassment.

Kissing her gently on the forehead, he stood. "You can have the master, I'll take the room next to it. Sweet dreams."

Damian retired to the second bedroom and Christine made a quick call to Mary Ann. A short while later, Christine stepped out of the shower and toweled off with a rich, thick, rose colored towel. Less than twenty-four hours ago, Christine had declared Damian Ware a part of her past, and here she was, spending the weekend with him in a lavish suite twenty-five hundred miles from home. She could probably be labeled psychotic.

Stepping into the bedroom, she was glad to see the items had been delivered as requested. The lavender silk short pajama set, a matching robe, black lacy underwear, a bra, and toiletries were laid out neatly on the bed. Hanging in the closet was a short, yellow sleeveless linen dress with matching sling back sandals. The desert air had been warm, even at midnight, and the winter clothes she flew in with would never do.

Getting into bed, she listened carefully for any sounds coming from next door. Closing her eyes, she wondered if Damian was asleep. She heard him shower earlier and silently visualized his naked body drenched in hot, steamy water. She understood his gesture of taking the other bedroom, but there was no denying the desire she saw reflected in his eyes. She knew they mirrored her own. It was just his way of letting her know that when their relationship moved to the next level, it would be her choice.

Damian laid staring at the ceiling. He knew he should be bone tired, but he was too keyed up to sleep. He was the last person who would have placed him in Las Vegas this weekend, but the idea was too good to pass up. All that talk about taking risks and gambling prompted him to think of this city. It took nothing but one phone call and a two hundred and fifty thousand dollar line of credit at the casino to secure the plane, the limo and the room. He chuckled as he recalled his conversation with Lester just a few short hours ago, asking him to make all the arrangements.

Hearing the shrill of his cell phone, he grabbed it on the third ring. Looking at the caller ID, he was shocked. It was on rare occasions when his Dad called his portable phone.

"Hi, Dad," he said, "Is everything OK?"

"I was just about to ask you the same thing," he answered with concern. "Lester called me."

Damian knew immediately what this call was about. Lester had been a family friend longer than he had been his accountant and he probably wanted to alert his father as to what was going on. Normally, he would have been angry at such an outright betrayal, but he understood why Lester would be concerned. As his accountant, Lester would not have felt comfortable asking probing questions about his personal life. He would just carry out Damian's instructions. But Lester knew Carlton Ware was a different story. Lester called his dad out of pure concern for Damian.

Carlton Ware, and his wife Charlotte, loved both their two sons dearly, but they also bore witness to their emotional turmoil when their relationships went sour. Brandon reacted by declaring himself a bona fide playboy and Damian dealt with his pain by blocking himself off from developing any type of relationship with the opposite sex. What Carlton heard from Lester last night would not have surprised him if he was referring to Brandon. This type of stunt was right up his alley, but for Damian, this was completely out of character. "What are you doing in Las Vegas, and who are you with?"

Damian smiled. He had no doubt that Lester had told him all of the details of his request. Damian was actually surprised it took him this long to call. "I told you about my new office and the woman who owns the design firm I'm using."

"You told me you were spending time with her, but I had no idea you would do something like this."

Damian had purposely kept his developing feelings for Christine to himself, only sharing some of his deepening feelings for her with his brother. It was mostly due to the fact that he didn't trust his feelings. The last time he followed his feelings, he got burned. What he was feeling for Christine excited and scared him at the same time, and he just wasn't ready to share them with the world, including someone as close to him as his father. But now, standing in a luxurious suite in the most exciting city in the world, with a woman who had taken over his heart, Damian was ready to talk to someone, and he was actually glad that his father called. "Let me get off this cell phone. I'll call you right back."

Damian spent the next twenty minutes telling his father the details of his blossoming relationship with Christine, leaving nothing out. After his monologue, Carlton continued the conversation by asking some very pointed questions about Christine. At any other time, Damian may have been offended with such probing questions, but this time, he wasn't.

He knew Carlton was aware of the crazy financial requests Damian had made of Lester years ago, as he attempted to fit into the world that surrounded Danielle; the lifestyle of the rich and famous. Danielle was a card-carrying member of the entertainment world's "can't miss a thing" club. She had a passion for fame that drove her to be at every movie premiere, every awards show and every top fashion show she was not participating in. Lester was always weary of how she could continue to maintain that lifestyle. While it was true that she was making upward of $25,000 per show, she was spending at a much higher rate. Damian had even suggested she use Lester to handle her financial affairs, but she flat out refused, putting her full trust in her manager to handle all aspects of her career. Lester advised Damian to be careful, as someone who spent money like that would be looking for a back up when the well ran dry.

However, putting his father's mind at ease, he explained that this excursion was totally his idea and his feelings for Christine ran deeper than anything he had ever experienced.

"Are you really going to gamble away a quarter of a million dollars son?"

"Dad, I'm gambling something money can't buy . . . my heart."

After a moment of silence, Carlton was convinced that Damian was in complete control. "She must be a very special woman," his father said.

"Believe me, Dad," he said, feeling his heart swelling with love. "She is."

Ending the call, Damian fell off into a restful night of sleep.

The next morning, Christine awoke to the smell of fresh-brewed hazelnut coffee. Stepping into the bathroom to freshen up, she looked longingly at the spa tub. It conjured up images of the time she and Damian soaked in his hot tub. She made a silent promise to herself that she would get in a good soak before she left. Maybe she could get Damian to join her.

Gazing in the mirror, it still took her by surprise at times to see the short, wavy hair crowning her head. Using the mousse provided by the hotel, she ran a small amount through her hair. She was still amazed at how easy it was to care for short locks. All those years she spent dealing with perms, rollers, wraps, and blow drying. She didn't miss any of it. The new style gave her a feeling of total freedom and flexibility. She couldn't believe how much power she had given to Henry, allowing him to have influence over every thing she had done.

During her childhood years, nothing she did seemed to please him. Henry had instilled a deep feeling of unimportance as he was went from one extreme to the other. He would either be putting her down, or ignoring her. He never acknowledged her accomplishments in school, nor did he offer encouragement. He made her feel unwanted, unloved and unappreciated.

Christine wondered if that was part of the reason she was so driven. Was she still trying to prove herself worthy of his love? Was she chasing the approval of someone who could never give it to her?

She thought of her mother. If it hadn't been for Ruth trying to make things bearable, she doubted if she would have survived those younger years. Christine realized it took courage to recognize and help foster the talent Ruth saw in her daughter. Providing fabrics and sewing supplies, Ruth cultivated Christine's gift, letting her create the designs she drew on paper. During her second year in high school, Ruth bought her a second-hand sewing machine. Christine, ecstatic over the surprise gift, began to spend her days cooped up in her room creating her own designs.

It was during that summer Christine began her redecorating project. She made her own drapes and matching comforter, painted her room using three different shades of purple, and stenciled flowers around the walls to create her own border. Ruth spent several Saturday mornings taking her to local yard sales buying small knickknacks of all kinds. But she didn't allow her mother to see her work in progress. Finally, when the room was complete, she presented her hard work to her mother.

"Well, Mom," Christine asked nervously, "what do you think?"

*Ruth entered the teenager's bedroom and carefully scanned the room. She saw the four throw pillows covered in shades of purple, yellow and orange they had bought for one dollar each, meticulously arranged on the wooden chair. The five dollar chair looked completely different now that the stains and tears had been replaced with a new printed fabric in shades of lavender. The large window on the far wall was draped with swag curtains that hung just below the midpoint. The borders stretched across the entire room and she purposely ignored the slight crookedness of the stenciling. The bed was covered in the simple seamed comforter and the many stuffed animals she had collected over the years. A proud mother smiled at her daughter.*

"I think it looks beautiful."

*Christine released a breath she hadn't realized she was holding.* "You mean you really like it?"

*Stepping farther into the room, she turned a full 360 degrees.* "You are a very talented young woman. You remind me of my mother. She could take a vision in her mind and create it with her hands." *She hugged her daughter tightly.* "You can do anything you want to do. You have the talent to take whatever you dream and make it a reality. No matter what anyone says, always know that I love you and I believe in you."

Snapping back to the present, Christine cleared her throat

and wiped her wet eyes. How she loved that room. It was her shining accomplishment and it gave her the inspiration to dream of a career in interior design. She recalled the feeling of peace that enveloped her when she spent time in her room. When she shut that door, it was as if she became a separate entity, no longer a part of that house. She was free from the abuse, the slander, and the drunken rages perpetuated by Henry. It was her private haven.

Hearing a knock at the door, she quickly blotted her eyes once more, and made her way across the room. Damian leaned casually against the doorjamb, looking cool in beige linen pants, matching button-down shirt and loafers. Stepping forward, he said, "I just wanted to see if you were ready to eat, we can . . ." Stopping in mid sentence, he stepped forward and took a closer look. "You've been crying."

Turning quickly, Christine answered, "It's no big deal, just give me a minute. I can't wait to have some of that fresh coffee I smell."

Moving to her side, he turned her into him. "Don't tell me it's nothing. Anything that brings even one tear to your eye is something." Searching her eyes for an answer, he pleaded quietly, "Please don't shut me out."

"I was thinking about my mom," she started quietly. "It's funny. When I was growing up, she seemed so weak and lost to me. But now, I'm remembering things about her that showed how much she truly cared for me." Taking a deep breath, she did nothing to prevent her tears from falling. "I missed so much by judging her and not loving her, and now I'll never be able to tell her how sorry I am."

Gently taking his hands to her face, he whispered, "Don't be so hard on yourself. I'm sure she knew how much you loved her."

Inhaling the clean, fresh scent of her hair, his body grew warm from the inside out. She felt so right in his arms, and he was slowly losing his fight to control the fire that was smoldering on the inside of him. He retreated two steps.

Christine, feeling the immediate loss, took a step forward and wrapped her arms around his neck, molding her soft curves to the contour of his hard body. Pulling him closer, she reached up to meet his lips. Hungrily, she pressed her body into his, searching for the comfort only Damian Ware could provide.

Her kiss was powerful and demanding, leaving no part of his mouth untouched. Shocked at her eagerness and the passion that engulfed her, she was hopeless to stop her assault. She sensed the awakening of flames within her that had been dormant her entire life.

Damian's response was instant and intense, forcing her lips to accept his thrusting tongue, unleashing at full force the undercurrent of passion that had been there since the day they met. Feeling her knees weaken, she leaned further into him, the thin material from her silk nightclothes offering no barrier. Her nipples, taut beneath the thin fabric, pressed firmly into his chest, and caused his arousal to be full and complete.

His hands began an intimate exploration of her body. First massaging her neck, then making their way to her shoulders, pulling down the slim spaghetti straps along the way. Continuing his motion, he outlined the tips of her breasts with his fingers. Hearing the moan released from her lips, he swept her up in one smooth motion and walked over to the bed and laid her down. Standing beside her, the only sound echoing through the room was their deep, uneven breathing. Looking at her swollen lips, her bare shoulders and her breasts peeking out over her top, Damian didn't make a move.

"Stop me now," he said calmly. It would damn near kill him, but he would walk right out of the room if she wasn't ready. He wanted no regrets.

Without answering him verbally, she crossed her arms in front of her, grabbing the bottom of her nightshirt, and with a boldness she didn't know she possessed, lifted it over her head in one smooth motion. "Who said anything about stopping," she said seductively.

Kicking off his shoes, he laid beside her, engulfing her completely in his embrace. He began with a trail of slow, drugging kisses. First her forehead, then her eyelids, followed by the back of her ears. He smoothly moved to her neck, down her shoulder blade, and finally to her breast. Gently sucking the swollen nipple of one, while the other enjoyed the gentle caress of his hands. The soft sounds Christine emitted only served to encourage him more.

Sliding his hands down over her flat stomach, he reached the top of her pajama bottoms and slowly slid them down, followed by her underwear. Pulling back, he looked her straight in the eye and smiled. "You are the most beautiful woman in the world, inside and out."

Kissing her deeply, he broke away and continued, "One of us is overdressed."

With a tentative smile, and a slight hesitation, she reached out to undo the buttons on his shirt. Discarding the item to the floor, Christine pressed her hands against his chest and gently rubbed his sensitive spots. Hearing his sighs of pleasure, Christine became courageous in her motions. Sliding her hands down his torso, she slowly began rubbing his hard maleness. He leaned his head back and moaned. Excited at the power she possessed over him, she helped him out of his pants and briefs. Staring at his perfect, bronzed body, Christine had a moment of hesitation, and he saw it. It was the same look she had in the hot tub at his beach house.

"What is it?"

Recovering quickly, she said with a sly smile, "Now who's asking too many questions?" Stroking his cheek, she whispered, "Just make love to me."

Reaching for his wallet, he retrieved the small foil packet.

Needing no more encouragement, he released the passion that had been festering below the surface these past months. Positioning himself above her, her looked her in the eye and

entered her. Her warmth enveloped him and then he abruptly
stopped, his questioning gaze searing into her. She answered
him silently by raising her hips to meet him. Holding her
tight, he pushed through the barrier. He cursed under his
breath at the pain he saw reflected on her face. Waiting a
few moments, they began to find their rhythm. They moved
to the imaginary beat of music made just for them. Skin to
skin, heart to heart, and soul to soul.

Encouraging her with whispered words of endearments,
he stroked her body with love and tenderness. Hearing a
moan of ecstasy escape from her lips, he soon followed with
his own release, amazed at the height of passion that she had
taken him to.

They laid silently for several moments before he moved
beside her and drew her into his arms.

"Why didn't you tell me?" he asked solemnly.

"Because you didn't ask," she answered lightly and with
a smile.

"Touche."

Gently stroking her arms, he asked, "Why me?"

Looking up into his eyes, she answered with confidence,
"Because you said you would never hurt me, and I believe
you."

Leaning up on his elbow, Damian gave her a serious look.
"Christine, after my disastrous affair with Danielle, I closed
myself off to everyone and totally submerged myself in my
work. I thought that there was no way I could risk another
relationship. But you have touched my heart and I care for
you more than I ever thought possible."

It was on the tip of her tongue to ask what happened to
end their relationship, but she bit it back. Danielle and
Damian looked like the perfect couple in the newspaper article she read and the curiosity was eating away at her, but
she figured he would tell her when he was ready. Even after
all he had just confessed, she wasn't naive enough to believe
that just because they had shared a bed, he was obligated to

open up his entire life to her. Christine also noted that he confessed no words of love, but that was OK. What she felt for Damian was more than she ever thought possible. He came into her life at her darkest moment and offered her comfort, friendship, and understanding. She loved him with her entire being, and right now, that was enough for her.

Later that afternoon, Damian sat in the suite, flipping channels on the television. Christine had only been away from him a few hours, but it felt like an eternity. They had spent the entire morning in bed, sharing stories of their lives, until hunger drove them to the kitchen. Eating a late lunch of Caesar salad and grilled chicken, Christine left in the trusted hands of Mary Ann to complete her shopping for the remainder of their visit. Damian had awoken early and completed his shopping, before he went to wake Christine.

Thinking of their lovemaking caused Damian to shiver in excitement. Feelings he had never felt before moved him in unexplainable ways. Coming together with her in the most intimate way caused a plethora of emotions to swirl in him. Passion. Excitement. Desire. Devotion. Intensity. *Love.*

That last word stuck in his mind, and his heart. Walking over to window, he gazed down onto the street and watched thousands of people move up and down the strip. A feeling of contentment surrounded him. He had fallen completely in love with Christine Davenport. He tried to pinpoint the moment it happened. Was it when they joined as one? Did it happen when she fell asleep in his arms on the plane ride here? Could it have been when she expressed her jealousy at seeing him at the restaurant with another woman? Or was it the weekend they spent at his beach house? Maybe it happened when he held her in the gazebo at her company's reception? Closing his eyes, he realized that he felt a strong connection to her the moment he sat beside her on that park bench outside the hospital. Was she ready to accept his love?

Christine entered the suite an hour later followed by a bellman carrying a multitude of shopping bags. Per her instructions, he went directly to the master suite and laid the items across the bed. Returning back downstairs, Christine stepped in front of Damian who attempted to give the man a tip. Handing over a large bill, Christine thanked him and shut the door after he left.

Returning back to the living room, he went to her, arms open. She stepped around him.

Confused, Damian watched her take a seat in the chair, opposite him.

"I want to talk to you," she said flatly.

"What's going on?" he asked, "Did something happen with Mary Ann?"

"As a matter of fact, something very interesting happened on my shopping trip. After deciding on several items, I took my selections to the register. They would not accept my credit card. I was told that all purchases were covered by you."

Folding her arms across her chest, she continued, "I insisted on paying for my own clothes, at which time, Mary Ann informed me that the instructions from the hotel manager were for all purchases to be charged to Mr. Damian Ware, and that she could not accept any other form of payment."

Rising, Christine began to pace the floor. "I am not a woman for sale. Do you think you can just buy me? That I would be so easily influenced by material things? I am very capable of buying my own clothes and shoes."

Watching him give no reaction to her words, she glared at him in frustration and continued, "I am an independent woman. I don't need anyone to take care of me. I told Mary Ann that I understand her instructions, so I'll go ahead and charge it to you, but I will be giving you a check for the total amount."

Damian watched in amazement as she continued her tirade. She barely noticed when he moved in her path, causing her to bump into him. Looking up startled, he took advantage of her being off balance and kissed her. Immediately she responded. The electricity flowing between them ignited a flame on the inside. Breaking the connection, he smiled. "I'm learning that this is the only way to shut you up."

Christine silently berated herself for being so easily distracted. Momentarily losing her train of that thought, she stepped away from him. "I want to pay you back for the clothes."

"No."

"Yes. I'll write you a check," she said, reaching for her purse.

Exasperated, he sighed, "I won't cash it."

"I don't owe anybody, and I won't start now!"

"A gift does not come with a price."

"Everything comes with a price. I learned that from Henry. The few times he gave my mother something, he would always throw it back in her face when he wanted her to do something. That taught me that everything comes with a price. Nothing is free."

Standing directly in front of her, he lifted her chin to look in her eyes. "Is that what you think, Christine? After what we shared this morning, do you really think my love comes with a price?"

Startled at his admission, she whispered, "Did you say love?"

Pulling her to him, he said, "How could you have doubted my feelings for you? You have awakened a part of me I thought died many years ago. I remember telling you in your office that love is sharing, caring, giving, taking, trusting, happiness, joyful, and definitely sexually satisfying. Well," he said, stepping back and gazing into her eyes, "I feel all those things with you. I love you, Christine Davenport."

"You've changed my life," she said softly. "You make me so happy. When my mother died, I was so full of anger. I was angry with my father for the way he treated my mother and me. I was angry with my mother for allowing it. After Henry died, and my mother and I began to repair our relationship, that anger began to subside. But then she died, and I've had to deal with her will, Henry's mistress and my half sister. But since you've come into my life, you've forced me to look past all of that and see what life has to offer. To put away the things of the past and enjoy my life now. I've had more fun and done more exciting things since I've met you, than I have my entire life."

Reaching up, she gently touched his cheek with the back of her hand, "But I can't completely change all at once. So many things have become such an intimate part of me. My independence, my feeling of having to do everything on my own, without help from anyone. Just be patient with me."

Damian nodded in understanding. She lived a childhood nightmares are made of, and he knew it embedded a way of life for her that could not be easily erased. She had yet to confess words of love to him, but he believed deep inside that she could not have given herself to him and not loved him. It would take time to win her completely, and he would give her all the time in the world. "Don't worry, I'm a very patient man. Now," he said, wanting to lighten the mood, "it is almost five o'clock and I've made dinner reservations for seven. After that, I thought we could hit the casino."

Christine laughed, "Sounds like we have a big night ahead of us. I think I'll go up and rest and bit, but I'll be ready at seven." Kissing him lightly on lips, she headed for her room.

# TEN

Standing at the bottom of the spiral steps, Damian checked his watch. Glancing up, his breath caught and he blinked twice. The soft glow illuminating from the dimly lit chandelier surrounded her in an angelic halo. She glided down the steps dressed in the elegance of black and white. The white, silk-shell blouse was tucked neatly into black and white striped silk pants that swung loosely at the ankle. The black t-strapped sandals with the three-inch heels were accented with sparkling white rhinestones. Her hair, completely slicked back, served to highlight her evening makeup and large white earrings. When she stood directly in front of him, he smiled. "You look fabulous."

Her eyes lit up at his compliment. "You don't look too bad yourself," she said, taking in the black Versace suit with a crisp white shirt with a Chinese collar.

Holding out his arm, "Shall we go?"

They enjoyed a leisurely dinner at the hotel's finest restaurant, which was extremely intimate, with seating for only eighty-six people. They feasted on smoked salmon, lobster bisque soup, house salad, and slow roasted duck in an Asian sauce, accented by a great bottle of wine. The service was impeccable, the view was breathtaking, a jazz band played perfectly in the background.

Placing her dessert fork down, Christine exhaled. "I don't think I could eat another bite. Everything was absolutely wonderful. Who would have thought that my Thanksgiving would be so wonderful? I can't remember the last time I ate this much. I'll have to work out twice as hard next week."

Standing, he offered his hand. "Why don't we start working off some of this food now. Dance with me."

Reaching out, she laced her fingers with his and allowed herself to be led to the small dance floor. Wrapped in his arms, Christine rested her cheek against his chest and locked her hands behind his neck, stroking his nape. As he gently swayed her back and forth, the feeling of desire became almost unbearable. He hummed softly, his warm breath sending tingles throughout her body. As he moved his hands slowly up and down her back, Christine totally relaxed. Feeling the pressure of his thigh against her, she was lost in a world of fantasy.

Damian swallowed deliberately as they moved to the sounds of the saxophone. The smell of *Tiffany* lingered in the air, mixing with her wonderful, natural scent. It was exhilerating and intoxicating, and his ability to contain the passion boiling on the inside was fading quickly. Being this close to her and unable to make love was pure torture. Feeling that he was about to lose control, he stepped back and smiled, "I think it's time we hit the casino."

Christine felt the energy as soon as they entered the gaming floor. Lights flashing, bells ringing, money dropping, slots turning, dice rolling, people yelling out in victory, and others moaning in defeat. The colors were vibrant and the air was filled with excitement. Her eyes widened in anticipation as she took it all in.

"Where do you want to begin?" Damian asked, feeling the energy himself.

"I've never gambled in my life," she said with a grin, "but I'm ready to give it a try."

"Well, we'll find a blackjack table and get you started. Remember, tonight is all about taking risks."

Finding a table toward the end of the casino, Christine sat on one of the stools after a five minute lesson from Damian.

Handing her a hundred dollar chip, he stood behind her as the dealer dealt the next hand.

"A hundred dollars! I can't bet this on one hand, I'll probably lose it!"

"It's only money Christine, remember that. It can't give you love, it can't keep you warm at night, and you can't take it with you when you go."

"OK. Besides," she continued with a wicked grin, "it's your money."

The next hour, Christine learned that even blackjack came with rules. Hands above the table, tap the table when you want a hit, and never, ever take a hit when you have nineteen. That one she learned the hard way.

"Do you think you have the hang of it now?" Damian asked, pleased at the laughter they were sharing.

"Are you kidding, what am I up, five hundred, six hundred bucks?"

"Actually, you're up nine. I think you're ready to be promoted." Gathering up her winnings, he led her to the other end of the floor. Walking up to the roped area, he spoke quietly into the employee's ear standing guard. The rope was pulled back and they entered.

This room was less crowded and much quieter than the main floor. Stepping up to the blackjack table, he motioned for her to take a seat.

"This looks a little out of my league," she said nervously.

"You'll do just fine."

Taking away the chips she had accumulated during the previous game, he handed her a new stack.

Looking down, she almost choked, "Are you crazy?"

"Christine, darling, don't hold up the game," he said, indicating the dealer was ready to deal the next hand.

"I can't play with these chips," she said, suddenly scared of playing.

"It's only money, Christine. It doesn't matter if you win

or lose, only that you're in the game. It's OK, honey, place the bet."

Turning back to the dealer, all eyes were impatiently resting on her. Throwing one chip on the table, she breathed deeply as she received two cards. She couldn't believe she just placed a five thousand dollar bet! Lifting the two cards, she squealed in excitement. Damian laughed as he saw her queen of hearts and her jack of spades. Just like that, she was up five grand. After winning about forty thousand, she lost the next ten hands and decided to call it quits.

Back on the main floor, Christine eyed all the slot machines and wondered how her luck would fare there. "I think I want to try the slot machines. I've never played them before."

Glad that she was having a good time, Damian led her to high roller slot area. "Your wish is my command."

Stopping at a row of slots, Christine laughed, "I should have known better than to think you would let me play the nickel or quarter machines."

"You told me to show you how to live in the moment, to not place value on things. So, here are your chips. Let's see how the one-armed bandit treats you."

Playing the hundred dollar slots, Christine realized that after about an hour of play, she had gone through almost four thousand dollars, only winning back a few hundred. But she was enjoying herself. Never in her life had she felt so free. All her life she was concerned with having all the things she didn't have growing up, but Damian was showing her that what you have is not as important as who you are and who you share it with. She was freeing herself from the bondage she held herself in. Suddenly, she didn't want to be in the casino any longer. She had a sudden urge to give to Damian what he had given to her. Pulling the handle one last time, she turned to Damian. As her eyes grew dark with desire, she leaned into him and whispered, "I'm ready to call it a night."

Without giving him a chance to respond, she walked past him, heading for the elevators. Reaching the twenty-ninth floor, she walked ahead of Damian and opened the door. By the time he entered the suite, she was standing in the living room, swinging her sandals in her hand.

"Damian, I had such a great time tonight. As a matter of fact, I feel like dancing."

Damian moved toward her, and stopped when she pushed out her hand.

Giving a wicked grin with a twinkle in her eye, she said, "You misunderstood me, sweetheart. I dance, you watch."

He stood motionless and his eyes followed her shoes as she dropped one on the floor, and then the other. Even her toes were sexy! Walking over to the stereo, she turned on some jazz and sashayed to the middle of the floor. Wiggling her hips from side to side, she slowly walked up a few steps and stopped, sliding down her slacks, stepping completely out of them. She held them out with two fingers and he swallowed hard as she dropped them to the ground. Heading to the top of the steps, she unzipped her blouse completely and let it fall to the ground. He exercised every ounce of self-control he had as he stared at her black lace panties and matching bra. Still moving her body in time with the music, she summoned him with her forefinger. Reaching the top of the stairs, she smiled wickedly at him and led him to the master suite.

This time, it was she who said, "One of us is over-dressed . . . again." Standing in front of him, she pulled his jacket down and threw it onto the chair. Unbuttoning his shirt, she spread her hands across his bare chest and heard him moan in pleasure. When she reached for his belt buckle, the feelings of desire threatened to overtake him.

Laying him on the bed, Christine began an exploration of his body with her mouth, leaving no place untouched. She wanted to brand him with her touch, making her a permanent part of him and he a permanent part of her.

"You're killing me, baby. I don't know how much more I can take," he said breathlessly.

After taking a moment to protect them, she placed herself above him, and slowly eased herself down. She was a glowing image of passion, fire, and love, and he filled her with an amazing sense of completeness. Their hands searched each other's pleasure points, their passion growing by the minute. Moving in exquisite harmony with one another, their bodies found a tempo only known to them. As they reached the threshold of pure ecstasy, they both released cries of pleasure.

Minutes later, neither moved, both recovering from the soaring heights the journey had taken them to. Still laying above him, Christine felt a lone tear fall down her cheek. He felt it when it hit his chest.

"What is it sweetheart?"

"That was so beautiful. I never thought I could have this. Henry told me that no man would want me and that I was destined to live alone. But you came along and I've never felt so alive." Sitting up, she smiled in contentment. "I love you, Damian."

Kissing her forehead, he wiped the tear from her cheek. "I love you, too, sweetheart."

They laid in each other's arms silently, listening to the beats of each other's hearts, until sleep overcame them.


The bright rays of sunlight danced its way through the bare trees and into the luxury hotel room, signifying a bright, but cold day. Danielle Olivia paced the floor nervously, her breakfast left untouched. Tightening the belt on her robe, she checked the digital clock beside the bed. Even though she had been up for hours, it was just after seven A.M. She had been trying to find a way all week to get time alone with Damian, but she had been completely unsuccessful. Taking a seat on the bed, she tapped her hands nervously against the small table. She had to find a way to talk to him today. It was Friday and time was running out.

She knew she had messed up when she left his house last weekend after insulting his date. But she couldn't stop herself. Feeling an immediate and unexpected bout of jealously at the fact that he was planning to spend the evening with another woman, she couldn't help but wonder why he would choose that woman over her. Periodically keeping tabs on Damian, she knew he had yet to get seriously involved with anyone. She was counting on him being unattached. Her plan counted on it. Now this woman had changed everything.

And who was this woman who had seemingly wormed her way into Damian's heart? Asking Tanya about her had revealed nothing. Tanya's loyalty to Damian was unwavering and she refused to discuss his life with her on any front. It was sickening. Now here she was, back in town over a week and she was no closer to resolving her dilemma than she was when she stepped off the plane. She had five days. Five days to convince Damian Ware to take her back and marry her, or she would lose everything she'd worked for.

That was easier said than done. She knew she had hurt him deeply when their engagement ended, but she thought he would have gotten over it by now. They say time heals all hurts, and it had been years.

She had not thought that he would welcome her with open arms, but she did not expect the pure hatred reflected in his eyes that night she showed up on his doorstep. His look had told her that she had a lot of making up to do. But she had to do it. She had to convince him of how sorry she was, how much remorse she felt for what she did, and that they deserved to give each other another chance. She had to find a way to get him to listen to her. Whenever she wanted her way, a soft word or a slight pout would have men fawning at her feet. But she could see that this situation was different. Rethinking her strategy was necessary if she was going to get Damian Ware to do exactly what she wanted.

Trying to contact him by phone hadn't worked. Every time he answered, he immediately hung up. When she showed up unexpectedly at his house again, she didn't make it past the door. Figuring her best bet was to show up at his office, she was met at the door by Tanya, who politely informed her that if she showed her face at either the corporate office or one of the construction sites, she would have her arrested for trespassing.

Initially, she had laughed in her sister's face. Tanya didn't have the guts to do it. Growing up, Tanya may not have liked the things that Danielle did, but she never went against her. But as her laughter died down, she took a closer look into her sister's eyes and felt a chill. Tanya was dead serious. That's when Danielle knew her plan was in serious trouble.

When she left after their blowup, she knew she had burned her bridges, but she had been in tougher situations and her beauty, charm, fame, and fortune usually got those bridges rebuilt rather quickly. But thinking about the cold reception she received from Tanya and Damian upon her arrival back in town, she realized she may have a longer road ahead of her than she originally thought. They weren't impressed by beauty, they were immune to her charm, they didn't seek fame, and her fortune was now in question. Picking up the phone, she dialed Damian's number. She had to keep trying.

A few moments later, Danielle slammed the receiver into the cradle with a loud bang, chipping one of her ten perfectly manicured nails. Where was he? Rising, she walked over to the window. What was she going to do? Reluctantly, she realized she'd have to try Tanya again. If there was one person Damian Ware would listen to, it would be his darling friend and confidante, Tanya Kennedy. Picking up the phone again, she dialed her sister.

"What do you want, Danielle?" Tanya asked, after identifying the caller.

"Is that anyway to talk to your loving sister?"

"You fly into town unannounced, show up unexpectedly

at your ex-fiancé's house, insult his girlfriend, and you want to know why I'm not falling over in excitement to talk to you?"

Danielle thought better of agitating her sister any further and decided on another approach, "You're absolutely right, Tanya. I've been insensitive and selfish and I owe you and Damian an apology."

Removing the phone from her ear and looking at it strangely, Tanya was silent, unable to believe those words were coming out of her sister's mouth.

"Tanya, are you there?"

"Yes, I'm here. It's just that I don't ever recall you apologizing to anybody for anything."

"Well, this is a new me. I've made some mistakes in the past, but I want to try and set things right. As a matter of fact, I was hoping we could get together today. Maybe I could meet you somewhere for lunch." Danielle held her breath, anxious for her sister to accept her invitation. This new girlfriend of Damian's had put a definite monkey wrench in her plan, so she had to move quickly on her sister. Tanya was her last hope to get to him.

"Sure, Danielle, I'll meet you. Just tell me when and where."

Tanya smiled in amusement after she hung up the phone. What game was her coldhearted sister playing now? No way did she believe for one minute that Danielle had magically turned over a new leaf, especially after that stunt she pulled at Damian's house. No, girlfriend was definitely up to something and she thought it wise to meet her, not so that they could make amends, but because she had to find out exactly what her sister had up her sleeve.

A few hours later, Danielle sat impatiently at the small table located in the back of a café. She had specifically chosen an out of the way location, for fear of being recognized. A year ago she would have thrived on the attention, but now, the last thing she wanted to do was put herself on display.

Until she got her issues resolved, she needed to keep the lowest profile possible.

Checking her messages in Paris, she knew that time was running out. Collectors were hot on her trail and she had less than a week or she was going to lose it all. She wasn't even sure how she was going to settle her hotel bill. It's amazing how when you're on top of your game and in the prime of your career, everybody is falling over themselves to be a part of your life, anyway they can. But when the well runs dry, the so-called friends follow suit. When all her troubles started, she was dropped like a hot potato, and now she was left to stand alone and pull herself out of this.

It was true, they tried to warn her. Her parents and Tanya tried to tell her years ago to slow down, take it easy, don't be so quick to live life in the fast lane. Michelle Ford, her agent since the beginning of her career, warned her that as she got older, the modeling jobs would slow down and she should begin setting up a back up plan for when she could no longer work the runways. Even Damian and his accountant, Lester, sat her down to guide her on planning her future. But she didn't listen. And now here she sat, years later, trying to rebuild bridges that she had possibly burned beyond compare, to get herself out of the well she had dug for herself.

"Sorry, I'm late," Tanya said, hanging her full-length cashmere coat on the hook beside their table and taking a seat.

Ordering drinks, Tanya decided to cut straight to the chase. "What exactly are you up to, Danielle?"

Taken aback by her bold question, Danielle took a moment to recover. Taking a sip of her water to buy time, she slowly placed the glass back on the table. "It's like I told you over the phone, I'm here to repair the damage I've done so that you and I could be a family again."

Tanya's lips curved in a slow and thoughtful grin. "That's the biggest piece of crock I have yet to hear you dish out. Now, I'll ask you again, what's really going on?"

Looking offended, Danielle replied, "I'm sorry to disappoint you sister, there is nothing going on. I'm not the same person I was then."

"I've only heard from you a total of four times in the past two years. On each of those occasions it was because you needed me to do something for you. You didn't ask about my life or my career, and you never asked about Damian. But now, you expect me to believe that you want to become an intimate part of our lives." Pausing while their waiter placed their two ice teas on the table, she then continued, "I'm not buying it."

Danielle lowered her eyes and placed her hands in her lap. Taking a deep, slow breath, she answered, "I know that you don't believe me. I've done things in my life that I am truly ashamed of. I understand why it would be difficult for you to see how much of a different person I am today. But I want the chance to show you and Damian. I want another chance at being your sister and at being a friend to him."

Tanya studied the woman sitting across from her. Dressed in simple black wool pants and a gray pullover, her long hair was pulled back into a simple ponytail. The jewelry and make-up she wore was understated, creating a vast contrast to her normal attire. Danielle was a person who thrived in creating a stir. Always wanting to be the center of attention, she dressed, acted and reacted like a person taking center stage.

Growing up in a small town in Georgia, both women were anxious to leave and head for the sophistication of a big city. When Tanya was seventeen and Danielle was fifteen, a New York modeling agency came to their local mall, doing open auditions. Out of the one thousand hopefuls that showed up, Danielle was the one who won the contract and a chance to make it big in the biggest city in the fashion world.

Even though their mother was skeptical, she packed up her last born and sent her off under the watchful eye of Michelle Ford. In less than three months, she had shot her first cover for a major magazine, introducing herself to the world as Danielle Olivia. That was the beginning of a transformation. The once sweet, considerate and kind sister who grew up helping her mom bake fresh bread and home-made pies and hanging out in her older sister's room and talking non-stop about her hopes and dreams, had become self-centered, conniving, arrogant and someone her family and friends could not recognize. Now she sat looking humble, asking for another chance to right some of her wrongs. The problem was, some things you could never make right. No matter how hard you try.

"Danielle, I agreed to meet with you to find out what you really want. All that talk about making amends, setting things right . . . it's too late. The damage you've done is beyond repair."

Holding her agitation in check, Danielle held back her initial curt response. The bottom line was that she needed Tanya to get Damian to listen to her. Sighing lightly, she replied, "Please, Tanya, just give me a chance. Talk to Damian for me. Get him to at least listen to me, if for nothing else, to apologize for the past. To put it to rest."

Tanya pondered her words carefully. Distraught after the fiasco Danielle created when she left, she watched as Damian tried to pull himself out of the pain he was experiencing and not only put his life back together, but put his business back together. She knew he still harbored anger toward Danielle, as demonstrated by his reaction when she showed up at his house. Maybe if he talked with her, got everything off his chest, he could put her behind him once and for all. "OK, Danielle, I'll see if he'll talk to you."

Trying to contain her overwhelming excitement, Danielle toned down her smile. "Thank you, thank you, Tanya. Do you think you can call him now, maybe I can see him to-night."

"He won't be back until Sunday."

"Back?" Danielle said, raising her eyebrow.

Realizing she had said too much, Tanya backtracked. "I'll let you know when he can see you."

Christine laughed as she tried to lick the ice cream dripping at breakneck speed down the sugar cone and onto her wrist. The blazing, desert heat was unforgiving, and at three o'clock in the afternoon, it seemed to be at its peak. Both were dressed appropriately in walking shorts, cotton shirts, and sandals as they took a seat on a wooden bench.

The past few days had been glorious. Damian and Christine were awed by the magnitude in which the various hotels on the strip entertained their clientele. They gazed out onto all of Las Vegas atop the Stratosphere, watched the pirates fight at Treasure Island, and even braved the roller coaster that soared high above the ground at New York, New York. Earlier that day, they boarded a four-seater helicopter and their breath was taken away as they soared over the Grand Canyon.

Taking another lick of her cone, Christine sighed. "I'm really going to hate leaving here. I can't tell you how much fun I've had."

Placing his arm around her shoulder, Damian answered, "I know exactly what you mean. But we can come back anytime you want."

Christine replied thoughtfully, "I'd like that. This place is an escape. There are so many things going on in my life right now. I can't believe those conniving women want half of my mother's money."

Hesitating a moment, Damian replied, "Have you ever looked at this situation from their point of view?"

Appalled at his question, Christine's eyes widened in amazement, "They have no point of view. I'm not going to have my mother pay for Henry's mistake. All those years of working, saving and investing for the future and they think they can just show up and take it all away. I don't think so."

"But the law may look at things differently. Your mother did use funds from his paychecks to invest."

Standing, Christine threw the remainder of her ice cream into the trash and answered incredulously, "I don't believe this. You think I should hand over a half-million dollars to total strangers?"

Realizing the conversation was spiraling out of control, he reached out to her and was hurt when she stepped away. "All I'm saying is that they don't have to be strangers. Maybe you should look past your mother's money and look at the lives of the women your father hid from you."

"And maybe you should mind your own business." Turning away from him, Damian watched as she walked down the strip and out of his sight.

Shaking his head in bewilderment, he slowly rose and followed behind her.

Arriving back at the hotel, neither spoke as they entered the suite. Going straight to her room, Damian followed, determined to deal with this issue now.

"Christine, I didn't mean to upset you. I was just trying to help you."

"I don't need your help," she replied, taking a seat on the bed.

"You're being difficult again."

Turning her body to face the window, Christine ignored him.

"Do you always act like a spoiled brat when someone doesn't agree with you?"

Still receiving no response, Damian continued in a calm tone, "I'll take that as a yes."

"You don't know what you are talking about," she spat. "My mother worked her butt off for over twenty years and I'm supposed to just give it away?"

Taking her hand in his, he was relieved when she didn't snatch it away, "All I'm saying is think about what I said.

You'll have to face them sooner or later. Why not meet them on your own terms?"

Christine thought about Mr. Murphy and his assumption that she only thought of herself. Was she being selfish in her refusal to entertain the thought of sharing the money with her half sister? "All right, I'll think about it." Seeing the satisfied grin on his face, she quickly added, "But I'm not making any promises."

Leaning over, he gave her a kiss on the lips. "That's all I ask."

"You're good for me," she said thoughtfully. "Since you've come into my life, feelings I buried under hurt and anger have shot to the forefront of my thoughts, forcing me to deal with them. And in doing so, I've let go of a painful past and embraced a bright future."

Damian thought of his parents who had been married for thirty-six years and still flirted with each other. The love he remembered being reflected in their eyes when they looked at one another was the same expression he saw on Christine's face and he felt on his.

"We have one more night in this lively city, and I propose one more bet . . . this time we risk everything. Are you game?"

Monday morning found Natalie Donovan racing down the corridor to her office. She was already fifteen minutes late for her nine A.M. meeting and had yet to print out the documents she needed. Throwing her briefcase onto a chair, she began to boot up her computer. Pacing the floor, she listened to the sounds of her system coming to life.

Hearing her phone line ring, she debated on answering it. Already late, she didn't need a reminder call from Marshall Lewis. Marshall, a thorn in her side ever since he became a partner in her firm two months ago, was full of demanding ways and sexual innuendos. She considered reporting him to Human Resources. His influence had grown over the years, and even if she got reassigned to another partner, the stigma of the scandal would remain with her throughout her tenure.

Deciding to chance it, she answered, "Natalie Donovan."

"Natalie, it's me."

Sighing loudly, Natalie said, "Not now, Mother. I'm late for a meeting."

"I want talk about the money. I was thinking of buying . . ."

Cutting her mother off, Natalie said, "I don't have time. Good-bye." Hanging up the phone, she pushed the button to send all calls straight to voicemail.

For the last month, all conversations with her mother revolved around the money and she had had enough. Margaret could only think about the money, but for Natalie, the entire situation only served to bring out all the questions she spent a lifetime suppressing.

Hearing stories as a young child from her mother of a man who didn't want her, Natalie decided early on to block Henry Davenport and his other family out of her mind. But now she found herself wondering about the daughter he chose over her. What did she look like? What did it feel like to grow up with a mommy and a daddy? Did Henry take her to ball games or meet her dates when they came to pick her up? Did her give her an allowance or attend school functions with her? Did Christine have the childhood she only dreamed of? A childhood filled with fond memories of a Daddy and his little girl? Did he have a nick name for her? Maybe it was Precious, or Kitten? Did they spend Saturday mornings watching cartoons together or going to church on Sundays?

Mostly, Natalie wondered if there was a strong family resemblance between them. As a child, Natalie had fought the battle of weight, and only began to win that fight during her sophomore year in college. Had Christine had the same struggle? Going from a peak size of twenty, she was now comfortable and confident in her size twelve. Her hair, jet black, like her mother's had been, sat neatly in a tight French roll.

Snapping her mind back to the present, she pulled out her compact and checked her makeup. Dressed conservatively in a dark brown pantsuit with black stripes around the wrist and collar, she portrayed the corporate accountant that she was.

Hearing the familiar beep on her computer, she pulled up the needed reports and pushed "print."

Working for a large accounting firm, she had dreamed of branching out on her own and starting her own consulting firm. Her clients were rich, powerful people who could probably fund small countries. But she knew there was an entire population of smaller, minority companies, that needed her services as well. And that's where she wanted to focus her attention. Many people could start a business and run it successfully, but they often fell short in the areas of accounting and taxes. She wanted to make sure that what people worked so hard to build, would not be damaged by lack of knowledge and mismanagement.

Unfortunately, that dream was still in the clouds, as it took capital to start her own CPA firm, and while she had managed to put away money and invest wisely, she was still well short of meeting the needed goal. Her mother was in constant need of money, and she found herself supporting two households. While she tried not to let bitterness seep into her heart, she sometimes resented her mother's lack of initiative. Instead of being proactive in her life, she blamed others and lived with an expectation that the world owed her something. Sadly, until the world paid up, she only had Natalie.

Reading about Henry's death in the obituaries, her mother had insisted that they attend the funeral. Margaret wanted to finally see the wife and child that he had chosen over her. It was after the funeral that her mother overheard a conversation between Ruth and an older gentlemen about a significant amount of money she had set aside for her daughter, so that if anything happened to her, her daughter would never have to worry about money.

Margaret was furious. Believing Henry had accumulated wealth over the years, but would not send money to take care of his other daughter, sent Margaret into a tailspin. Undecided about what to do with the information, she stewed over it for months, constantly calling Uncle Paul about her rights and how she could get her hands on some of that money.

Soon after, Ruth passed away and Margaret became more determined than ever to get a piece of the finances that she believed should have been hers years ago. Initially, Natalie was dead set against staking any claim to the money. But she began to think about all she could do with a half million dollars. She could pay off all her mother's debt and set her up with a monthly stipend and she could pay off her school loans and have enough money to begin her own CPA firm.

Retrieving her documents off the printer, she headed to her meeting, hoping her reprimand for being tardy would be short and sweet. She couldn't wait to get her hands on that money. While her mother had plans of cars, houses and vacations, Natalie had an entirely different agenda. She was going to quit her job and start her own business. She hadn't heard back from her Uncle Paul regarding their offer, but she was determined to get what was rightfully hers. Henry owed her that, and she planned to collect.

# *ELEVEN*

"Thank you, Mr. Murphy for your help. I would like to meet them, preferably in a social setting. I do understand that it will be best if you are present as well as their attorney, but I don't want a formal, stiff event. I want to meet in an atmosphere that will lean toward the sociable. Perhaps a restaurant instead of a conference room?"

Mr. Murphy was thrilled at this phone call. He was glad to see that Christine was moving toward accepting the situation and seeking out a resolution. Initially, their conversations about the money and her parents were laced with anger. Over the past month, he'd seen a steady change in her attitude. In fact, that day she sounded the happiest he'd ever heard her.

"That sounds fine. I'll see what I can arrange." Hesitating a moment, he decided to take the chance. "You sound different today, Christine. There's something in your voice that speaks of joy. Did something happen over the long holiday weekend?"

Wanting to keep her newfound feelings of love close to her, she just answered, "Let's just say things are looking up."

"With your business, or personal?"

"Both," she said gaily. "My business is doing fantastically and my love life is on the upswing. Now, if you'll excuse me, I have an appointment waiting."

After he hung up with Christine, Douglas reached into his wallet and pulled out a small photograph of Ruth. The day they met to set up investment funds for her daughter, the restaurant had a portable picture machine, and for one dollar, it would spit out six pictures. She thought it was silly that he wanted a picture of her, but he convinced her, after threatening to back out of the arrangements they just made.

Staring at the dark eyes smiling back at him, he said, "It looks like its finally happening, Ruth. I think your precious daughter is falling in love."

Placing the photograph back into his wallet, he opened his desk drawer and pulled out an envelope. Sealed tightly, he turned it around in his hand. He had no idea what Ruth had written to her daughter, he only knew he had promised to follow her strict instructions that it was not to be given to her until the day she married. Ruth called it her "special gift." Feeling his emotions about to takeover, he placed the letter back into the drawer and slammed it shut. Picking up a file, he got back to work.

Natalie opened the door to her apartment and threw her mail onto the small table in the foyer. Noticing the handbag on the floor, Natalie leaned against the door, closed her eyes and inhaled deeply. She was not in the mood to deal with her mother. Lately, every time they got together, the only topic of conversation was the money. It was as if she was possessed with making plans on how she was going to spend the money.

Last week she was talking about the new Mercedes Benz and this week, she had become fascinated about taking a vacation around the world. She had already typed up her resignation from her administrative position at a local bank, and planned to turn it in as soon as an agreement was reached. And frankly, all her talk about money was getting on her last nerve.

"Natalie," Margaret said, coming down the hall, "I was hoping you would get here soon. I called your office, but they said you left for the day. Where did you go? That was hours ago."

Heading for the kitchen, Natalie responded, "Mom, I gave you a key for emergency situations only. What are you doing here?" She purposely ignored her question. She was not ready to share the plans for her own business or the fact that she had met with a real estate agent to scout out a location.

"Is that anyway to talk to you mother?" Margaret answered sarcastically.

"Look, Mom. I've had a very rough day at the office. My boss is on my back and I have a ton of work I brought home that I need to catch up on."

"The money is . . ."

Her last band of patience snapped, Natalie yelled, "The money . . . the money! Is that all you can talk about? Well, I have had enough. I don't want to hear another word about a house, a car, a vacation or about Christine Davenport. Besides, you're planning to spend money that's not even coming to you. Or did you forget that I'm the one entitled to that money. The check they write will be written to me."

Margaret stood staring at her daughter. "How dare you speak to me that way? I struggled to raise you on my own, and now that I have a chance to get something for it, you treat me like this."

Natalie rubbed her temples to fight the onset of a headache just as the phone rang. "What now?"

Picking up on the third ring, she listened as her Uncle Paul informed her that Christine Davenport had declined their settlement offer, but wished to meet.

After confirming a date and time, Natalie hung up and told her mother of the latest development. Seething with anger, Margaret cursed Christine and her family.

"I can't believe that greedy wench declined our offer," Margaret said.

Natalie silently agreed with her mother. As Henry's

daughter, she had just as much right to that money as anyone, and when they met on Friday, she would tell her that.

Checking her makeup one last time in her compact, she snapped it shut and got out of her car. Dressed in a long, straight black skirt, with a gold and black sweater, Christine hummed as she made her way to the front door. The last time she made this walk, she was greeted by Danielle. This time, there would be no ex-fiancé, no snide remarks and no argument. Together, she and Damian were hosting a dinner party at his home with their closest friends and she planned to enjoy every minute of it.

Opening the door before she could knock, Damian took one look at the love of his life and exhaled a slow whistle. "You look absolutely gorgeous."

Handing him a bottle of her favorite wine, she entered the foyer and took her first look at the house. "Oh, Damian, this is beautiful."

Watching her admire his home caused a stir in him. When he first laid eyes on this house, he knew it would be the place where he would raise his family, and seeing Christine standing in his entryway with a look of love reflected in her eyes, his happiness was complete. He knew he would have that family with her.

Who would have imagined that fate would have their paths cross again, after their strange initial meeting? Walking into that reception and seeing her face made him realize that his promise to focus on his business was not enough, he needed someone special in his life . . . he needed her.

"I'll give you the five cent tour after dinner. But first, how about a proper hello?" Pulling her gently to him, he embraced her with tenderness and devoured her with his mouth. Probing deeper, he pressed his body into hers. Immediately, his desire grew. If he didn't stop himself now, he would suggest they skip dinner and head straight to his master suite. But he pulled away. Their guests would be there at any moment. They had all night. First they would feast on the fabulous meal he prepared and then they would feast on each other.

Placing his hands over hers, the corners of his mouth curved upwards. "If we don't stop now, our friends will find us in a very compromising position."

Pretending to pout, Christine responded, "I guess we can eat first . . . you will need your strength later."

He laughed, with a sparkle in his eye. "Is this the same woman who less than two months ago wouldn't even let me kiss her? I think I've unleashed a monster."

Christine's snide response was caught on her lips as they were interrupted by the ringing of the doorbell.

Greeting her best friend and fiancé, introductions were made and they headed for the family room where hors d'oeuvres were waiting. Asking everyone to dress for dinner, Nathan looked distinguished in a black suit and Stephanie looked stunning in a Chanel velvet dress. The oversized sofa and chairs, the glowing fire and the bookshelves lining the walls, gave off the feeling of warmth and comfort. Nathan and Damian talked sports, while Stephanie and Christine sat on the sofa, enjoying the fresh baked bread and crab dip.

"Christine, you have been full of surprises. First, you take off for Las Vegas at the spur of the moment, and now you're hosting a dinner with Damian. What's going on?"

Hearing the doorbell, Christine rose to follow Damian to meet their next arrival. "I promise I'll fill you in later."

As Stephanie watched Damian and Christine leave the room, she stood and joined Nathan by the fireplace. The concerned look on her face did not go unnoticed.

"What's the matter, honey?" Nathan asked, "You look like you lost your best friend."

Gazing in to his eyes, she reflected on his words and sighed, "I think you may be right."

Brandon held his breath standing outside his brother's

house. This was the opportunity he had been waiting for and he planned to take full advantage. He would finally get a chance to talk to Tanya and clear the air between them. The inner torture he'd endured when previous attempts to talk to her had failed, constantly reminded him of what he had lost due to his foolish behavior. But he couldn't blame her.

He remembered the look on her face when he confessed to sleeping with another woman. What a fool he had been! He gave up the one thing he now knew made his life complete. And he'd been paying for it with loneliness ever since.

Taking a deep breath, he greeted his brother and Christine when they opened the door. Following them to the family room, he could hardly contain his excitement. It would be a challenge, but he was prepared to find a way to get Tanya to listen to him and agree to give them another chance.

Tanya parked her car and cut off the engine. Sitting for several moments, she needed time to get her emotions under control. When Damian invited her to dinner that night, he warned her that Brandon was going to be there.

Over the past year, Damian had always played a neutral friend to her and a loyal brother to Brandon, and he went out of his way to avoid having them together. But he said that night was special and he wanted both of them there.

Tanya knew it had to be important to Damian to ask her to set aside her personal feelings for one night, so she hesitantly agreed to be there. Now that she sat less than thirty feet from seeing the man that had once been the love of her life, she wasn't sure she would be able to make it through the evening. Not because she was still in love with him, but because she wasn't sure all her anger was gone, and she was liable to punch his lights out.

Stepping out of the car, she prayed that civility would rule tonight. There was no reason she couldn't handle one dinner . . . four hours . . . maybe three, if she skipped coffee and dessert.

Damian opened the door and saw the look of apprehension on Tanya's face.

"I can see this is hard for you," he said, wondering if he made the right decision in having them both over for dinner.

Faking indifference, she replied, "It's only dinner, Damian. Your brother doesn't effect me either way."

After hanging her coat, she followed Damian into the family room where Christine, Stephanie, Nathan and Brandon admired the artwork hanging on the wall.

Tanya made eye contact with Brandon, and was pleased when her inner feelings of disgust stayed hidden behind her smile. As long as the group kept the conversation going, she would be just fine.

Opening a bottle of expensive champagne, Damian poured everyone a glass. After everyone was served, he stood beside Christine, placing his arm around her shoulder.

"Christine and I are thrilled that our closest friends could join us this evening. As all of you know, we spent this past weekend in Las Vegas, and we had the time of our lives. It was there that we laughed together, cried together, and fell in love with each other."

The room was silent with expectation. No one made a sound as Damian raised his glass. "Welcome to the home of Mr. and Mrs. Damian Ware."

Complete silence surrounded the room as the guests digested the weight of his announcement. Stephanie was the first to find her voice.

"Married! You guys went to Las Vegas and got married? How? What happened?" she exclaimed, focusing her attention on Christine. Wasn't this the same woman who proclaimed less than three months ago that marriage was the last thing she would ever commit to?

Lovingly gazing into his wife's eyes, he said, "We realized we loved each other and wanted to spend the rest of our lives together, so we contacted our host at the hotel and he made all the arrangements. We wanted to surprise you guys tonight and have you share our first dinner as a married couple. But we're planning a reception for all our friends and family next month."

Brandon stared speechlessly at his brother. The past few months, Damian constantly talked about his budding relationship with the interior designer, but marriage? Did his feelings for her really run that deep, or did they get caught up in the excitement of Las Vegas, eventually to grow to regret the decision they had made?

Tanya moved swiftly toward the couple and gave both of them a huge hug. "I knew you two were meant to be together. This is wonderful, congratulations."

That started a round of hugs and kisses.

Moving toward the door, Damian announced, "If everyone will follow me into the dining room, dinner is served."

As they made their way to the dining room, Stephanie stood back and gently touched Christine's hand. Allowing the others to go ahead, the two women stayed in the family room.

Stephanie's look of concern and confusion did not go unnoticed by Christine. Hoping to avoid this conversation, she knew exactly what her best friend was going to say. Christine couldn't blame her. If the roles had been reversed, she would have been doing the same thing.

"Before you say anything, Stephanie, I want you to know that I love him very much."

Setting her champagne glass down on the coffee table, Stephanie sat on the sofa and Christine followed. Placing her hand over hers, she squeezed it lovingly. "I know you do, Christine, but are you really ready for marriage? Not long ago you told me marriage was not for you."

"I know what I said, but in my heart, I know I made the right decision."

"I don't doubt your heart, but I'm concerned about your mind. There's so much going on with you right now . . . the will and meeting your half sister. You've always handled things on your own. Are you ready to open up and share your life with Damian?"

"Damian has nothing to do with those situations. I'll deal with them on my own."

Stephanie remembered the look of love she saw in Damian's eyes and said, "Is Damian going to go along with that?"

"He'll have to," Christine answered with confidence. Rising and heading for the dining room, she said, "Let's go have dinner."

Conversation was plentiful around the table as Christine and Damian relived their trip and Stephanie and Nathan talked about their upcoming wedding. As dessert was served, Tanya thought this the perfect time to bow out graciously. Thrilled for Damian, and taking an instant liking to Stephanie and Nathan, she still could not overshadow the tension that hung between herself and Brandon. Excusing herself, she rose and signaled for others to remain seated.

"Don't get up. I can see myself out." Walking around the dining table, she said her good-byes and headed for the front door.

Brandon rose to follow and Damian said, "Brandon, let her go."

"I can't big brother. Not this time."

Retrieving her coat from the closet, Tanya said a prayer of thanks that she had made it through the evening without a scene. When she walked into the family room and saw Brandon standing next to the bar, his smooth skin, playful eyes and quirky grin immediately touched her to the core. People say that time heals all wounds, but in that instant, all the hurt and anger she felt the day he confessed his betrayal resurfaced with a vengeance.

She should have known better than to trust him, especially since she had heard about his philandering ways from Damian when they met in college. People never believed that a man and woman could be friends and not end up in bed, but that was the case with Tanya and Damian. They never crossed that line, and had developed one of the most enduring friendships she'd ever had.

When Damian started his business, there was never a doubt who would handle his contracts. It was during their first year in business that Tanya was introduced to his brother, Brandon Ware. Already aware of his escapades with the ladies, she had no qualms about turning him down after he turned his charm on her. She had no time for an immature, womanizing player, no matter how sexy he was.

But he pursued her with a vengeance, and in the end, she gave in. His charm, success, great looks, and his affirmation that he no longer wanted to play the field, sucked her in. And for a while, it was everything she dreamed love would be.

While Damian picked up the pieces from his failed relationship with her sister, her relationship with his brother was blossoming. Walks in the park, late night dinners, and nights on the town were a staple for them. Romantic getaways to the Carribean, the west coast, and cozy east coast hideaways, provided the perfect backdrop as they opened up their inner selves to each other. She found herself falling deeply and completely in love. He had stolen her heart, and he told her she had done the same.

But it was all a lie. In the end, his true colors emerged and he committed the ultimate betrayal. He confessed to her at her office, which prevented her the chance to vent her anger at him. It was only by the grace of God that she didn't throw every heavy object in her office at him. But she managed to remain calm, simply telling him to walk out that door and never, ever put himself in her space again, for fear that she would probably go to jail for her actions. It amazed her that she worked so hard to warn Damian about Danielle, but never took her own advice, and for that, she got burned.

Living the next few months in a fog, she finally pulled herself together, trying to convince herself that she didn't need or want him. And while Brandon made several attempts to contact her or apologize for his actions. The last words he spoke to her was that he spent the night with another woman. And now she was expected to spend an evening dining with him?

She thought she could do it, but seeing him in this social setting brought back all the hurt, pain, and feelings of betrayal, and, most annoyingly, the feeling of complete attraction.

Shaking those thoughts out of her head, she reached for the front door, reaffirming that the part of her life that involved Brandon Ware was over.

"Please, Tanya, can we talk?"

The touch of his hand on her arm sent a massive wave of awareness through her, warming her from head to toe. It had been so long since she last felt his touch. Closing her eyes, she reached deep for the strength to walk out the door and never look back.

"I can't do this," she whispered, and opened the door.

Stepping onto the stone porch, the cold bolt of winter air against her face was a welcome feeling. Breathing deeply, she cursed herself at being so affected by him. How much longer before he moved completely out of her system? Lord knows she had tried, dating several nice, eligible men. The problem was, no one compared to him. And she hated herself for feeling that way. Realizing tears welled in the corners of her eyes, she pulled her keys out of her purse and headed for her car.

"Tanya, wait," he yelled, jogging to catch up with her.

"Go to hell, Brandon," she said, not turning around and picking up speed.

Catching up with her before she could unlock the door, he stepped in front of her. "Please, Tanya, don't go."

Taking a deep breath, she wiped the last of her tears and stared him directly in the eye.

"Get out of my way before you get hurt."

"Just give me five minutes, that's all I ask."

"No." The desperation in his voice left her unaffected. The heart racing inside of her had grown hard and there was nothing he could do to change that. Pushing him out of the way with a brute force she didn't know she possessed, she opened the door and slid inside.

"I never slept with anyone while I was with you."

His words stung her like a queen bee. Stepping out of the car and slamming the door, the raw anger brewing on the inside of her was barely containable. The slap was hard, fast and lethal.

"How dare you stand in my face and tell me that bold face lie!"

Ignoring the sting on his cheek, he felt it was time to cleanse his soul. Taking a step forward, he repeated in a low whisper, "I never slept with anyone while I was with you."

This time, he caught her wrist before she connected another blow.

"Five minutes, Tanya. That's all I ask."

Jerking her hand away, she replied, "You have no right to ask for anything. Good-bye." Opening the car door again, she said, "If you get in my way, I will run you over."

Stepping around the door, he dropped to his knees, feeling no shame. He made a mess of their lives and this meeting tonight gave him the opportunity to make things right. Whatever it took, he would get her to listen to him. "I'm begging you, Tee, just five minutes."

Her head was spinning at break neck speed. Did he really have the audacity to stand before her and continue this charade? What did he hope to gain by all of this? What did he want from her?

Seeing the confusion play across her face, he reached up and touched her hand. "Five minutes, and then I'll walk away."

She wasn't sure if it was watching him get down on his knees, or hearing him call her by her pet name, but she gave in and allowed herself to give him the benefit of the doubt. "Four minutes and counting."

Rising, Brandon refused to waste one moment of his precious time. "I was scared. You were everything a man could ever want in a woman. You gave yourself completely to me and you loved me unconditionally. I had never experienced that before. All my life, women were a commodity, to be traded when a better one came along."

"Three minutes."

"But then you came along and shattered everything I thought I believed. And when you wouldn't give me the time of day, even though I was your best friend's brother, I knew you were something special. And when we finally got together, our passion, intensity and attraction blew me away. But when you confessed your love, I panicked. I didn't know what to do. I knew deep inside that I would probably end up hurting you, and that thought haunted me day and night. My track record was nothing to be proud of, and my thoughts became consumed with the idea that I would somehow, someway, destroy everything we built. So, in order to spare you the pain that would surely come, I figured it would be best to get out before I really screwed up. So I lied. I made it up because I believed I would eventually hurt you. But you have to believe me, I never cheated on you. Ever."

Seemingly unfazed by his confession, Tanya sat in her car, "Time's up."

"I love you, Tanya. Please forgive me. My life has been so empty without you."

Slamming the door, she drove off without looking back.

Brandon stood for several moments as the car disappeared down the dark road. Now he knew what it felt like to have a broken heart. Reluctantly, he walked back to the house, his body shivering from the cold air and the cold look he received from her before she drove off. He was met in the hallway by Damian, raw pain still etched across his face and Damian's heart went out to him.

"I screwed up, big brother."

Hugging him tightly, Damian said, "Give her time."

Later that evening, after the newlyweds said good night to their remaining guests, they put away the last of the dishes.

"I had no idea about Tanya and Brandon."

"It was an ugly breakup and I have always avoided getting involved. But tonight they both said they could set aside their personal issues and enjoy the evening."

Placing the last of the glasses into the cabinet, Christine said, "I hope they work things out. I really like them both."

Leaning against the sink, Damian pulled her into his arms, "Enough about them, I have something for you." Reaching into his back pocket, he placed in her hand a small, cool object.

Glancing down, an expression of bewilderment on her face, Christine asked, "A key?"

"Of course, a key." Realizing she was still confused, Damian's face became serious. "It's the key to this house. You'll need one as my wife."

Christine stared at the silver object and felt a moment of panic. What had she gotten herself into?

Damian watched intently as she twirled the innate piece of metal around in her hand. He knew that just because they had said "I do," didn't mean that she had put to rest all the demons that haunted her. Deciding not to press the issue, he smiled and said, "How about that tour?"

After showing her the basement and the first floor, they walked down the second floor hallway, "Damian, this is a lovely home."

Stopping in front of the double doors, he said, "That's a fine compliment coming from the top designer in the country."

Smiling, Christine responded, "Compliments will get you everything."

Opening the doors, he said, "That's my plan."

They entered the master suite and Christine's breath

caught. The room was aglow with the flickering of candles strategically placed throughout. Champagne chilled on ice and rose petals were sprinkled on the bed. The smooth sounds of jazz permeated the air and on a chair in the sitting area sat a large box wrapped in silver with a big bow.

Eyeing the present suspiciously, Christine experienced a moment of agitation. She hated gifts. For birthdays and holidays, Ruth would always be sure to have something special for Christine, but the first chance he got, Henry would ask her to do something for him and remind her that they just gave her a present.

That's why she made an issue of buying her clothes in Las Vegas. If she began to accept material offerings from Damian, what would it end up costing her?

*You're being silly Christine. This man is not Henry. His love is true . . . and free. Just accept it.*

"Go ahead, sweetheart, open it," he said, noticing her hesitation. After the blow up about the clothes, he knew exactly what was going through her mind. But if she was to ever love him completely, she had to trust him. He wanted her to understand that what he was offering did not come with a price. His love, commitment, and adoration was hers . . . free and clear.

Walking over to the chair, she picked up the box and pulled on the bow. As she continued to unwrap it, she got into the spirit of the moment, and found herself tearing away the wrapping paper. Lifting the lid to the white cardboard box, Christine moved away the tissue paper and felt the emotion swell in her. It was a collage representing their time in Las Vegas. Running her fingers slowly over the glass frame, she vividly remembered the moments represented in the postcards and pictures before her. The private jet, the strip, the hotel, and the suite. There was even a one thousand dollar chip.

In the center of it all was their wedding picture. Dressed in a white suit with a floor-length skirt, she stared carefully at the couple. As she stood in his arms, smiling into the camera, she looked relaxed. Taking a closer look, she identified something in her that had escaped her all her life.

With her education, her career, and her thriving business, she thought she was doing OK. She didn't understand until this very moment that she was just going through the motions. Doing what was right, trying to live out her dreams, because she believed her mother had failed to do so. But at this very moment, she stared at the couple in the picture and saw happiness. For the first time in her life, Christine Davenport Ware was truly happy.

Standing beside her, Damian whispered in her ear, "Do you like it?"

She turned to him and the look on her face was the only answer he needed.

"It's beautiful. It seems as if I had to go two thousand miles to find myself. But it was worth the trip. I love it, Damian, and I love you." Leaning up, she kissed him passionately on the mouth.

"We belong together, Christine. Nothing will ever change the love I have for you."

Pushing all thoughts of doubt from her mind, Christine responded with passion and they spent the night moving to a beat only the two of them could hear.

Early the next morning, Damian awoke to the annoying ringing of the phone. Glancing at the clock on the nightstand, he sighed and wondered who would be calling him at five o'clock in the morning. Not wanting to wake Christine, he grabbed the receiver.

"Hello," he answered quietly.

"Welcome back!"

Sitting up with force, Damian felt his blood pressure rise at the voice on the other end of the line.

"What the hell is your problem? Don't you ever go away?" he said in a hushed whisper. "I thought I made it clear the last time we saw each other that I want you out of my life."

Danielle switched her phone to the other ear. She took a moment to gather her thoughts. While she wanted to tell him that was no way to talk to her, she knew she needed him on her side. Taking a deep breath, she spoke in a soft, sweet voice, hoping to invoke sympathy. "Please, Damian, I know I made some mistakes in the past, but I really need to talk to you. I promise you, if you just give me thirty minutes, I won't bother you again . . . unless you want me to."

Rolling his eyes heavenward, he wondered how long before Danielle would stop this charade and leave him alone.

"Please, Damian, believe me, all I want to do is talk to you and make things right before I move on." Danielle paced the floor as she listened to the silence on the other end of the phone. If he turned her down this time, she wasn't sure what she was going to do. Time was running out. She stood to lose everything.

"If this is what it's going to take to get you to leave me alone, then fine. Thirty minutes."

Breathing a sigh of relief, Danielle spoke before he could change his mind. "I'm staying at the Hilton, room 1205."

"Forget it, I'm not going anywhere near your hotel room. Meet me at The Coffee House, twelve-thirty."

"Thank you, Damian," she said.

"Thirty minutes, Danielle, and then I want you out of my life."

Danielle hung up and jumped around her room in delight. This was the chance she was waiting for. There was a time when Damian could deny her nothing, and she believed that with a little encouragement from her, it could be that way again.

She knew she had hurt him deeply, but she had messed up before and always managed to get him back. Granted, that was five years ago, but she stilled looked great and she hadn't forgotten the buttons to push to get him to do exactly what she wanted. Picking up the phone again, she ordered breakfast. For the past week, she could hardly eat, but suddenly, she had a taste for waffles, eggs and orange juice.

Damian hung up the phone and laid back down. What was Danielle Olivia up to now? Tanya updated him on the lunch the two had shared while he was out of town. They knew Danielle too well to believe that this was about atoning for her sins. Every move she made was calculated and for her benefit. He would give her thirty minutes and that was it. Looking over at Christine he smiled. There was nothing his ex-fiancé could say or do to ever cause him to leave the woman laying next to him.

"Please tell me that wasn't the wicked witch of the west!"

Laughing, Damian answered, "I didn't know you were into name calling. I never would have guessed."

Sitting up, Christine answered, "She brings out the worst in me."

Sliding over to her, he wrapped his arms around her waist, and began nuzzling at her neck and ears. "I don't want to talk about her."

"But you are meeting her today?"

"She promised me that if I gave her thirty minutes of my time, she would leave me alone once and for all."

"And you believe her?"

"No, but I can always hope for a miracle," he answered sarcastically.

"I'm being serious, Damian," she said pulling out of his embrace. "How can I compete with a runway model and actress who travels the world and has millions of adoring fans, mostly men?"

"That's a moot question because there is no competition. That song ended years ago and I have no intentions of ever going back. You are the woman in my life. For now and always. Nothing Danielle could do or say will ever change that."

Christine believed him, but her curiosity got the best of

her. "What happened between you two? According to the reports I read, you two were 'couple of the year' candidates."

Hesitating a moment, Damian decided to tell the secret that destroyed his relationship with Danielle. Up until the day their relationship fell completely apart, he was sitting on top of the world. His business was thriving and he was in love. The only thing that could make his life complete was the family he and Danielle planned to start right away.

He should have paid more attention to what Tanya was telling him and what Danielle was doing, but he chose to ignore the warning signs. Tanya cautioned him on several occasions that her sister was self-serving and career-oriented and no matter how much she claimed to love him, those two things would always come first and second and he would remain a distant third. She even went so far as to run down a list of the men who had fallen before him.

There was Todd Anderson, the pilot, who gave up his job at the airlines to spend more time with her. There was Edward Carlys, the corporate attorney, who almost lost his practice because he catered to her every need. Finally, there was Richard Highland, the all-pro offensive lineman for the Dallas Cowboys. Now that was painful. Never before had Tanya witnessed a two-hundred and fifty-pound man cry like a baby. But he did, the day he found out she left him to live in Spain for six months, with no intention of returning to him.

When the dust settled from a Danielle tornado, the results were always the same. The men in her life ended up broken and alone. All of these men spent the better part of their relationships working to keep Danielle happy and she ended up dumping them for a new assignment, a new commercial or a new man.

But he ignored the stories. He told Tanya that this time it was different. That Danielle was different. She was kind, considerate, and had made many compromises in their relationship. She had agreed to move to the east coast permanently and start a family as soon as they were married. There was no way she was going to hurt him. He believed in her love for him and he knew that they were on their way to building a solid future together. How wrong he had been. But to Tanya's credit, she never once said *I told you so*.

It was soon after he bought the house that Danielle flew in from New York after taping a pilot for a sitcom. She was extremely excited about this show because she could tape on location in New York and commute between the city and her new permanent home outside of Washington, DC.

Planning a special celebration for the two of them upon her return, he made reservations at her favorite restaurant, followed by dancing at their favorite club. He met her at the door, but she begged off a night on the town, claiming exhaustion from a long day and a two hour delay on her flight back home. All she wanted was a good night's sleep. Seeing the weariness in her body, he readily agreed.

A few hours later, Damian was working in his study when the phone rang.

"Hello?"

"Hello, may I please speak with Danielle Olivia?"

"I'm sorry, she's unavailable at this time, is there a message?"

The woman on the other end hesitated a moment before continuing, "It is quite imperative that I speak with her."

"She's resting right now. She's had a very long, hard day, and I do not wish to disturb her."

The woman exhaled with relief, "She asked us not to call, because she planned on contacting us when she arrived back home, but the doctor became concerned when he hadn't heard from her. But if you say she's resting, I guess everything is OK."

*Doctor? Why would Danielle need to call a doctor? She never mentioned anything about being sick.*

"I'm sorry miss, but I didn't catch your name."

"This is Nurse Charron. And you are right, I'm sure it

was a very difficult day. The doctor was concerned about her traveling so soon after the procedure. Could you please ask her to contact Dr. Taylor tomorrow to schedule a follow up visit?"

Procedure? What procedure did Danielle need and why didn't she tell him about it? The feeling in the pit of his stomach signaled something wasn't right. What was she hiding from him?

"Is there a number for Dr. Taylor?"

After getting the number, he thanked the nurse for checking on Danielle, and promised that she would call the doctor in the morning.

"Are you her fiancé?"

"Yes, I am," he said, feeling a small measure of relief that she knew of him.

"Danielle said your work kept you from being with her today, I know it must have hard for you, unable to hold her hand during the abortion."

The room began to spin and Damian fell back in his chair for support. Closing his eyes tightly, he prayed that what he just heard was a cruel joke. His mind began to work double time to concentrate on the words this woman was speaking to him.

"But everything went fine. She should be up and about tomorrow." Still getting no response, she continued, "I've held your time long enough. Good-bye."

Damian held the phone so tight, his knuckles began to change colors. Slamming the handset into the receiver, the rage in him was boiling to a point of explosion as he tried desperately to make sense out of what he just found out. There was only one person who could give him the answers to his unanswered questions.

Taking the stairs two at a time, he worked on getting his emotions under control. There had to be a plausible explanation for that phone call. He didn't know what it was, but there was no way Danielle could have aborted their child without telling him. Was there?

Entering the darkened room quietly, he eased over to the bed and stared down at the sleeping figure. Could someone have had the day that she had and still sleep with a look of contentment and peace. Reaching for a chair, he scooted beside the bed and decided to take a moment to gather his thoughts.

That moment turned into hours, and as the sun began to rise, he was no closer to making sense out of what he learned than he was when he climbed the steps to confront the woman he thought was completely devoted to him.

Danielle stirred and slowly opened her eyes. She was obviously taken aback when she saw Damian seated right beside her, staring intently. Propping herself up on pillows, she gave a tentative smile and said, "What's going on? Why are sitting up here, just watching me?"

Leaning forward, Damian folded his hand across his lap to speak, but he had yet to find the words to articulate what was going through his head. He searched her face carefully, looking for a sign that would give him clarity. Some women needed time in the morning to make themselves presentable. Not Danielle. With a clean face and flat hair, she was beautiful.

"Damian," she asked, concerned by his total silence, "you're scaring me. What's going on?"

"You got a call last night. I didn't want to wake you."

Danielle immediately thought of her family. Things had been extremely strained between her sister and parents over the past few years. They refused to understand what it took to be a success in a business that depends so heavily on image and perception. There were certain sacrifices that had to be made and decisions that had to be carried out if she was going to be competitive in this industry. Sacrifices and decisions that neither her parents nor her sister approved of. But through all of their differences, she still wished them no harm, and the way Damian was acting, she thought he had bad news about one of them.

Reaching out, she covered her hand over his, and was visually surprised when he jerked his hand out of her touch, stood and walked over the window.

"Why, Danielle, why?"

Getting out of bed, she started toward him. "What are you talking about, Damian? Who called last night?"

Turning to face her, he looked for any indication in her expression that less than twenty-four hours ago, she laid on a table and took the life of his child without telling him.

"It was Nurse Charron. She called to check on you after you failed to call when you arrived last night."

The color drained out of her face as she realized the implication of that phone call. "Damian, I can explain . . ."

The small thread that was holding his fury in check snapped, and he threw his hands up and yelled, "Explain . . . you can explain. . . . Well, please Danielle, go right ahead. Explain to me how you could abort our child without talking to me?" After the words were out of his mouth, the next thought caused him to physically falter. "It was my child, wasn't it?"

"How could you ask me that," she said softly.

Not moved by her tone, he answered, "So you admit it. You have no other explanation about that phone call last night?"

"You have to understand, Damian. I was up for this series, I just signed a one year contract with Cover Girl."

"Cover Girl? I thought you told me you weren't renewing that contract to give us more time together," he asked incredulously.

"You don't understand, Damian. I was prepared to turn them down, but they came back with an offer twenty percent higher than their original. And once I agreed to the deal, I found out I was pregnant. At this point in my career, my image couldn't take me having a baby."

"You made this decision because of your image. We were getting married in a few months. We agreed to start a family right away," he cried in total bewilderment. "How could you do this?"

Placing her hand on his chest, she gently stroked him. "We'll still get married in a few months. We'll just put off the family part for a while."

"You lied to me, Danielle."

Removing her hands she stepped back, "Damian, don't be so melodramatic. You've made tough business decisions before. I know you can understand why I had to do it."

Reeling from her callous response, he stated, "I can't trust you."

"Let's just move past this. We'll get married in a few months, I'll do the series and a few more modeling jobs, maybe one or two feature films, and then we can have a family. As many little kiddies as you want."

Damian heard Tanya's voice running through his head. All the warnings, all the examples she gave of Danielle's self-ishness, and the offers to be there for him when it fell apart. Because Tanya knew it would.

"I'm going to the office for the day. I don't expect you to be here when I get home."

"What are you saying, Damian? You're kicking me out because I made a decision about my body? Because I want a successful career?"

"No, Danielle, I'm throwing you out because you lied to me. You've broken our bond of trust. You told me you wanted to cut back on your work schedule. I didn't ask you to. You should have talked to me. Told me that you wanted to renew the Cover Girl contract. We could have worked it out to-gether."

Christine watched Damian's expression as he retold the story that tore him apart. She gently used her thumb to wipe away the lone tear that fell down his cheek.

Folding her hand in his, he continued, "When I returned

home, she was gone. Tanya and my brother were there to pick up the pieces with me. It was a terrible time for me. Her lies and deceit never even seemed to phase her. Her sitcom didn't get picked up and she headed to Paris. I hadn't heard from her until that night she showed up at my house."

Christine listened with understanding reflected in her eyes. She could only imagine the pain he must have experienced at finding out that someone he loved, someone he put his faith in, betrayed him.

"What do you think she wants?" Christine asked.

"With Danielle, one never knows, but it probably has to do with her career or money," he answered, pulling her to him, "but enough about that woman. I'd rather take care of the wants of the woman right here with me."

And he spent the next hour doing just that.

# TWELVE

Waiting for the elevator, Danielle checked herself in the mirror on the wall. Running a mental checklist, she wanted to make sure she didn't forget anything that would give her even the slightest advantage over Damian. The light floral scent of Damian's favorite perfume wafted through the air, and she could stop traffic in the stunning candy-apple red Vera Wang suit with black trim. The skirt stopped about eight inches above her knees, giving him a fabulous view of her legs, one of her features he had always admired the most.

Patting her French roll, she confirmed that not one hair was out of place. He told her he loved the sophisticated look the updo gave her, and that pulling the pins out and watching her hair cascade down her shoulders excited him beyond words. Finishing her look with the diamond and ruby earrings he had given her for her birthday, Danielle was ready for battle. By the end of the day, Damian would be back in her life and her life would be back on track.

Danielle sat impatiently at a small table in the back of the restaurant. It was a quarter to one and she hated to wait. When he arrived, she would love to let him know exactly how she felt about his tardiness, but she needed his help, and the last thing she wanted to do was alienate him any further. She would swallow her pride to get the one thing she needed and wanted . . . Damian Ware.

Entering the small coffee house, Damian spotted her right away. Rising, she walked to meet him and gave him a hug, which he did not return. Feeling the stiffness in his body, she retreated.

Damian had to admit, she could take a brother's breath away with her smooth skin, long legs and perfect smile. But that was the extent of her assets. While she had the body of a goddess, it was a complete facade. It was only a covering for a cold, empty, hollow woman who didn't have a sensitive, caring bone in her body. And to think, he had been ready to commit his entire being to her, mind, soul and body. Now, looking at her, he felt nothing for her. He questioned whether he would be angry, upset, sympathetic, or even forgiving. But standing in front of her, he felt absolutely nothing. He would make sure that by the time this meeting ended, Danielle Olivia would no longer be a part of his life.

"Thank you for meeting me," she said, with her head slightly turned downward. "I know that you didn't want to see me, but I appreciate you taking the time." Sitting down, she dramatically crossed her legs, giving him the perfect view of long, bronze legs. "Please," she continued, pointing to the chair opposite her, "have a seat."

Damian smiled at the ploy and sat down. She was pulling out all the stops.

Touching her ears, she slowly ran her fingers over the teardrop earrings. "Do you remember the night you gave these to me? We were spending the weekend at my house in Malibu. It was my birthday and we had just enjoyed an intimate dinner on a private beach. We laughed, we danced, we shared a bubble bath, and as we climbed into bed, you handed me a small box and told me that this gift was from the bottom of your heart."

Not in the mood to head down memory lane, Damian stood up. "Either get to the point, or I'm leaving."

Panic crossed her face for a moment, but she quickly recovered. It was time to try another tactic. "OK, I'm sorry. Please don't leave. It's just that seeing you again and wearing these earrings caused me to remember the good times we had. You do admit, that even though it ended on a sour note, we did have good times."

Returning to his seat, Damian relented that much. "Yes, Danielle, we did have some good times together. But all that is in the past. Those good times could never out shadow your actions that led to the demise of our relationship."

"I know. So I propose that we start fresh. We were good together once, we could be great together again."

Damian stared at her with a look of bewilderment. "What are you on? You must be crazy. You stroll back into my life after all this time and expect us to get back together?"

"I know it was hard for you after I left. Tanya told me that you cried on her shoulder at the thought of losing me. All I'm saying is that you should give us a chance to recapture what we had."

Interrupted by a waiter, Danielle ordered an espresso while Damian ordered nothing. He didn't get the feeling that he would be there that long.

Leaning forward and revealing enough cleavage to gain attention, she whispered, "I was good for you and you were good for me. I know I messed up, but I want to make it up to you. We loved each other, and deep inside, I know that some of that love still remains. Give our love another chance. This time, I'm ready to be all you want. Just tell me what you want me to do and I'll do it."

"What about your career. Are you ready to give all that up?"

Danielle secretly smiled. It was working. She could see in his eyes that the idea of being with her again was beginning to appeal to him. If he was asking about the very thing that stood in their way last time, he was obviously open to the idea of a reconciliation. Handling the situation with care, she answered, "I was a fool to put my career before you. I see the error of my ways now, and I'm ready to commit fully to you and the family I want with you."

Moving toward her, Damian cut his eyes downward, gazing at the product she was pushing. "Are you saying that you are ready to give up your career to become my wife and the mother of my children?"

Danielle adjusted herself, and a little more of her poured into his view. "You are still the love of my life and I am willing and ready to give up my life in the entertainment world."

Damian smiled and took her hand. Gently stroking her palm, he gazed into her eyes.

Danielle tried to contain her excitement, as she watched his fingers move back and forth. When they were dating, this was their secret signal for wanting to make love.

They remained silent as the waiter delivered her drink.

She decided to go in for the kill. "I'm ready to sell my house in Malibu and my condo in New York. I'll have my belongings sent here and we can begin again right away."

Still holding her hand, Damian spoke in a low, but lethal voice, void of any emotion. "Do you take me for a fool? That was the biggest piece of bull I've heard in a long time. I don't think this reconciliation idea is based on you having a revelation to do what's right. I think it has to do with the fact that your business manager siphoned off millions of dollars from you, including making bad investments. I think it has to do with the fact that the pretty Porsche you drive is one week away from being repossessed.

"No, I have it. Maybe it has something to do with the fact that you already sold your house in Malibu to pay off some of your debt, and your New York apartment has been on the market for months." Removing his hand, he sat back in his chair and continued. "Now, you have exactly five minutes to end this charade and come clean, and then I will get up, walk out that door and expect never to see you again."

Shocked beyond words, Danielle's mind began to work overtime.

"I know that look. You want to know how I knew? After your lunch with Tanya, we figured you were up to no good, so I made a few phone calls this morning. Thinking I was going to help bail you out prompted a whole lot of people to talk to me about your situation."

Defeated, Danielle felt her fame and fortune slip away from her. She decided to appeal to the part of Damian that had attracted her to him in the first place, his true chivalry. He was totally dedicated to his friends and family. Pulling a tissue out of her purse, she dramatically dabbed the corners of her eyes. "You're right, Damian. It's all gone. The money, the investments. If I don't do something now, I stand to lose everything. Please try to understand."

"I understand you wanted to use me," he answered with disgust. "You haven't changed one bit."

"Please, Damian. I know you probably hate me, but I'm asking for your help for old time's sake. I really need the money."

Rising, he snickered in her face, "You must be out of your mind."

"You don't understand, I don't have a place to live, my car is about to be repossessed and I haven't gotten a call from my agent in months. My last modeling contract expired over six months ago. You wouldn't turn your back on a friend in need."

"There's just one flaw in your analysis of me, Danielle. You're not a friend." Standing, he put on his coat and said, "Good-bye Danielle. I have to get home to my wife."

*A wife! When did that happen?* Watching him walk out the door, Danielle cursed out loud, causing several heads at nearby tables to take notice.

"What the hell are you looking at?" she asked to no one in particular. Gathering up her purse, she dropped a few bills on the table and stormed out. What was she going to do now?

Later that week, Tanya and Damian sat at the conference table in his office reviewing the report from inspectors on the other three buildings the electrical contractor worked on. All three had substandard wiring and would have to be replaced. Pinching the bridge of his nose, he knew it would take months and an army of lawyers before the contractor would begin to replace the wires, all the while placing those buildings in danger of catching fire.

"Damian, did you know that Justin was the foreman on all these jobs?"

"I never thought about it."

"It just seems weird that those wires got installed without any knowledge from our people. I know the subcontractor uses his own laborers, but don't we require our foremen to ultimately be responsible for the work?"

Damian digested what she said. "I can't believe Justin would have anything to do with this, but we have to check it out. I'll call the police tomorrow. But as for now, we'll replace the wires."

Tanya looked up from the spreadsheets in surprise, "Damian, that could run us a half million dollars," she said.

"I don't care, it's my name and reputation on the line. Find me a contractor—a real one—this week and get them started on this project in the next thirty days."

Gathering up the data and heading for the door, Tanya replied, "I'll get right on it."

"Tanya, before you go, I want to talk to you about the other night."

Sighing, she said, "Don't worry about it. You can't be held responsible for your brother's action."

"He told me that he lied to you about sleeping with another woman. Do you believe him?"

"It doesn't matter whether I believe him or not. It's over between us."

"You know I've never put myself in your business, but I stopped by his house yesterday and he looked awful. He says he really misses you."

"Look, Damian, we've been friends a long time, and one

of the main reasons it's been that way is because we've respected each other's privacy. I'm asking you to butt out."

Valuing their friendship, Damian resigned himself to the fact that whatever happened or didn't happen between Tanya and his brother, was none of his business. "Fine, have a good weekend."

After Tanya left, Damian rang his wife and Christine answered the phone on the second ring.

"Hey baby, I was calling to see what time you would be home tonight. I thought we could go shopping for our wedding rings and then have dinner."

Filing some papers into folders, Christine cradled the phone between her neck and her shoulder. It was almost five o'clock, and if she was going to make the six o'clock meeting with Mr. Murphy and the Donovans, she needed to leave now. "Damian, I'm sorry, but I have other plans."

Feeling a little rebuffed that he was unaware of her schedule, he asked, "A late meeting with a client?"

"Actually, I'm meeting the Donovans tonight. Hopefully we can settle this issue once and for all."

Silence filled the phone lines. Did he hear her correctly? She planned to meet the cause of her emotional turmoil? Why didn't she say something sooner?

A little pang of guilt crept into Christine's heart. Stephanie had warned her to not only tell him about the meeting, but to invite him to it. He was her husband, and Stephanie was positive that he would want to be there and offer his support. But in Christine's mind, this was her family's business, and she could handle it on her own.

"Damian, I know I should have told you. But it never seemed like the right time. Besides, this is my business. I can handle it."

"I didn't say you couldn't handle it," he said, working to remain calm. "I just thought, that as your husband, you would include me. I want to be there for you and support you."

This is exactly what Christine had hoped to avoid. "I appreciate your concern Damian, but I won't be late and I'll tell you all about it when I get to your house tonight." Getting no response, she added, "I promise."

Hanging up the phone, Damian paced his office in frustration. How long was Christine going to continue to hold onto her independence? It had been a week since their return from Las Vegas, and Christine had yet to use the key he gave her. Always ringing the doorbell, she claimed she left it in the car or at the office. Why didn't she just put it on her keychain?

The other issue was her house. When he broached the subject of selling her house, she reacted with a vengeance asking why did she have to give up her house and why couldn't he sell his? He shut her up immediately when he agreed to sell his house, leaving a message for a real estate agent that very moment. But after further discussion, she agreed that it made more sense to sell her house and move in with him. But that had led to another fight. She had not brought over one thing from her house. She was stopping by her house on the way home from work to pick up clothes for the next day. He offered to make room for her furniture and personal items, and she waved him off, saying that there was no rush and they had a lifetime together to move her things.

But now Damian began to wonder if she ever planned to merge their lives. Just now, she referred to their house as "his house." Never once had she indicated that it was their home. It was like dealing with Danielle all over again.

Retrieving his briefcase from behind his desk, he turned out the lights and headed home. It had been a long week, and he intended to spend the weekend relaxing, but he knew that what he had in mind would be anything but. This weekend, he was going have it out with Christine Ware.

\* \* \*

Paul and Natalie arrived at the restaurant a little before six. Spotting Margaret at the bar, they joined her while they waited for their table.

"This meeting will probably not result in a settlement, but it will open the door for discussion and we will get an idea of where they stand and what they consider a fair offer," Paul said, ordering a regular ice tea with lemon. He never drank during business.

"The only fair offer is half," Margaret said, slamming her glass on the oak bar.

Paul and Natalie looked wearily at one another. Obviously, Margaret had no issue drinking before a business meeting.

"Mother, I need you to be calm tonight. You don't have to like them, but we do need to be professional. This is a business meeting and the better we all get along, the better chance we have of reaching an amicable agreement."

Waving to the bartender to freshen up her drink, Margaret smirked. "I don't care about getting along or being amicable. I just care about the money. Henry used me and never looked back, and now it's time for payback."

Just then the hostess interrupted. Their table was ready.

About ten minutes later, Christine walked confidently behind Mr. Murphy as they entered the restaurant. The hostess informed them that the rest of their party had already arrived. Moving through the tables at the Italian restaurant, Christine felt her heart rate increase as they made their approach. In less than one minute, she would come face-to-face with the woman and child who were a part of her father's history.

Natalie, Margaret, and Paul Donovan stood as they approached. As Christine and Mr. Murphy stopped at the table, an uncomfortable silence enveloped their space.

"Allow me to make formal introductions."

Everyone showed immediate relief at Mr. Murphy's offer. It was an awkward situation, and no one knew exactly what to do.

"I'm Douglas Murphy, attorney for Christine Davenport."

Hearing him say her former name, Christine's heart constricted as another pang of guilt settled in her. She had not told anyone she had married. Making Stephanie promise to remain silent about her recent nuptials at work, no one outside of that dinner party knew of her change in status. Not even her attorney.

After handshakes and polite hellos, they all sat down. Their waitress arrived a few moments later to take their drink orders.

Christine looked at the three people who had now become an integral part of her life. Margaret Donovan, dressed casually in jeans and a sweater, sat across from her with little makeup and slightly unkept hair that was pulled back in a loose ponytail. The lines around her eyes didn't look to be from laughter and the permanent frown on her face added at least ten years to her age.

Moving her focus from mother to daughter, Christine studied her half sister for the first time. Dressed in a stylish taupe pantsuit with a matching scarf around her neck, she looked for any resemblance to her father. Her hair, jet black, hung in a bob cut, framing her bronze face. Her high cheekbones, highlighted with a berry blush, were shaped like those of a model. But when she focused on her eyes, that's when she saw it. Henry. She had his eyes. The high arched brow, the long lashes, and the deep brown center could only have been attributed to his genes.

The only difference was that Henry's eyes had always been filled with anger, hate and sadness. When she looked into the eyes of her half sister, she saw none of those things.

"As you know," Mr. Murphy began, "we are here to discuss the estate of Ruth Davenport. In her will, she left everything to her sole heir, her daughter, Christine."

"But she is not the sole heir," Margaret interrupted, her eyes narrowing in anger. "That no good father of hers had another heir. My daughter. She has a right to that money and we mean to get some of it."

Christine looked closely at the woman her father bedded and felt her anger rise. *How dare she use that tone with her?* She was the one sleeping with a married man. "Henry had nothing. It was my mother who worked and saved for the future. MY mother! You have no right to that legacy."

"Ladies, please," Paul said, pleading for civility. "This is not going to solve anything."

Margaret gave a snide chuckle and said, "The only thing that will solve this problem will be little miss prissy over here writing us a check for five-hundred thousand dollars."

Standing, Christine said, "Who do you think you're talking to. You little two-bit tramp. Do you still get your kicks from sleeping with married men?"

Reacting immediately, Margaret stood and lunged for Christine. Paul and Doug rose immediately, preventing a violent confrontation in the middle of the restaurant.

"Christine," Mr. Murphy said, shocked at her words and behavior, "what has come over you?"

Realizing the spectacle she was making of herself, Christine sat back down.

The restaurant manager arrived a few seconds later, concern for the welfare of his other customers clearly reflected in his expression, "Is everything all right here?"

"Yes," Paul assured him, "Everything is just fine." He assisted Margaret into taking her seat.

"Mr. Murphy, Ms. Davenport," Paul started.

"It's Ware," Christine said, realizing that her outburst at Margaret was not only her frustration about the money, but her guilt over keeping her marriage a secret.

"Excuse me?" Paul and Douglas said in unison.

"Ware," she said, suddenly feeling a warmth inside her at sharing her secret. She loved Damian with all her heart. How could she not want the world to know? "Ware is my name. I married Damian Ware over Thanksgiving and my last name is now Ware."

Douglas stared openly at Christine, his eyes wide with

utter surprise. Immediately he thought of the letter. Ruth had given him strict instructions to give it to her after she was married.

"Mrs. Ware," Paul started again, "I have taken the liberty of calculating child support that would have been due my client, had your father paid."

Christine leaned forward with interest, "My father never paid any child support?"

"You just said he had nothing, sweetie," Margaret said sarcastically, "what was he going to pay with?"

"Margaret, please," Paul said with pleading eyes, "let's just try to get through this."

"Fine," she said waving the waiter over, "but I want another drink."

Not wanting to agitate his sister any further, he let her request for another drink go unchallenged. Unfortunately, Paul had no idea how many she had before they arrived.

"As I was saying," Paul continued, "it is undisputed that Henry Davenport is the father of Natalie Donovan, and he has paid a total of three-hundred and twelve dollars toward raising his daughter."

Christine looked at Margaret, and slowly turned her head to face Natalie. It was at that moment that she remembered Damian's words in Las Vegas. She had never considered the situation from their point of view. It had to be difficult raising a daughter alone. Henry was no "Father of the Year," but Christine always had food and a place to live. Had that been the case with her half sister? She knew money could never replace her childhood, but was Christine right in not sharing the inheritance?

Completely distracted by these thoughts, she forced her attention back on Paul.

"So as you can see, if you include eighteen years of back child support and college expenses, the amount is quite high. Not to mention how much has been left from his estate.

We're prepared to settle for two hundred and fifty-thousand dollars."

"The hell we are!" Margaret screamed, glancing in astonishment from Paul to Natalie. "This was never discussed with me. That heifer had Henry, a house, a car, and money to save for a rainy day. We had NOTHING. If you think I'll take one red cent less than half, you are out of your mind!"

"Margaret, please," Paul started.

Christine stood, and before he could finish she pierced her gaze on Margaret. "How dare you talk about my mother like that. You know nothing about her. All you can see is dollar signs. Well you can forget it. There is no way you will ever get your greasy palms on that money."

Grabbing her purse, she turned to Douglas and said, "This meeting is over." She walked out of the restaurant.

A few hours later, Damian paced the floor and glanced at his watch. Ten forty-five and no sign of Christine. Her meeting was at six o'clock and he had yet to hear from her. Calling her cell phone, he got her voicemail but didn't leave a message. Where could she be?

Arriving home around five-thirty, he spent the first few hours allowing his frustration to grow at her blatant disregard for their relationship, but now that he was worried about her, he set aside some of that anger and replaced it with compassion. He knew it would be hard for her to accept marriage. She had reminded him constantly since they met that the relationship between her parents was mentally and physically abusive. Her father, domineering and filled with rage, was the only example of a husband she had. But she had to know that he was different. Why couldn't she understand that the words that he spoke to her were true? He loved her, cherished her, and wanted to spend the rest of his life showing her just how different he was from her father.

Moving to the foyer, Damian glanced out the window. Still no sign of her. Where could she be? Suddenly it hit him. Grabbing his coat and keys, he headed out.

* * *

Christine stepped out of the tub and wrapped herself in the soft towel. She hadn't relaxed in her tub since she had returned from Las Vegas, and it felt strange. Her house used to bring her comfort, but now she felt like a stranger.

Close to eleven o'clock, she was mentally drained and physically tired. After she left the meeting, she headed to her house in a fit of raw anger. The nerve of that woman speaking about her mother that way. *And to think, I was beginning to contemplate a settlement!* Wanting to just crawl into bed and call it a night, she reached for the phone to call Damian. Surely he would understand if she wanted to stay in her own house tonight. But before she could complete the call, the doorbell rang.

Damian saw the hallway light come on and swore under his breath. *Why was she here?* As she opened the door, he formed his mouth to ask her. But when he gazed into her eyes, he saw the mist and immediately embraced her.

"What is it, sweetheart? What happened with the Donovans?" he asked, gently stroking her neck. God, she felt good in his arms.

"Oh, Damian," she said, "I know you're concerned, but I really don't want to talk about it." Stepping back, she wiped her tears, and continued, "It's my problem, I'll deal with it."

Releasing his hold, Damian remained calm, even though her statement ignited a spark of anger. "Christine, you're my wife. I want to help. Let me help you."

Walking into the family room, he glanced around. Nothing had been packed or boxed up. The spark just caught. *Why won't she move her things?*

"It's OK, Damian, I can take care of it."

Exasperated, Damian replied, "I know you can take care of it. But you don't have to do this alone now. I'm here for

you. I'll always be here for you. You know that, don't you?"
He watched her body stiffen and her eyes gaze downward.

Reading her body language, he asked again, "You do know that I will always love you and be here for you."

Still getting no response, the burning on the inside of him grew to a flame, and trying to keep his growing anger in check, he pleaded, "Christine, please answer me."

Feeling the effects of her entire life fall upon her shoulders, she yelled, "What do you want from me? I have had to depend on myself all my life. Just me. My father beat my mother and belittled and demeaned me until I had no hope left. But I managed to survive, no thanks to anybody."

Stepping toward her, he flinched when she took a step back. He felt like he was at the end of his rope.

"When are you going to stop singing that song to me?" he asked.

"You have some nerve," she screamed. "You have no idea what my life has been like. You have no right to judge me."

"I'm not judging you, Christine, I'm trying to love you."

"I don't need your love," she said defiantly.

Her words stung his heart and pierced his soul. Buttoning his coat, he said, "I'm sorry to hear that Christine, because the only thing I need is your love."

At that moment, Damian knew there was nothing more to say. She had come to him with a wall around her heart, and over the past months, he believed he had broken through. When they took their vows as man and wife, he never doubted the love he saw reflected in her eyes. He knew she loved him, but she just didn't know how to let go of the past. And as much as he wanted to, he couldn't do it for her.

When they returned from Las Vegas as man and wife, he began to notice the wall being rebuilt. She was scared, and he understood. Her fear had nothing to do with her love for him, so he tried to show her compassion, trust and love, but she continually threw it back at him. How much more could he do? Feeling his anger turn to pain, he knew that until she was ready to accept her past and put it behind her once and for all, their relationship was doomed to fail.

Turning to leave, he knew that she would not stop him. Her pain was too deep and raw. Stopping one last time, he turned to her and said, "I'm not your father."

# THIRTEEN

Christine wrapped the delicate dishes carefully in the newspaper. Placing them into the box, she made sure that there was no chance of one of them breaking. It was packing day, and the kitchen was the first room to be boxed up.

"Put those mugs in the box in the corner. I'm donating them to charity," Stephanie said, placing another empty box onto the counter. "We both have completely furnished houses, so I'm taking as little as possible."

Christine nodded and continued her task. She had arrived early that morning with warm bagels and cream cheese. She promised Stephanie she would help her pack, and even though she really wanted to hide from the world that day, she could never let her friend down. She only hoped that she could get through the day without Stephanie realizing how much pain pierced her soul.

After Damian left, she had dragged herself to her bedroom and flung herself across the bed. In the silence of the night, she felt strange. It had been almost two weeks since she last stayed in her own bed, and she couldn't get comfortable. Emotions swirled around her head like a midwest tornado. Anger. Resentment. Fury. Rage. Love. Amazed that in all that confusion, she could feel his love, she held onto it as her saving grace. But when she awoke that morning, she pushed that feeling aside. She had married him because she loved him, but she just didn't know if she was capable of being his wife.

"Coffee break," Stephanie said, setting two cups onto the table.

Not stopping, Christine answered, "If we take a break now, we may never get back on track."

"Sit," Stephanie replied sternly.

Surprised at her tone, Christine turned to her friend. In that moment, she understood the meaning of a sister. They may not have been blood related, but Stephanie knew her like the back of her own hand. There was no hiding anything from Stephanie Jackson.

Over coffee, Christine told Stephanie everything that had happened yesterday. The meeting with the Donovans, going home instead of Damian's house, and finally, the blowup with her husband and his retreat. As she told her story, the tears flowed freely and the pain grew.

"Oh, Stephanie," she cried, "what am I going to do?"

After several moments of silence, Stephanie stood, shrugged her shoulders and said, "Get over it."

Christine jerked her head up and widened her eyes in confusion. "What did you say?"

Turning her back on her friend, she picked up a saucer and continued her packing. "I said, get over it."

Standing herself, Christine couldn't believe her ears. "What do you mean?"

Stephanie prayed for strength and now understood what parents meant by the phrase "tough love." Not turning around, she said, "So you had a tough life. Who hasn't? I lost my parents before I started high school. My grandmother smothered me until I thought I would suffocate to death. My first year in college, I drank so much, it's a wonder I don't have liver damage."

Appalled at the audacity of her words, Christine said, "You have no idea what I've been through."

*"Through,* Christine. That word says it all. Life is made up of good things and bad, but either way, you move through

them. But you seem to be stuck. When are you going to move forward?"

The room was silent, except for the sound of the paper being wrapped around a delicate glass. Christine walked over to the box she was packing, and continued. Neither spoke as they continued to put the items into the boxes.

Monday morning found Christine sitting at her desk, trying to concentrate on reading resumes. She had put off finding a replacement for Stephanie and now found herself in a crunch. With just a few weeks left, she knew that her business stood to suffer if she didn't hire someone soon.

But her mind wandered constantly, as she contemplated the Donovans, Damian, her parents and Stephanie's words. Having stayed at her house all weekend, she realized how much she missed her husband and his home. But he hadn't contacted her all weekend, and her heart ached from being apart from him. Was this separation for the best?

At the ringing of the phone, she shook off those thoughts and focused on business.

"Christine Ware." *That name sounds so right!*

"Christine, this is Natalie Donovan."

Surprise was an understatement. After the fiasco at dinner on Friday, she thought the only contact she would have with her half sister was in a courtroom.

"Are you there, Christine?"

Clearing her throat, she answered, "Yes, I'm here. What can I do for you?"

"I'm in the lobby of your building. I wanted to talk to you."

Weary of her motive, Christine asked, "Should we be talking without our attorneys present?"

"Probably not, but it won't take long."

Knowing this wasn't the most legally sound decision to

make, she threw caution to the wind. "Come on up. The receptionist will direct you to my office."

It was probably less than five minutes from the lobby to her office, but it seemed like an eternity as she waited for Natalie. Curious about her visit, Christine wasn't naive enough to think it wasn't about the money, but what exactly did she have to say about the money?

Walking over to the window, Christine stared down at the pond, almost frozen over from the winter weather. She thought of Stephanie's words, *How am I supposed to move through this?*

Turning from the window at the sound of her name, Christine thanked Debbie, her receptionist, and motioned for Natalie to take a seat. Dressed for the corporate world in a gray suit, Christine realized she didn't even know what she did for a living. And it was at that moment that she understood her selfish behavior. Only thinking of the pain she had been through, she never once stopped and considered that others in the situation were hurting too. Maybe instead of dealing with her own situation, she needed to reach out and help others with theirs.

Christine took a seat in the chair next to Natalie. Natalie raised an eyebrow, obviously taken aback by her not sitting behind her desk.

"I know this visit is unexpected, but I wanted to talk to you," Natalie started.

"You have Henry's eyes," Christine said, staring into them. "Did you know that?"

"Uh, no, I never noticed," Natalie answered, startled by the unexpected comment.

"How often did you see him?"

Not expecting this line of questioning from Christine, Natalie wondered what was going on. "I only saw him a few times. I wouldn't know if I had his eyes."

"I see."

Realizing her questions were over, Natalie continued.

"Christine, the reason I came here was to apologize for my mother's behavior. She has been angry and bitter for a long time, and while I can understand why she has those feelings, I cannot condone them. She had no right to speak that way about your mother."

"What do you do," Christine asked, "for a living?"

Again, taken aback by her questions, she hesitated, but answered, "I'm a manager at a CPA firm. Why?"

"How did you pay for college?" Christine asked, genuinely concerned about her half sister's life.

"Forgive me if I sound rude, but why are you asking me all these questions?"

Sighing, Christine covered her face in her hands.

Natalie wasn't sure what was going on, but she could tell that she was upset. She did what naturally came. She reached out and rubbed Christine's shoulder as a way of comfort.

Raising her head at Natalie's touch, Christine smiled at the feeling of comfort she received from that gesture. It was as if she were being consoled by family.

"Henry . . . our father . . . was a no good, dirty, bastard."

Removing her touch, Natalie sat straight, "Excuse me?"

"Have you ever wondered what your life would have been like if you had a father. Maybe you thought your mother would have made something more of herself and that she wouldn't be so bitter now. Perhaps you thought about learning to drive, or your first date or your prom. How proud he would have been when you graduated from college. Have you ever had those thoughts?"

Feeling a lump in her throat, Natalie shook her head "yes." In fact, those thoughts swirled in her head constantly since the entire episode with the will started.

"Did you think that our father was doing all those special things with me?"

Natalie sniffled and continued to nod.

"Well, let me tell you, you and your mother were better off without him."

Over the next hour, Christine told Natalie about their father and the trail of pain and suffering he had left behind. When she finished, the box of Kleenex she kept on her desk was empty.

"Thank you for sharing that with me. I understand now why you have been so adamant about that money being your mother's legacy and fighting us so hard on our claim."

Interrupted by a knock on her door, both women turned to see who it was. "Christine, I . . ." seeing two sets of red eyes staring at her, Stephanie, said, "I'm sorry, I can come back later."

Standing, Christine walked behind her desk and waved Stephanie in. They hadn't spoken since Christine left her house Saturday night after helping her pack.

Christine made introductions and saw the surprise on Stephanie's face when she realized Natalie was her half sister.

"I didn't mean to interrupt, I just wanted to know if you had any more résumés for me to review."

Suddenly, something Natalie had said earlier jumped to the front of Christine's mind. Believing that they both wanted to get to know each other better, she said, "Natalie, are you happy at your firm?"


Later that afternoon, Christine flipped through the pages of a catalogue for an upcoming auction. The owners of the bed-and-breakfast she was redecorating wanted Victorian furniture in two of the bedrooms and she wanted to select the pieces she planned to bid on in advance. But she found it hard to concentrate.

What a day! She had set aside her anger and preconceived notions about Natalie and found a common ground. In fact, they discussed her coming to work at her firm after Stephanie left. Wanting to call Damian, she picked up the phone several times, but she hung up before he could answer. What was she going to say?

Picking up the phone again, she dialed Mr. Murphy's number. Getting his voicemail, she left him a message to contact her immediately. It was time to move on and put this contestment behind her.

Her phone immediately buzzed after she had placed the receiver back into the cradle.

"Christine, a Mr. Murphy is here to see you."

This had been a day of unexpected visitors. "Send him in."

They sat at the conference table. "I was hoping you were still here. I know of Ware Construction Company through my business circles and called there yesterday. Damian told me that I could reach you at your home. I thought you two were married?"

Not wanting to rehash her dysfunctional relationship with her husband with her attorney, Christine decided to change the subject, "I just left you a message at your office."

Seeing through her bad attempt to change the subject, he let it go, for the moment. "What about?"

"I want to settle with the Donovans."

"I know, Christine, I'm reviewing their offer now."

"You don't understand. I want to give Natalie half the money."

Douglas stared at Christine for a long moment, and then slowly, the corners of his mouth turned upward. It was finally happening. She was finally letting go of the past and moving forward . . . for good.

"I'll draw the papers up."

"That's all you have to say? No lecture on how no court would ever award them that much?"

"You're the client, if you say settle, I settle. Now," he continued, "back to Damian."

"There is nothing to discuss. I moved too fast and it wasn't meant to be."

Reaching into his pocket, he pulled out an envelope. "I think you're lying to herself. I see the love you have for him in your eyes."

He placed an envelope onto the table. Christine saw it was addressed to her, in her mother's handwriting. Sucking in her breath, she reached out and lightly touched it. Confused, she asked, "What is this?"

"Your mother asked me to give it to you after you were married."

Rising, Douglas prepared to leave. Pausing at the door, he saw that she had yet to pick the envelope up.

"Your mother and I never had a romantic involvement. But believe me, it wasn't because I didn't want to. She was married, and even though her husband didn't deserve her, I respected their vows. But if I had to do it all again, I would have grabbed hold of your mother and never let her go, showing her what true love and happiness are all about.

"Don't make the same mistake I did. Don't let Henry stop you from loving someone and finding true happiness."

After he left, Christine pondered his words while she fingered the letter. Nervously, she opened the letter and began to read.

*My dearest daughter,*

*If you are reading this letter it is because my prayers have been answered and you have found forgiveness in your heart, which has allowed you to love another. I know it must have been a tough journey, but I'm sure the man you have chosen is patient, kind and understanding. You are a priceless jewel and I know your husband treats you as such.*

*I never meant for your childhood to be so painful, but I did the best I could with what I knew. But now that I've grown older and wiser, I realize the emotional scars that Henry and I must have left with you. I know that money can never make up for the challenges you*

*faced as a child, but it's a token of the love I have
for you.*

*Please don't be afraid to let those who reach out
to you, help you. I rejected help from Doug early in
your life, and I often wondered how different things
would have been if I actually had packed you up and
run off with him. But I didn't, and I will forever wonder what could have been.*

*But as for you, your journey is still continuing. Let
your husband love you. He will never leave or forsake
you. I know, because I know you. You would never
give yourself to a man who was anything less.*

*Finally, there is no shame in professional help. In
the year after Henry died, I began seeing a psycholo-
gist to help me understand, not just myself, but how
to help you live a full life. My last session with her
included writing this letter to you. You are a strong
and beautiful woman and I just wanted you to know
that you were loved. I found peace in my final days,
live with your peace now.*

*Have a wonderful life.*
*Love always,*
*Mom*

Christine read the letter three times, as the tears streamed
down her face. Her journey was complete. The weight that
she had carried around was finally lifted. She walked to her
desk and picked up the phone. She knew exactly what she
needed to do.

Damian left the construction site in frustration. The police
had found out that large deposits of cash had been made to
Justin's bank account. After questioning by the police, he
confessed to helping the electrical contractor steal money by

switching wires. Damian couldn't believe the betrayal by one of his own men.

And on top of that, it had been exactly one week since his blow up with Christine and he had not heard one word from her. Stephanie had called him Monday night to assure him that if he could just give Christine a little time, everything would work out. How much time was he supposed to give her? He loved her with his body, mind and soul, and each day they were apart was like a tearing in his heart.

But he didn't know what to do. He knew she needed to come to him, free from doubt and fear. Maybe he should try one more time and as he headed home he made a decision. It didn't matter what Stephanie said, he was going to change clothes and go over to Christine's. He wanted his wife back, and he was going to get her.

Damian pulled into the driveway, and he abruptly slammed on the brakes. *What is going on?*

The entrance was blocked with a big truck and he couldn't get to the garage or see the front door.

Walking around the side, he peeked into the back of the truck and saw that it was empty. Hearing his front door open, he watched two burly men wave good-bye to someone inside and stroll toward him. Acknowledging him with a nod, they jumped in the cab of the truck and started the engine and drove off.

Opening the front door, he called out. "Hello?"

"Damian, you're home!"

"Christine?"

Seeing her after being apart for a week sparked desire throughout his entire body. In one smooth motion, he was at her side, kissing her hard; thigh to thigh, chest to chest. It didn't matter that they hadn't resolved their issues. It was just good to have her back in his arms again. "Oh, baby, I missed you."

Stepping back, she smiled. "I missed you, too. I've been

so selfish and I finally realized it. I'll tell you everything over dinner. Believe it or not, I'm cooking tonight."

Growing serious, Damian stepped back and asked, "Are you here to stay?"

"You tell me."

For the first time since he walked in the house, he took a look around. There was stuff everywhere. Furniture, two televisions, a stereo, paintings, and clothes. Reality hit him like a ton of bricks. "The truck?"

"Yep, my house is empty. Everything has been moved here." Growing serious, Christine stroked his cheek softly and said, "I'm sorry I doubted your love for me. I can't imagine living my life without you. The time we were apart almost drove me crazy. But it won't happen again. You make me happy. You give me peace. You would never hurt me. And I love you."

Hugging her tightly, he spun her around and laughed. His wife was finally home.

# EPILOGUE

The party was in full swing and the dance floor was packed. It was New Year's Eve and the Tidewater Room was filled with joy and laughter as Damian and Christine decided to celebrate their marriage while ringing in the New Year. Moving to the sounds of Marvin Gay, the happy couple swayed in each other's arms.

The past month was filled with many changes for them. Christine began to develop a relationship with her sister, and even though Margaret Donovan wanted nothing to do with her, Christine still held out hope that one day, they could at least be civil to each other.

Natalie, now working for Davenport & Associates, took part of her money and set up a non-profit organization to help small companies, charging half the rates that other firms would charge for their services. Thrilled that her dream was finally becoming a reality, she planned to open up other locations around the city.

Nathan and Stephanie danced and admired the couple they were here to toast. Just arriving back from a vacation in St. Lucia, they were looking forward to their Valentine's Day wedding. They laughed as they watched Douglas Murphy and Cynthia Vanderpool shake their groove thing on the dance floor.

Brandon stood at the entrance staring across the room at Tanya. Jealousy coursed through his veins as she stood in the arms of another man. He physically cringed as the man whispered something in her ear and she responded with a smile. Deciding that he needed to talk to her again, he headed across the floor.

"Don't do it, little brother."

Brandon stopped as he felt the touch of Damian.

"I love her, Damian."

"I know you do, but you can't push her."

"Who is that jerk she's with anyway?"

Laughing, Damian replied, "That jerk is running for congress."

Resigned to the fact his brother was right, Brandon said, "Look big brother, the party's been great, but I'm gonna get out of here. Happy New Year."

Exiting the ballroom, Brandon never saw the disappointment on Tanya's face when Damian stopped him from coming to her.

Dear Readers:

I hope you enjoyed reading about Christine and Damian. I would love to hear from you. You can write to me at P.O. Box 1263, Alexandria, VA 22313 or e-mail me at doreenrainey@prodigy.net. If you are online, please visit my Web site at www.doreenrainey.com.

Finally, if you or someone you know is a victim of domestic violence, help is available from the National Coalition Against Domestic Violence at 800–799–7233.

Take care,
Doreen

# ABOUT THE AUTHOR

Doreen Rainey lives in the suburbs of Washington, DC, with her wonderful husband. She is a graduate of Spelman College with a BA in English and currently works for a CPA firm as a Human Resources Manager. FOUNDATION FOR LOVE is her first novel.